Taken

A Kiss Me Killer Novel

By Jenn Maples

This story is dedicated to my partner Paul and our daughter Amie.. for being there with me through this and encouraging me to keep going. I Love You xxxxxx

To my 3 best friends, Firstly to Carly.. you Nutter, you have kept me sane so many years and you continue to do just that, your my best friend and the one I can always count on, I Love you Red xxx

To Cerys, for the laughs, the insanity of our late night phone calls, and the fun you brought to my life, you mean the absolute world to me, you and Johnathan are my life, I Love You Millions xxxx

and to Julie, you have been so important in my life. You have given me the Opportunity to clear my mind and let my dreams flow. I can't ever thank you enough for that, so this one is for you chick. You mean everything to me, I Love You Always.

Here's to many more years of friendship, laughter and weird jokes. Thank you for always being there.
Jenn xxxxxxxxx

Prologue

Screams echoed in the dark dank cellar as The Kiss Me Killer picked up his knife and smiled at his next victim- Grace Garrett felt the fear in the pit of her stomach and prayed that her Partner and best friend would find her soon, The Kiss Me Killer was angry and she knew he was ready to kill her any second.

"Please, don't do this. If you let me go they will stop hunting you I swear it, just please let me go" Grace begged

He sneered and laughed at her request, it was an angry laugh, he was pissed, at her- and at her partner, but she didn't know why.

Tears rolled down her cheeks as she closed her eyes and thought of the one she loved so much, the memory of the day they met fresh in her mind, the bittersweet memory now like a lead weight in her stomach as she realised that they might not find her in time to stop him.

"You think i'm going to let you go? After what you did I don't think so- you are going to pay for what I saw you do!" he snapped as he thrust his face into hers, rage and hatred evident in his eyes.

"I don't know what you mean, you cant get away with this" she sobbed as her body began to sag with exhaustion and fear.

"Liar!" he screamed and dragged the knife across her skin in a jagged X over her left breast.

"Aggghhhh, Please stop," she screamed in tears, he laughed at her cries of pain.

"What the Fuck do you want from us? Why are you doing this?" she begged, once again she was rewarded with the knife cutting another jagged X on her right breast.

"You know why- she belongs to me and you took her from me, for that i'm going to make you suffer the worst fate, say Goodnight Grace, you will never see her again, now she's all mine Bitch" he lunged at her with the knife and she screamed with all the strength she had left as she pulled against the restraints that tied her to the metal table, she thought of Molly and her beautiful smile, and how much she loved her, and how she would be devastated when they finally found her body on the side of the road.

Grace closed her eyes, conjuring up the image of Molly and their last night together, their laughter, echoing in the bedroom as they made love for the last time, the feel of her fingertips still tracing over her skin.

"I Love You Molly, Forgive me" Grace whispered as the knife cut deeper with each Jagged X.

"Bitch, she's mine!" he snapped and struck her hard around the face, her eyes rolled back into her head, and darkness took her under. Silence filled the room.

Chapter One

2 Months Earlier.

*"What the Fuck! I'm getting a new Partner? Why?" Molly James asked
her boss, Lieutenant Owens just nodded his head and sat back in his
reclining chair and smiled at his best Detective, he cared for her
dearly, but she was hard to work with when her mood was low, as it
was all the time now, it was no secret through the precinct that Molly
was unhappy, everyone could see the evidence in her tired eyes,
concern for her was the No 1 topic of discussion in the Homicide Squad
room.*

*"Because you need some help out there Molly, your'e not sleeping and
that's starting to show on your face, I wish you would talk to the
department shrink, or even talk to me, i'm really worried about you-
your my best detective and the only one I trust to keep the yahoo's out
there in line, but something is seriously wrong and you wont talk to
anyone, so I got you a new partner that will hopefully take some of the
strain off of you and maybe even get you a new friend to talk to"*
*Molly shook her head in frustration and slumped into the chair in front
of the desk, her head hurt.*

"I don't need to talk to someone, i'm fine John, really," Molly sighed.

*"Yeah like that was even convincing, what's going on Molly? Please just
talk to me, i'm not the only one who's worried, the whole squad is
worried for you, now talk to me please just talk" a knock on the door
interrupted them, and John growled in frustration.*
"What?"
the door opened and his assistant poked her head in.
"Grace Garrett is here"   "Send her in" John answered.
*Molly turned to look at who was entering the room and felt her breath
catch in her chest, her new partner was just a few inches taller than she
was, with hair that looked like Golden Caramel that reached past her
curvaceous hips, and bright blue eyes, and the most plump lips she'd
ever seen, she was absolutely stunning, beautiful beyond Molly's wildest*

dreams, Molly's hair was light brown and reached the middle of her back, with light ocean blue eyes Molly was just as stunning as her new partner, Molly fought the urge to grab her and kiss her and instead held out her hand as the woman smiled shyly at her and reached out to shake it, the moment their hands touched they both pulled back when a flash of attraction hit.

"Hi Molly, John has told me so much about you, looks like I'm your new partner" Grace said softly, Molly gave her a nod as she stood up and looked Grace in the eyes, Molly could smell vanilla shampoo and the hint of Lavender lotion, her stomach fluttered as she committed the scent to memory, oh boy- this was going to be torture.

"I'll show you to your desk, this way" Molly headed for the door and Grace followed with a wave to the Lieutenant before she closed the door, John was smiling as he watched them through the window, he hoped this plan worked, if this didn't work, nothing would.

"This is my desk, this one here is yours, you can add pictures of your family or husband if you like, most of the guys here have pictures of their wives or girlfriends, kids" Molly mumbled as she sat down and looked at the message slips from the front desk.
Grace sat down in the chair and stowed her bag in the bottom drawer, and plugged her cell phone into the socket on top of the desk. She smiled at Molly and rested her chin in her hands, "I'm not married, not dating, and no kids, does an Orchid Count?" Grace chuckled, when Molly barely gave a shrug, concern slipped across her face, John wasn't lying, this woman was really miserable, Grace decided to try and get her to open up.

"so do you have pictures of your husband or kids? I bet they are beautiful like you" Grace knew she wasn't married, and had no kids, but she needed to break the ice somehow.

"I don't have anyone, doesn't matter anyway" Molly shrugged as the phone rang on her desk,

"Detective James"

Grace frowned at her reply, and picked up her cell to send a msg.

Grace: John what the hell happened to this woman, i'm really concerned for her!

John: I don't know, everyone is worried about her, I don't think she will last much longer if she stays this miserable, can you help her?

Grace: I'm going to try, John, but I think she hiding from something, whatever it is it's eating her alive, she's afraid

John: I cant lose her Grace, she's like a daughter to me, I've known her all her life, help her please.

Grace: I won't let her go John, I swear I will do everything to help her, I promise.

"There's been a Homicide, dead body in Golden Gate Park" Molly said as she hung up and grabbed her gun and badge from her desk drawer and slipped her cell phone into her jacket pocket.
Grace retrieved her bag and cell phone and pasted on a smile, trying hard not to let her new partner know how much she was worried for her.
"lead the way Partner" she trilled happily, Molly just nodded and left the squad room with Grace by her side.

They arrived at the crime scene 20 minutes later and fought the way through the mob of reporters blocking their path, Molly was grumbling as the reporters tried in vain to get their Attention, the local Officers who were tasked with keeping the vultures back. once they had the car safely behind the crime scene tape Molly switched off the engine and sighed deeply, Grace looked at her with concern and placed a gentle hand on her arm, she could feel her body trembling beneath her fingertips. That's when she noticed the dark circles under her eyes, Molly was exhausted and she looked so fragile.

"Are you ok, Molly?" Grace asked carefully. Molly just shrugged with a

frown.

"It doesn't really matter anymore, it's too late for me!" Molly said as she climbed out of the car and Grace followed, she was really scared by her answer. they walked over to where the body was being examined by the medical examiner, forensic techs were searching the area for evidence.

"Is this what I think it is Hallie?" Molly asked as she bent down to look at the body, the dead woman was no more than 27 years old with hundreds of Jagged X's all over her body, and clear evidence of strangulation.

"Yep- the same Jagged Cuts all over her body, finished her off by strangulation, and he kissed her on the lips again, just like the first 4 victims" Hallie answered as she ran a swab over her lips and then got to work photographing the wounds.

"Son of a Bitch, I want this Fucker before he kills another woman" Molly snapped, Hallie raised an eyebrow as she saw Molly's new Partner.

"Hallie Sanderson, M.E, nice to meet you" she smiled, Grace smiled back and gave a small wave.

"Grace Garrett, Molly's new Partner, care to fill me in?" she asked. Hallie sighed and handed the camera to her assistant who carried on with the photographs.

"we've been hunting a Serial Killer who killed 4 women, he abducts them, tortures them by cutting hundreds of jagged X's all over their bodies, then strangles them and kisses them on the lips as they die, so far we haven't found any DNA hair or fibres, the only DNA he leaves is when he kisses them on the lips but his DNA isn't in the database so either he hasn't killed before these women started turning up or he's just never been caught"

Hallie looked over at Molly and saw the dark circles under her eyes.

"Molly, when was the last time you slept Honey?"

Molly shrugged and brushed off the concern. Hallie looked to Grace who gave her a worried frown, Grace could see that Molly's friend was concerned for her as much as she and John were, she was desperate to *help her now more than ever.*

"What time was she killed?"

"About 1am, I will know more when I get her on my table, i'm hoping he made a mistake that way we can catch The Kiss Me Killer before any more young women end up on my table, i'll let you know what I find"

"Ok, thanks Hallie, which way was she brought in?"

Hallie pointed up the hill to where an area is taped off with a tent next to it. Molly nodded and headed toward it, Grace turned to follow, but Hallie reached for her arm.

"I'm scared for her, Grace, Molly's health is getting worse, if we can't get her some help then i'm scared that we'll lose her. Please- I can't watch her die" Hallie declared with a frightened gaze after her friend.

"I know, i'm going to do everything I can to help her, I just hope i'm not too late" she replied and hurried after her partner.

Molly was stood outside the tent when Grace caught up to her, Molly watched with awe as Grace's hair flowed behind her like a silk blanket, she suddenly pushed the thought aside and focused on the crime scene inside the tent.

A lone red shoe and several drops of blood lay on the ground inside the crime scene tent, there was also a tooth, Molly and Grace looked at the scene and tried to hash it out.

"So he brought her here from where ever he killed her and her shoe came off, several drops of blood and a tooth are left here- did he have trouble carrying her or wasn't she completely dead yet?" Grace speculated

Molly caught onto what Grace was saying and nodded her understanding.

"He strangled her, maybe he thought she was dead but she hung on and tried to escape- lets run that theory by Hallie and see what she thinks, she may be able to confirm that once she has the woman on her table," Molly knelt down to look at the tooth and blood drops, and she noticed

something strange, directionality.

"Look at these blood drops, look at the direction, they were made while

running" Grace said as she stepped closer to Molly, she looked over her partners shoulder and pointed out what she saw as Molly had noticed it. Molly looked up into her eyes and nodded her agreement, this was the first mistake The Kiss Me Killer had made.

"He Fucked up-i wonder what else he fucked up on" Molly wondered out loud as she stood up.

"Lets head back to the station and try to make a timeline of this

woman's death, maybe we can pinpoint where he fucked up" Molly said. Grace nodded with a smile.

Molly was about to make her way to the entrance of the tent when she suddenly went dizzy, she swayed on her feet as she looked at Grace,

"Molly?" Grace asked as she suddenly went pale, Grace was worried

as she reached for her and tried to steady her, "Are you ok Honey?" Molly collapsed, Grace caught her in her arms before she hit the ground.

"Molly, Molly can you hear me- oh my god Molly please wake up," Grace cradled Molly in her arms and gently stroked Her face trying to wake her up.

"HALLIE HELP" Grace cried out as she caressed Molly's cheek,

"C'mon Molly wake up for me Honey please wake up, please-MOLLY" Hallie rushed through the tent entrance and gasped when she saw Molly unconscious in her Partners arms.

"What happened?" "I don't know she just collapsed and she wont wake

up"

Hallie turned to her assistant, "Claire call an ambulance, Now" Claire nodded and quickly called an ambulance while Grace and Hallie tried to wake her up.
Molly started to stir but she wasn't responding by the time the ambulance arrived, Grace reluctantly moved aside while the medics worked on her.

"Her pulse is weak, we need to get her to the hospital now" the paramedic said as they placed an oxygen mask over her mouth, "I'm coming too" Grace said as she followed them into the ambulance and reached for her small hand.

Grace was by her side as they took her into the ER at San Francisco Memorial Hospital, she watched with fear as they quickly removed her shirt and began compressions, while the Nurse in charge checked for a pulse, tears were running down Grace's face as she watched them work, they were attaching monitors to her body and the beeping sounds filled the room.

"I can't find a pulse" one of the nurses said, "Her heart stopped, get the paddles- charge to 300-Clear"

Grace felt her stomach drop as she watched them get the Defibrillator and begin to shock her, she jumped when John turned up at her side and pulled her into his arms to comfort her, he looked on with horror, it seemed that Molly's health was in more danger that they realised.

"What the hell happened?" he asked as Grace sobbed, her body shaking in his arms. "I don't know, she collapsed at the crime scene, her pulse was weak, now her heart has stopped" she cried.

"we got a pulse, intubate her and keep up compressions" Grace breathed a sigh of relief and watched as they put a tube down her throat to help her breath, then attached the tube to a machine that would help her maintain her breathing while they ran tests.

Suddenly the machine began to beep, her heart stopped again, "Fuck, No" John said as he watched with sadness, he was afraid that Molly was dying.

"Charge to 350-Clear"

Grace felt her heart thumping wildly as Molly's body jerked as she was shocked once again to get her heart started, she was praying with everything she had that Molly would make it. "We got her back" a nurse called out.

"Get a Fluid IV in, and call ICU, tell them i'm bringing her up, she needs to be closely monitored and kept heavily sedated"

Grace moved forward with a hopeful look. "Can I come with her?" she asked softly.

"Are you family?" The Nurse asked with a pointed look.

"She's my Girlfriend, I'm all she has" Grace lied, John was proud of her for that lie.
The nurse softened as she smiled at her.

"Normally id say no, but she needs someone with her, follow me, you're in for a long wait though" Grace shook her head and looked at Molly.

"I don't care, I'm not leaving her side"
Grace followed the nurse as she and another nurse wheeled the gurney up to the ICU and got her settled in a side room.

8 Hours went by and Grace was sat by her bed holding her hand as she watched her with tenderness. A nurse walked in with a cup of Coffee and a sandwich from the cafeteria. "Here, you need to eat,the doctor will be here in a few minutes to talk to you"

"Thank you, god I hate seeing her like this" Grace said as she ran her hands through her hair, she was beyond tired, but she refused to leave her side.
A few minutes later the doctor walked in and greeted her with a sad smile.

"Miss Garrett, I'm Dr.Havens, Molly's Doctor" he said as he pulled a chair over to sit by her side. "Call me Grace, is she going to be ok?" she asked with a small shaky breath.

"Grace, Molly has a sever case of exhaustion, she has an empty stomach, and she's dehydrated, from what we can see from the test results she hasn't eaten in at least a week, her body is basically running on empty and she collapsed because of that, we have her on a Fluid IV Drip, a feeding tube and we've decided to keep her sedated until we can be sure that she's able to breath on her own without putting her heart through more strain, i've spoken to Lieutenant Owens and he says that you have been added to her medical files as her Emergency Contact alongside him, and that your decisions are to be considered first! Are you happy to continue with this form of treatment until she is stable?" Grace was shocked by all this, but mostly that she was on her medical files as an emergency contact, "Yes, do whatever you need to to save her, please don't let her die" she croaked as she squeezed her hands more, hoping that Molly could feel her there with her. "Don't you worry Grace, I won't let her die, she has a great chance of coming out of this unscathed, we just need to be patient" Grace nodded and leaned forward, she brought Molly's hand up to her lips and kissed her fingertips as she watched her chest rise and fall with the machine that was breathing for her, she was desperate to hear her delicate voice, to see her beautiful bright eyes as she looked at her.

"Molly, I don't know if you can hear me, but I need you to fight, please don't give up Honey, I need you to come back to me" Grace reached over and stroked her face gently, she could feel small movements of her hands as she slept deeply thanks to the sedatives, every once in a while her face twitched, Grace placed a small gentle kiss on the side of her lips next to the Intubation Tube, she held her cheek as she did so, and felt her heart break with sadness, she couldn't wait until she woke up.

Heavy! Molly felt heavy and she couldn't open her eyes, she could feel someone holding her hand. The touch felt soft and tender, almost, Intimate...she tried to reach for who was holding her hand, but she couldn't move her arm. She felt someone's lips on her cheek, the soft lips brushed against the side of her mouth, then up to her temple where the lips remained for a few minutes.

"Molly" Molly heard the soft gentle voice of her new partner, she couldn't understand what had happened, where was she? They had been at the crime scene...inside the tent when a wave of Dizziness had overtaken her, but what happened after that? She couldn't remember.

"Molly, Sweetheart please come back to me. I want you to get better Honey. Please don't leave me, I've just found you, I don't want to lose *you"*

Molly tried with all she had to open her eyes, but they were shut tight, almost like they were being forced to remain closed.
Where the hell was she?
Why couldn't she wake up?
Grace was still murmuring to her as she held her hand, then she felt Grace's fingertips gently stroking her hair, longing coursed through her veins as she tried again to open her eyes, to move her arms or even her hands, but nothing would move.

"Please wake up baby. I need you Molly...I wish you could hear me.

please My Darling, wake up" Grace was sobbing, she could feel the tears on her cheeks, the trembling of Grace's lips as they kissed her softly. Molly felt a sob deep in the pit of her stomach- she wanted to reach out to her and hold her, to kiss her and tell her that everything would be ok. But she couldn't get her eyes to open.

"Molly...I can't lose you, not now" Grace cried harder than before, it hurt to know that Grace was so upset, she craved to reach out for her, to brush away her tears and soothe her heartache.

"My Darling Molly- Come back to me please"

At 11pm that night John walked in with a takeout bag, he handed it to Grace and told her to eat, then dropped a small kiss to Molly's forehead.

"How is she doing?" he asked as he sat in a chair beside Grace. Grace sighed as she rubbed her tired eyes, she was dying for a shower, a hot meal that wasn't takeout and a soft bed to sleep in, and she wanted Molly snuggled up beside her so she could hold her in the safety of her arms. "She's holding her own, for now! Her breathing has improved over the last 4 hours, Dr.Havens said that if her breathing remains stable over the next 24-hours then they will ex tu-bait her and see how she does"

"Well thats a relief, Hallie sent a bag with some clean clothes for her, and she sent some for you too, why don't you go and take a shower in

that bathroom, I'll stay here with her" "Are you sure?" Grace asked as she looked at the private bathroom with longing, John pulled her up out of her seat and pushed her into the bathroom and pulled the door shut. A half hour later Grace emerged fresh from the shower, dressed in a pair of dark jeans and a long sleeved t-shirt, and a pair of boots, she'd left heir down and flowing on her shoulders as she took her seat beside the bed.

At 12am John left and made Grace promise to get some sleep.

The next day Dr.Havens was pleased to see that Molly was holding her own, so he requested the tube to be removed, with the cords for the machines firmly in place to monitor her condition, they waited as the tube was taken out, Grace held her breath as she prayed that she began to breath on her own.

"C,Mon Molly, Please Breathe Baby, Please Take a Breath" Dr.Havens looked to her with concern and placed a gentle hand on her shoulder, he could feel her trembling beneath his fingertips. Tears were streaming down her face as she waited, her heart pounding with fear.

"Please Molly, Breathe! Breathe Baby" she pleaded.

Suddenly Molly's chest began to rise and fall as her breathing filled the room, Grace began to sob with relief as she leaned over and kissed her temple with joy. Molly was alive and she was breathing on her own, it was the most incredible sound in the world to her.

"Thank God" Dr.Havens said as he breathed a sigh of relief.

"Now she's breathing on her own, we will reduce the sedation slowly, let her come round in her own time,i'm thinking she might need a bit more time to heal, she's a very lucky woman to have you here with her Grace,"

"Thank You so much for all you've done for her, I can't ever thank you enough" Grace said as she shook his hand great fully. "You Welcome, now sit down and talk to her, she will be able to hear you as the sedation wears off, it will do her good to hear your voice" Grace nodded and sat on the side of the bed, she pulled Molly's hand up to rest over her heart. She gently stroked her hair as she waited for each breath to fill the room, "I'm here Molly- can you hear me Honey? Please come back to me, I need you to come back, you're going to be ok, i'm here and I'm waiting for you to open your eyes" Grace said as she kissed her palm, and rested her forehead against hers.

"Molly, can you hear me honey?" Grace whispered in the dimly lit hospital room, she was sat beside Molly's bed holding her hand as she had been since she was rushed in, they had almost lost her. when she felt the small delicate hand moving in her own Grace almost sobbed, she held her hand tighter and kissed the fingertips with hope and longing.

"Mmm, Grace?!" Molly groaned and opened her eyes, Grace reached out for a glass of cool ice water and placed the straw against her lips.

"Here honey, sip slowly" Grace said as she used her other hand to lift her head up, after a few small sips of water Molly turned her exhausted eyes to her partner. The memory of Grace sobbing at her side made her chest feel tight, she wished she could reach out and touch her, she wanted to feel her just once, but she knew that didn't deserve her, Grace deserved happiness and love, someone who could make her laugh as they made love, Molly could never give her that- she was damaged goods, and she knew it.

"What happened?" Grace continued to stroke her fingertips through the soft silky hair as she shifted forward to be closer to her.

"You collapsed at the crime scene, you were unconscious we had to call

an ambulance"
Confusion clouded her memory and the feel of her fingertips stroking her scalp was making her feel sleepy.

"How long have I been here?"

"8 days, your dehydrated, exhausted and you haven't eaten in at least a week from what the doctor said, they had you on a feeding tube, and a breathing machine. basically your running on an empty tank, Honey your heart stopped twice in the emergency room, we almost lost you

Molly"

Molly sighed as she turned onto her side facing Grace, she loved the feel of her fingertips stroking her hair,

"stay with me, please" Grace nodded and took her small shaking hand in her own, she brought Molly's hand up to rest it over her cheek, then kissed the palm gently, Molly fought the desire to ask for those luscious lips to kiss her passionately.

"I never left your side for a second, I'm not going anywhere, sleep honey, I'm going to stay here by your side"

Molly closed her eyes and finally let sleep claim her.

It was 3:30am when Molly opened her eyes and glanced around the hospital room, she gasped when she saw Grace curled up against the side of the hospital bed, Grace had Molly's hand clutched tightly in her own as she slept deeply, Molly laid there and watched her sleeping for a few moments, then reached over and stroked the soft skin on her beautiful face, she shuffled over to the edge of the bed to be closer to her and rested her forehead against Grace's and breathed her in, she could smell Vanilla in her hair, and the lavender lotion that clung to her like a second skin, butterflies turned her stomach into a quivering mess, the feel of her breath on her face tore her apart and she couldn't stop herself from placing her lips over Grace's and kissing her softly, the kiss was sweet and tender, even though Grace was asleep she moaned softly and responded to the kiss, parting her lips and brushing her tongue against Molly's, a shiver rippled down Molly's back as she deepened the kiss a little, then pulled back, the taste of mint toothpaste on her lips.

Molly was tempted to kiss her again, Grace's lips still moist and plump from a kiss she would never know happened. "Grace" she whispered with longing against her lips and rested her head on her friends shoulder, emotion welled up in her chest as tears rolled down her cheeks, she cried herself to sleep.

The Morning Sunlight streamed through the blinds as Grace woke up *from a beautiful dream, she looked at the bed and realised that Molly wasn't there, the sound of the shower in the private bathroom instantly made her relax, she thought back to the dream she was having and smiled, she dreamt that Molly kissed her, and she could almost feel the touch lips, the taste of her making her ache to hold her, touch her-Make love to her.*

She only wished the dream was real.

Grace ran her fingertips over her lips and replayed the dream over in her head, a vague memory of Molly whispering her name in the night sent shivers down her back. Grace gasped as she wondered if the dream was just a dream or if Molly really kissed her, oh how she wished that Molly had kissed her.

The door to the bathroom opened and Molly walked out wearing a towel and headed for a bag of clean clothes dropped off by John, Grace gasped at the sight of her in just a towel, Molly dressed slowly as she asked about the investigation, avoiding eye contact as she fought the desire to grab her and kiss her passionately.

"So where are we with the investigation, the timeline of her death?" Molly asked quietly, exhaustion weighing her down.

"So far the theory that we came up with may have actually happened, the autopsy shows that she fought back, Hard. The techs confirmed that the blood drops were made while running and she lost the tooth while fighting her killer off, brain matter was found 5 feet away from where she lost her shoe, so she wasn't dead when he took her body to the park and she tried to escape"

Molly nodded as she turned to the bed to pick up the white t-shirt, Grace gasped when she saw the scars on Molly's stomach and chest, panic showing on her face as she walked around the bed and placed her fingertips over the soft skin of her stomach. "Molly, what happened?

Who did this to you baby" Grace asked as her fingertips travelled up her body to a scar directly over her heart, Molly shivered at her touch and fought against her feelings, wishing she could touch her too.

"who did this? Did someone hurt you?" Grace breathed as she stepped closer.

"I did it, it doesn't matter anymore, I'm not important, let's find The Kiss

Me Killer before he hurts someone else, I'm discharging myself, we have work to do!" Molly replied and walked away to find the doctor.

"Molly wait, please talk to me" Grace called after her, but her calls were ignored, Molly had shut her out- Grace ran her hands through her hair and sighed with frustration, once Molly had signed the paperwork Grace followed her out to the car and climbed behind the wheel, she kept glancing at her partner as she was driving and hoped she could eventually get through to her.

"Did you sleep at all last night?" Grace asked, she was looking for an indication that her dream had been real, Molly shrugged her shoulders and replied

"slept all night"

Molly's face was turning red, the flush of arousal in her cheeks, she saw Molly biting her lips, her breathing was deep.

Holy Fuck! Had the kiss really happened?

Chapter 2

Grace Pulled the car into the underground garage behind the
precinct, Molly had refused to go home and rest for a few days, she
made it clear that she wanted to go back to work, Grace took the keys
out of the Ignition and sighed, she turned to Molly, who was staring out
the front window absently, lost in her own thoughts.

"Molly"

Grace reached over and placed her hand on her face and turned her to
face her, she caressed her with tenderness and pleaded with her eyes
for Molly to talk to her.

"Talk to me sweetheart, I need you to trust me" she whispered as she
leaned forward and rested her head against Molly's, she breathed in the
scent of Molly's perfume, Jasmine clinging to them both as Molly
relaxed into her touch, and shivered with longing, Grace could feel her
trembling, fighting the arousal and need coursing through her veins.
Molly wrapped her hands around the nape of Grace's neck-holding on
with all she had as she fought her desire for Grace.

"Do you feel it Molly, I want you to trust me, trust me to protect you. I
know we don't know each other but I know you can feel what I feel,
open up to me darling, I swear I wont hurt you, I want to help you
Molly. Let me be the one to hold you and keep you safe, please let me
hold you" Grace breathed as she pulled Molly into her arms and ran
her hands through the long silky locks, arousal coursing through them
as their lips finally touched, they both gasped as the kiss deepened-
Molly moaned as she thrust her hands into Grace's hair and gave in to
the passion, after removing the seat belt Molly climbed onto Grace's
lap and wrapped her arms around her, Molly writhed in her lap,
rocking her sensitive body into her as she lowered her hands to cup her
full breasts, squeezing them with desire, she moaned into Grace's
mouth and delved her tongue deep inside in a passionate bid to taste
her sweetness, Grace kissed her back with all she had and slipped her
hand beneath the top she was wearing to feel the smooth skin she
craved to run her lips over, the feel of Molly sat on her lap made her
wish they were anywhere but at work.
Grace wrapped a hand around her waist as she pulled her sensitive

centre closer and lowered the other hand to the apex of her legs and pressed her fingers against her, making her cry out with a deep and primal need, she thrust her hips into Grace's hand and gasped as she felt her sex clenching with the need to come, Grace pressed into her harder and faster as she felt Molly getting ready to come, she was so hungry for her lips, her body and the feel of her shaking as she neared her release made her desperate to taste her as their tongues brushed against each others and they clung to one another, their heated breathes making the feeling more intense and sexually arousing.

"Molly" Grace gasped and took her mouth once more in a passionate kiss.

Molly finally pulled back and sighed, she held back a sob as she moved far enough away, shaking her head with sadness, tears fell down her cheeks as she said something that broke her heart, and Grace's.

"I cant do this, I don't deserve you! Find someone who deserves to be with you- to hold you, kiss you, to love you. I'm sorry but I cant do this"

Molly Mumbled and climbed out of the car and walked away, Grace sat there in shock as tears slipped down her cheeks, she felt her heart shatter as she realised that Molly was denying herself the release she so desperately wanted, she wasn't allowing herself to come, and that upset Grace so much, she watched Molly walking toward the elevator- Grace could see that her partner was trying so hard to hold herself together, her body shaking as she stepped inside the elevator car, as the doors closed Molly broke down and cried, her body curling in on itself as she sobbed with heartache, Grace jumped out of the car and ran to the elevator and tried to reach her as the doors closed, "Molly-Please don't shut me out"

but she was too late. she never wanted to let her go. "Molly" Grace cried out to her, the pained look in her eyes tore her apart as she sobbed into her hands, how was she ever going to reach her.

Molly stopped the elevator as she dropped to her knees and sobbed with devastation, she wanted Grace so badly, but she couldn't have her, she didn't deserve her, pain tore through her chest as she tried to pull herself together. She could still taste Grace's lips on hers, she craved her, but with a broken heart she'd walked away to give Grace the chance to find love with someone who deserved her. She set the elevator going and when the doors opened she wiped her eyes on her sleeve and headed for her desk and kept her head down and got to work, a few people stopped by her desk to welcome her back and wished her well, everyone knew that she had collapsed at the crime scene and she was mortified by that, but she smiled as best she could and thanked them before she got stuck into her work.

An hour passed before Grace walked out of the elevator and over to her desk and sat down.

Sneaking a glance at her partner Molly felt so damn guilty at the pained expression on her face, a single tear escaped from Grace's eye and she quickly brushed it away.

"The Victims name is Kaitlyn Downs, 27 years old, she was kidnapped after leaving work 2 Months Ago, her mother reported her missing when she didn't show up for her usual weekend brunch, her apartment was empty and theres been no activity on her bank or credit cards, no sign of a struggle. Maybe she knew the person who kidnapped her, her mother is coming in to make a list of possible suspects, he could have made a mistake by taking someone who knew him, Hallie is taking a second look at her body, he could have left DNA on her body without knowing" Grace said with a hint of irritation, she then reached into her drawer and handed a file to Molly, she was pissed off and Molly felt awful.

"I'm sorry Grace" Molly whispered across the desk, Grace pushed away from her desk ignoring her apology, and walked over to a white board where the victims photos were lined up next to the first 4 victims, Lieutenant Owens walked out of his office once he realised that they were back in the squad room.

"Welcome Back Molly, you had us all scared for a while, we were putting together a big bouquet of Orchids for you, we didn't expect you out of the hospital so soon" John said as he placed his hand on her shoulder.

"she discharged herself John, she wont listen to the doctors or to me, she's so Fucking stubborn its driving me crazy." Grace snapped, John

glanced between Grace and Molly with concern and pulled up a chair.

"Is there something I should know?" John asked with worry.

Molly shook her head and walked over to the kitchen area to pour herself a coffee.

"Grace can I speak to you in my office," John said and headed for his door, Grace followed and closed the door behind her, she was fighting the tears that threatened to fall.

She sat down in the chair in front of the desk, he sat down beside her and took her hand in his.

"Tell me what happened Grace, I know something happened, Officer Miles called me told me that you were sat in your car crying for an hour"

tears fell and Grace blew out a frustrated sigh, she wiped her eyes with an angry swipe of her hand. "You have feelings for Molly?"

Grace nodded as more tears fell, "I'm in Love with her John, I'm so in Love with her it hurts, she keeps pushing me away, but i'm not giving up on her, I'll never give up on her" Grace stood up and tried to compose herself before she walked out of the office, Molly was stood outside the door with a frown on her face, she spoke with a subdued tone.

"the DNA on the lips matched the DNA from the first 4 victims, theres still no ID on the the first 3 women but the 4th victim I think I can ID her, she has a birth mark on her left thigh, shaped like a tear drop," Grace raised her eyebrows, and followed her back to the white board.

"who is she?" "Angela Harris, we went to school together, I haven't seen her since we were 17, I hardly recognised her, she's had a lot of surgery since I saw her. Kaitlyn Downs was also in our class, she and Angela were best friends, until Angela got jealous when me and Kaitlyn started seeing each other" Molly said so no one could hear her, Grace gasped as she turned to face her partner.

"So you can be with someone else but not me!" Grace breathed sadly, the pain evident on her beautiful face, Molly tried to reach out for her hand but Grace pulled away with a silent cry and walked back to her desk, effectively ending the conversation as she sat down and turned

away from her.

"What do we have ladies, fill me in" John said as he rejoined them in the bullpen in the middle of the squad room.

Grace cleared her throat and caught him and the rest of the room up on what they had learned so far, Leaving out the relationship between Kaitlyn Downs and Molly, she wasn't sure if anyone knew about Molly,

"You went to school with 2 of the victims? What about the other victims, could they be old school friends too?" Officer Davis asked as he took notes.

John got up from his chair and moved to stand in front of the white board.

"Wait, Wait- are you saying all this is connected to Molly?" John asked with astonishment.

"ME, why the fuck would someone be interested in me?" Molly spluttered as she joined her boss at the front of the room. Grace laughed Bitterly as she sat up in her chair to stare her straight in the eyes.

"The question is why wouldn't someone be interested in you? Someone you knew at one time is sending you a message, it doesn't matter if you never actually met this person. If you were in the same class the odds are this suspect has imagined a fantasy about the two of you and these women are being killed because they knew you! You need to find a school year book and see if the first 3 women are in there"

John nodded his agreement.

"We may just find this son of a bitch!"

Molly grabbed her house keys from her desk and headed for the elevator and pushed the button for the Parking Garage, she was heading home to find her copy of the High School Year Book, Grace appeared at her side without a word, when the doors opened she followed Molly inside and braced herself for the car ride to her partners house. The tension between them was thick with sexual attraction, Molly was very aware that Grace was by her side- she could just feel the heat of her body next to hers and she had to hold in a groan as Grace ran a hand through her long dark hair, pulling it down to hang over her left shoulder, the move sent a shiver of arousal through her stomach and down to her core.

Fuck! She thought as she stepped out of the elevator and headed to the car as quickly as she could, it didn't help that the memory of their passionate kiss here earlier this afternoon was still heavy between them- Molly had heard the conversation between John and Grace in his office, Grace had sat in her car for an hour crying and it broke her heart that she had done that to Grace, she'd caused her pain and that didn't sit well with Molly.

Grace climbed into the car with a small sigh and left the Garage to drive to the Town House Molly owned on a quiet tree lined street in Pacific Heights, once they entered the house they headed for the staircase and made their way up to Molly's bedroom where she'd said the yearbook was inside the closet, it was 11:45Pm and it looked like sleep wasn't happening anytime soon.

Molly pulled 6 large boxes out of the closet and flipped the lid off of them with a groan.

"The yearbook is in one of these" Molly said as they both sat down on the rug at the foot of the bed to start searching.

"What is all this?" asked Grace as she began to sift through all the books pictures and paperwork.

"All of this? Its what I could save from the fire at my parents house, I lost everything else" she replied sadly, Grace ached for her, John had told her about the fire that ripped through their house and killed her parents and baby sister when she was 11-years old, she had lived with her aunt until she was 18 and finished school, then went for The Police Exam and passed first time.

She had climbed the ranks quickly because she was good at her job and Homicide is where she wanted to be.

"I'm sorry about your parents, and your baby sister, it's not fair that they can't be here to watch the beautiful woman you have grown into, they would be so proud of who you are Molly, don't ever doubt that" Grace whispered as she reached over and held her hand, she squeezed her hand tightly and rubbed her fingertips against her soft skin.

A breath caught in Molly's chest and she shivered, Molly looked down at Grace's hand on top of her own and she sighed loudly, she turned her hand over so their palms were pressed together, their fingers enter twined and Grace held tight, she looked deeply into her eyes and saw that her eyes were alight with fire and longing, Grace moved closer and leaned into her to rest her forehead on Molly's shoulder, wishing she could take her lips and kiss her like they had earlier, Molly obviously felt the same as she gasped at the feel of her breath on her neck. she pulled her hand away and went back to searching the boxes, by the time they emptied the final box it was 12:58Am and the yearbook was no where to be found, and something began to bother Molly.

"It's not here, where the Fuck is it?" Molly growled as she shot to her feet and walked over to her dresser with Grace right by her side as she searched her dresser drawers, moving jeans sweaters in the bottom drawer, Grace gave a little gasp as she looked in the top drawer and found herself searching through silk nighties and lace underwear and bras, she longed to see Molly wearing the lavender lace panties and matching bra, but she pushed that fantasy down and tried hard not to imagine her moaning and crying out in pleasure as she traced her lips over every inch of her skin.

"It's gone, the yearbook was in one of those boxes, and the photograph

of me and my sister was in this dresser, It's also gone" Molly breathed with panic.

Grace looked round the room and felt the dread sinking inside her- this was so not good.

"Is there anywhere else it could be, somewhere else in the house

maybe?"

Molly shook her head and began to pace up and down the bedroom, worry was etched into her face.

"Grace, someone has been inside my house, the picture of my parents is

missing from my nightstand, my diary is gone too,"

Suddenly the sound of footsteps drew their attention to the spare room by the top of the stairs.

"Does anyone else live with you? Any pets or room mates?" Grace asked quietly, Molly shook her head, panic bright in her eyes.

"No, someone is in my house!" Molly whispered back through clenched teeth.

They both drew their guns and crept to the doorway of Molly's room. Grace placed a hand on her face and stroked her cheek gently, before tracing her finger over her lips with longing, she wished she could kiss her again.

"Stay with me, don't leave my side baby" Grace stated with a serious frown, she wasn't going to risk losing Molly to whoever was Murdering these women.

Creeping down the hallway with Molly firmly behind her, Grace checked the spare room and the family bathroom and closet. Then they began the slow walk down the stairs waiting for whoever the footsteps belonged too to make a move, the sound of movement in the living room made them stop.

"Who's there?" Grace shouted, suddenly the intruder growled and fired his gun in their direction 4 times before he made a run for the kitchen, where he threw open the back door and ran out into the night, Molly and Grace followed through the house and Grace ran out into the night after him, Molly almost sobbed as she watched Grace fade into the darkness, she feared that Grace would get hurt as she ran down the steps to search for her, she finally found her outside the gate at the bottom of the yard, she dragged her back toward the house as Grace frantically searched the darkness for the intruder. "Grace No, please I can't lose you, come back in the house please, I Cant't Lose You, I'm so scared Grace. I'm not letting you go" Grace followed her back into the house, and closed the door as they stared at the darkened yard, Molly threw her arms around her neck and held her tight, Grace wrapped her arms around her too and gently stroked her back with one hand, the other in her hair as Molly sobbed with exhaustion and fear. They were in shock at what had just happened.

"Is there anything else missing from your house Molly?" John asked as he paced her living room at 4:40am that morning, once they realised someone had been in her house Grace had called John and asked him to get over there now with a forensic team, they were looking for fingerprints fibres and DNA, they were sure it was The Kiss Me Killer

but they needed proof of that before they could confirm it.

"My diary is gone, the yearbook, a picture of me and my sister, and one of my parents, I can't see anything else missing right now, I just don't get it.....why has this Psycho picked me, what have I done to get his attention all of a sudden?" Molly raged, she was pissed that someone had violated her privacy by coming into her house and going through her things.

The sound of forensic techs tearing apart her house to search for clues made her even more angry, there were 15 cops in her house and she'd known all of them since the day she started, Molly was a quiet introverted social outcast and no matter how much the other cops in her squad room tried to make friends with her she's shut them out, several of the male officers had asked her out on a date over the years but she always ignored them and hoped they would go away- no one knew that she wasn't interested in men, no one but Grace.

She'd kept her sexuality a secret from everyone at work, even John didn't know, no one could know or everyone would treat her differently.

"You haven't done anything wrong Molly, you are not responsible for any of this...we just need to find the yearbook some other way so we can find out if the first 3 victims went to the same school as you, Kaitlyn and Angela." John said as he finally sat down, Molly could see he was wound tight, she'd never seen him so tense and she's known him since she was a kid.

Memories of John and her father taking her fishing and camping with his own family felt bittersweet, she wished her father was here now to give her advice, she wished her mother was here to give her one of her heartfelt talks, they always had a way to calm her down and make her see focus, that focus had shattered after they died, the only thing that kept her together was her drive to get onto the police force.

As she glanced around the room at the cops all pitching in to help solve this case before someone else got hurt, she noticed Grace wasn't there, she couldn't hear her downstairs and that meant that she was upstairs in Molly's bedroom, What the hell was she doing up there?

After searching the hall closet Grace found a suitcase and took it into the bedroom and laid it on the bed, frustration gnawed at her as she proceeded to pack a bag for Molly, there was no way in hell that she was staying here alone, not after some sicko had been in her house, although that wasn't the only reason, the mattress on the bed was still in it wrapping, meaning Molly had never slept on it, but the disturbance on the sofa made it clear that she had been sleeping there for some time- Molly was beyond exhausted and after what the doctor had told her she wasn't going to let Molly carry on with the way she had been living, Molly needed to sleep, eat and take care of herself, and Grace would make damn sure that she slept, she was so pale and it scared the hell out of her to see her fighting to stay awake.

With several pairs of jeans, slacks and t-shirts in the bag, she added some sweaters then opened the drawer with the silk nighties, she picked 4 different ones, along with a camisole top and shorts, then she selected some bras and underwear, including the lavender set she had lost her breath over earlier that night, she then walked into the bathroom to get her a bag of toiletries, she packed a razor, shaving gel, shampoo and conditioner, body wash and perfume, the Jasmine one she liked, and some deodorant, she opened the cabinet and found 3 pill bottles, they had been filled recently.

Molly was taking Prozac for Anxiety.

Naproxen for pain in her stomach due to scar tissue.

Temazepam to help her sleep, Fuck!, Molly was in more pain than anyone realised, what the hell had happened to her to make her abuse her body like this, the scars on her stomach and chest a frightening reminder that she had hurt herself repeatedly- but why? Had her parents death and her baby sisters hurt her so much that she began cutting herself as a way to cope.

Grace grabbed the medication and anything else in the cabinet that seemed important and added them to the suitcase, along with her phone charger and laptop, then zipped up the case and wheeled it downstairs, Molly frowned when she saw what Grace was holding and jumped to her feet.

"Grace what are you doing?" Molly asked with shock, Raising her eyebrows at the question she decided to go with the honest truth.

"You are not staying here alone, you can move into my place until this

Fucker is caught, and it's not open for discussion so don't bother trying, now get your ass in the car, its almost 5:00am and your exhausted, so am I, I packed everything you need let's go" Grace whispered sadly as she walked toward the front door.

"John!" Molly Pleaded with exasperation, John shrugged his shoulder and pointed to the door.

"Go, Now. We cant catch this asshole if your not able to focus enough to work, I have the team working on this while your getting sorted so just go with Grace"

Molly growled and grabbed her jacket off the sofa, then walked out to the car where Grace was waiting, sat on the bonnet with a guarded expression. Silence filled the air as they got into the car and drove to Grace's loft on the other side of town.

Walking into the very large spacious loft apartment in the heart of San Francisco Molly looked round and liked what she saw, the loft was decorated in soft Lilac colours with summery yellows here and there, the floor to ceiling windows gave a beautiful view of the Bay and the Golden Gate Bridge in the distance.
Grace locked and bolted the door and set the security alarm, then wheeled the suitcase to the Guest room right next to her own room. Placing the suitcase on the bed Molly opened it to see her medication on the top with her toiletry bag, Grace's face gave nothing away as she backed toward the door, "Get some sleep, i'm next door if you need me" the door shut behind her and Molly slumped onto the bed with sadness as she realised that Grace really was angry at her. Only she had no idea how to make it right between them, she cared for Grace more than she cared for anyone else.

"I hate my life" Molly mumbled and crawled into the bed once she had stripped off and fell into a deep troubled sleep.

Chapter 3.

   *Watching from afar, The Kiss Me Killer aimed the camera in the
direction of the house where she lived, his heart was pounding as he
tried to calm down after the near miss he'd had in that house earlier,
he'd gone there to go through her things and he hadn't heard them
come in while he was in the basement.*
*It pissed him off that he hadn't heard them in the house, because of that
Fuck-Up he'd almost gotten caught. He had to be more careful, if he
was ever going to get his Love where he wanted her then he needed to
pay more attention to his surroundings. her essence was all over that
house- the smell of her perfume, the spot on the sofa where she slept
held an indentation of her body, while he was in there he had laid in
that spot and felt himself grow hard at the thought of being with her.*
*He'd seen her being carried out of the crime scene tent after she
collapsed, he wondered what caused that, the lack of sleep perhaps? Or
maybe that she hadn't been eating very much lately, he'd been watching
her closely.*
She'd lost so much weight, and she looked too pale.
*He'd wanted to pay her a visit while she was asleep in the hospital, but
that new partner hadn't left her side for a second, it angered him as he
watched the bitch holding her hand- he was fuming when Molly had
leaned over and placed her lips over her partners, how dare she kiss
someone else, she belonged to him, and him alone, she would pay for
that mistake.*
*He'd followed them as they left the hospital and drove to the parking
garage, he couldn't park in there so he used a blind spot where no one
could see him and the cameras couldn't spot him.*
*He watched the heated discussion in the car, the partner reached over
and placed her hand on her face, turning her to look into her eyes, the
conversation turning heavy with tension as Molly leaned closer to the
woman by her side, the pained expression on both their faces soon
turned into one of arousal, Molly thrust her hands into her partners
hair and took her mouth in a passionate kiss, she ripped the seat belt off
and climbed out of her seat and into her lap where their passionate
clinch turned even more urgent, he could see Molly writhing on her lap
as she tried to get closer, wrapping their arms around each other.*
*Anger seared his insides, he hated that bitch for taking his woman away
from him, he would kill her slowly so she suffered, yeah, he would cut*

off a souvenir to remember her by, once he had Molly where he wanted her then he would give her the gift so she could see what he had done for her, she would appreciate that.

He watched from his private spot as the bitch put a suitcase in the car, the house was filled with cops now so he couldn't spend anymore time in there, but where was his woman going with a suitcase?

He followed them across town at a discreet distance and wondered where they were leading him, when he finally saw them entering an apartment building he punched the dash board, hard.

She was staying with the bitch, and that was a huge mistake- now he wanted to kill her for the fucking hell of it, how dare she take his Molly away like that!

He smiled with hatred, and formed a plan, one to make it clear who was boss here, let the games begin!

It was still dark outside as Molly tossed and turned in a restless sleep, when the sound of moaning woke her up, it sounded like Grace was having a bad dream, climbing out of the bed she grabbed a silk nightie from her bag and slipped it on, she then left her room and walked over to Grace's door, which was partially open, Molly was about to knock on the door when she saw that Grace wasn't having a bad dream- she was awake and deep in the throes of ecstasy, her hand was beneath the sheets, her chest breathing heavily as she touched herself, a thin layer of sweat coating her skin as she gasped softly, Molly watched her, wanting nothing more than to run to her and lose herself in Grace's arms,biting her lip Molly felt her breath catch in her throat, the feeling of arousal making her crave the sweet release she would find in Grace's arms, but she didn't deserve this beautiful woman, or the passion they could share.

Molly backed away from the door intending to go back to her own room, but the sound of moaning made her stop.

"Molly-oh Molly" Grace gasped, Molly turned and walked back to her doorway, stepping into the room she felt her core throbbing with need, her desire for Grace was making her whole body hum with arousal. her startled breathing making Grace's eyes shoot open when she realised that Molly was watching her. the sheet fell from her grasp and Molly saw her beautiful full breasts, Molly swallowed deep as she felt

her core flush with need, there was no way she could walk away from her now, she needed her desperately, her whole body throbbing with the need to bury her fingers deep inside her heat.

"Molly" Grace breathed as she sat up, panic in her eyes, she was afraid that Molly would never forgive her for this.

"Oh god Molly, I'm sorry" she whispered with fear, Molly walked over to the bed, her heart pounding in her chest as she did something that shocked both of them, she reached down for the hem of her silk nightgown and pulled it over her head, letting it drop to the floor at the foot of the bed, Grace gasped as she rose to her knees on the soft mattress, Grace was shocked by her move, "Molly?" she whispered with hope, she watched as Molly climbed onto the bed in front of her, Molly gently traced her fingertips over her naked body, she shivered as she hoped Molly was finally letting her in to her heart, Grace was breathing heavily as she opened her arms for Molly, when they finally reached out for one another and their lips met in a kiss so passionate, Molly guided Grace back on to the pillows and ran her tongue over her lips, her hands all over her body, tasting her sweet skin turned her on so much that she shivered in Grace's arms, Molly could smell her arousal, and she hungered for her.
Taking Grace's nipple into her mouth she kissed her with desire, Grace gasped as she reached for Molly and caressed her softly, she pulled her mouth to hers and delved her tongue deep and moaned with hunger. Molly rolled on top of Grace and the feel of Grace's soft skin made a fire burn in her veins, she kissed her so passionately as she felt Grace wrap her legs around her. Grace cried out as she felt her sex throbbing with need for Molly.

"My Molly-My Beautiful Molly" Grace whispered as she ran her tongue over her neck.

"I want you more than my next breath Grace, I'm aching for you My Darling, I'm Burning"

Grace kissed her again, she replied "Then Burn me My Darling, set me on fire, I'm Burning for you too"
Taking Grace's neck she bit hard enough to leave a love bite on her skin, Grace flushed with heat as she cried out in pleasure, their soft

fingertips tracing down each others bodies as they finally gave in to what they felt for one another, Molly sank her fingers deep inside her heated core as Grace took her lovers breast into her mouth and kissed her breast with passion, their lovemaking taking them to new heights as their lips touched, their hands caressed.

"Oh Molly, Baby don't stop, please don't stop"

"I Can't stop my darling, I've wanted you so much, I can't get enough of

you, I need you so badly" Molly said as she thrust her fingers deep inside her, Grace cried out and Molly gasped until they both climaxed together, their bodies damp with sweat, their breaths mingled as they kissed deeply, exhausted from the hottest sex of their life Grace wrapped her arms around Molly and kissed her lips.

"Where's your cell phone?" Grace asked softly.

"In my room on the desk" Grace jumped out of bed and ran to her room to retrieve her cell, she returned a second later and climbed back in beside her, she brought up the camera and pulled Molly into her arms, they kissed briefly and then smiled at the camera.

"These Pictures mean we belong together, you are so perfect My

Darling and I need you by my side Always" Molly kissed her tenderly and snuggled into her warm body, they were both feeling sleepy.

"sleep sweetheart, sleep here with me"
Molly nodded and they soon fell asleep as the dawn kissed the horizon.

Waking up in the arms of her lover, Molly felt a sense of peace that she hadn't felt in so long, they had fallen asleep as the sun was rising and had slept deeply, Molly hadn't slept this well in years, she rolled closer to Grace and kissed her soft shoulder, she smiled as the feel of her lips caused Grace to stir, her eyelids fluttered open, Grace smiled and bit her lip, then leaned over and kissed her lips tenderly.

"Good Morning My Darling" Molly whispered

"Oh Molly- last night was the best night of my life, I wanted you the

moment I saw you" Grace told her softly,

"I know, I wanted you too, so much it hurt"

they caressed each other as they shared a sweet and tender kiss.

"What happened Molly? Why have you been punishing your self for so long- John said that you have been so miserable that you hadn't been sleeping, working overtime, not eating much, everyone in the squad

room has seen the pain your in, what happened baby, you can tell me"

a flash of pain went through her as she pulled away from Grace and vacated the bed they had made love in for the first time.

"Please don't, I can't talk about that, ever! We should get dressed and

head to work, we have a killer to catch"

Grace was shocked when Molly walked away to her own room, locking the door behind her.

"Fuck" Grace shouted as she hit her pillow with anger, she was hoping that after last night that Molly would trust her enough to open up, she really wanted to help her, but that wouldn't happen if Molly didn't trust her.

Blood seeped down her stomach as Molly ran the razor blade over her already scarred skin, she bit her lips so hard that she drew blood, the metallic taste hitting her tongue, she muffled the scream that was almost bursting from her lips, tension radiating from her as she watched the warm water from the shower wash it away, she looked at the 3 new cuts she had made while she was in the shower, she eventually turned off the dual shower heads and stepped out, she grabbed some tissue paper and held it over the wounds while she searched for a first aid kit, Jackpot. There was a kit in the cabinet beneath the sink, she grabbed it and searched for some band aids and carefully dressed the first two cuts, but the 3rd cut was deeper than the others, and bleeding more than she realised, Fuck this one would need to be stitched up- perfect, Hallie was going to kick her ass when she saw this.

Despite the bleeding she dressed the wound as best she could and headed back to her room to dress for work, she winced at the pain in her stomach from her new wounds, but the old ones were causing her pain too, they had been for a while, she grabbed her pain meds and took one to try and make the pain more bearable, she then slipped the

meds into her jacket pocket before she headed out to the kitchen where Grace was making Coffee in two travel cups, she slid one over to Molly and offered a smile, Molly barely responded. "thanks"
after taking the cup she turned toward the door and headed out, Grace fought back a sob as she followed, they were back to square one.

The elevator ride up from the Parking garage was filled with silence, the mere memory of last night almost didn't seem real, they kept glancing at each other as they waited for the doors to open.
"What the fuck happened to your lip?" Grace asked as she noticed a bead of blood on the plump lip she'd kissed with passion.
Molly shook her head and pulled away as Grace reached for her.
"Nothing, don't worry about me" was her cold response, That was it, Grace had taken as much as she could, she pushed the stop button on the elevator and the car juddered to a halt, Grace grabbed Molly and pushed her up against the wall, Molly gasped at the move, her heart began to thunder in her chest, excitement coursed through her veins as she hoped that Grace would kiss her, but the feeling of shame was still in the back of her mind. Arousal was making Molly crave the passion that they had shared only a few hours ago. Grace took Molly's lips in a crushing and passionate kiss, Grace reached down for her legs and lifted them to wrap them around her waist, she held one hand against her ass, the other one she slipped between them and stroked her through her jeans, Molly gasped at the intense pleasure that was coursing through her veins, she kissed her back with everything she had, feeling so much emotion as she slipped her hands beneath Grace's top so caress her breasts, Grace hissed as she fought back the urge to come, she didn't want to until Molly did, she needed her to come so badly so she could join her.
"I don't care what it takes Molly, i'm not going anywhere, i'm here and i'm with you, I'm never going to leave you- I'm here, right now. Feel me touching you Molly, I want you more than anything in this world, you have me sweetheart, body mind and soul"
Molly sighed, and gasped. She thrust her hips into Grace's hand, moaning and gasping as she felt her Sex begin to clench against the

pleasure. Suddenly the depression began to invade her mind, and she felt like her heart was breaking, with a devastated sob Molly pulled away as she removed her legs from her waist. "I'm not good enough for you, you deserve more than me" she set the elevator going and hoped that she could walk away with dignity.

Chapter 4

 Walking into the squad room Molly and Grace both frowned at the Buzz of activity, the phones were ringing constantly, the white board that held the photos of the murdered women now had names above the pictures, a second white board was at the side, there were 3 new pictures on there.

"Fuck! This doesn't look good" Grace whispered as they walked into the bull pen where their desks were situated, John was there with Hallie, and about 15 other cops who were answering phones, taking notes and trying to locate families.

"John?" Grace said as they headed over to their boss and the M.E.

 "I hope you two got some sleep- because we have a shit storm brewing, we identified the first 3 women, i'm sorry Molly but they were also in your class at school, Elizabeth Marks, Tanya Jacobs and Stacy Ellison, they were friends with the last two victims"

Grace sighed and rubbed her tired eyes, it was going to be a long fucking day.

Molly began pacing as she thought back to these girls in school, she remembered them now, mean girls who liked to torment the ones they felt threatened by, Kaitlyn was the only nice one out of them all.

"What the Hell is going on? I don't get what this has to do with me- Kaitlyn was the only nice girl in the group, Angela became jealous when me and Kaitlyn started hanging around together"

John saw an opportunity to get Molly to open up and admit her sexuality, he'd known for a long time that she wasn't into men but he had never asked her directly if she had a girlfriend, he knew that she would come to him when she was ready- but that day had never come and she'd obviously been suffering with her sadness and her silence, that's why he'd stole Grace from The Missing Persons Unit. He'd known her for 6 years, she was a great cop.

After months of them meeting for coffee and talking about Molly trying to find a way to help her, Grace finally agreed to transfer to Homicide and be her new partner.

"So you and Kaitlyn were close?" John asked, Molly nodded and ran

her hands through her hair, none of this made any sense.

"Molly"

Grace walked over to her and place her hand on her partners shoulder,

"It's ok Honey"

John looked between them and suddenly he saw the love bite on Grace's neck, elation surged through him as he hoped that Grace had been able to break through her walls.

Molly looked at the 3 pictures on the second white board, the skeletal bodies barely resembling a human being.

"Who are these 3?" she asked as she tried to rein in her emotions,

Grace shot a panicked look at John as she felt the trembling beneath her hands, John saw it too and began to worry.

"Baby your shaking, John!"

John jumped up from his seat at the front of the room, Grace led Molly to John's chair and sat her down, kneeling in front of her Grace took her face in hers and rested her forehead against Molly's, Molly reached up and cupped Grace's hands which were holding her face, she breathed in Grace's scent and the memories of their LoveMaking made her tremble with need. John and the whole squad room was watching them with anticipation, Molly had been asked out by half the single cops she worked with over the years, but she had ignored that and never gave them an answer.

Now everyone was watching as Grace knelt down in front of her and caressed her face tenderly, tears were falling down Molly's cheeks onto Grace's hands, Grace gently wiped them away with her thumbs as she kissed her forehead.

"Breathe My Darling, breathe- it's ok he won't ever hurt you, I wouldn't let him, neither would John or Hallie, take a deep breath baby, Molly I know your scared but I need you to be in this with me, we have to catch this fucker but we can't do this alone" Grace stroked her cheeks and looked deeply into her eyes, John and Hallie both exchanged a hopeful glance, Grace brushed her fingertips over the soft lips she was craving to devour, As Molly took a deep breath she found that she couldn't stand not having Grace's lips on hers, her Desire for Grace was too strong and she needed to kiss her with all she had. Molly surprised them all by leaning forward and placing her lips over Grace's, it was *the softest sweetest kiss, silence filled the room as everyone watched with awe as their kiss deepened, Grace stroked her tongue against hers and wrapped her arms around Molly tightly, John was beaming with pride, Hallie wiped the tears that were streaming down her face and the whole room erupted into applause, the sound of her colleagues cheering her on gave her the courage to take Grace into her heart.*

"I'm In Love With You Grace" Molly cried as she buried her head into her neck, Grace smiled as she ran her hands through her hair "I'm In Love With You Too, I thought i'd lost you when you collapsed. I was so Fucking scared Molly. Please don't ever do that again" Grace gasped as she threw her arms around her neck.

Molly wrapped her legs around her waist and Grace stood up, taking Molly with her as she spun her around with happiness, it made her heart soar as Molly smiled at her with so much love, her eyes shining brightly as their lips met and they kissed again.

"You too make a beautiful couple, congratulations" John said as he hugged them both, Hallie kissed Molly on the cheek and gave Grace a hug, "Thank you for saving our girls heart, I'm so happy for you both" Hallie said gratefully, Grace smiled back as she pulled her lover into her arms and kissed her tenderly.

"You don't have to thank me Hallie, I fell in Love with her the moment I met her, my beautiful girl,"

"Ok everyone lets get back to work," John called and everyone went back to what they were doing, after they all came over to Congratulate them both and offer their unconditional support.

"I hate to do this but we have found 3 more victims, they have been identified by dental records, you knew them Molly"

Molly turned to John with a shocked expression, a feeling of dread settled in her stomach.

"Tell me"

"Dana Thompson, she was a teachers aid at your school, these last two are male, the only deviation from his signature is with these two, Tom Rhodes and Phil Jeffries, Dana Tom and Phil all vanished when you

were in school, the police report states that they probably all ran away together, no bodies were ever found and no sign of foul play, do you remember them?" John asked, Molly turned to the white board and looked at the pictures of their remains, a chill suddenly made her shiver.

"Yeah, Yeah I remember them, and I'm not sorry they are dead, Dana was a teachers aid- she was also a predator, she held me down while Tom and Phil raped me repeatedly for 8 hours, then she raped me with the barrel of her fathers gun, she said if I told anyone then she would put that gun inside me and rape me again, then pull the trigger"

Grace gasped and covered her mouth to hold back the sob that threatened to overtake her, no wonder she had been so scared all her life, she had been horrifically beaten and raped by someone who was meant to help her, and the two boys in her class who hurt her were no better, the savage sexual assault had traumatised her to her very soul.

"My Poor Beautiful Baby, I wont let anyone hurt you ever again" Grace whispered as she kissed her softly.

Molly smiled at the tender gesture, and melted into her arms, "I know darling, I love you too"

"Molly someone who knows what happened to you is committing these murders, these 3 were the first to die, what they did enraged someone so much that they killed them and buried their bodies, in Golden Gate Park, the only reason we know is because a woman walking her dog called it in when her pooch dug up a bone half a mile from where the other bodies were discovered"

Molly pointed to the photos of the first 3 victims, she hated to think of them as victims after what they had done to her.

"Can you confirm that The Kiss Me Killer is responsible for their deaths?"

Hallie nodded as she stepped forward, she cleared her throat and picked up a case file from the desk.

"Dana, Tom and Phil all have Jagged X's all over their bodies, Dana was strangled and kissed on the lips as she died, the men however were not strangled, this is the deviation from his M.O- he gave both men a Penectomy, placed their crown jewels in their mouths then cut their throats"

Grace all but gagged as she pictured the brutal way they died, even if they did deserve it for what they did to her girl, "Well that message is loud and clear, in a sick way this creep is trying to avenge your rape"

"But I never told anyone what they did to me, no one knew, so who the hell is doing this and why? I don't want some psycho killing people because he thinks he's god, what happened to me was their fault, I should have reported it so they could pay for what they did, but I was too scared. So why now has this asshole started killing the girls who where mean to me?"

"God Complex- he thinks you two have a sexual relationship and are deeply in love, he's been watching you Molly, he knows that you have been unhappy and now he's taking to killing anyone from your past who hurt you, these fuckers hurt you in the worst way possible, and he killed them in the worst way possible, these girls humiliated you and bullied you in school, so he's killing them in a bid to make you happy, he thinks you want him to kill-"

"My God, is this an old boyfriend, a past love interest?" Hallie asked,

Molly shook her head and turned to face her friends, "No, I've never had a boyfriend, I dated Kaitlyn for 4 months, but Angela got jealous and caused us to split, it wasn't serious, a teenage crush, I've never fallen in love until now," Molly reached for Grace and held her hand, she soothing feel of her skin making her stomach jump with excitement. "I fell in love with you Grace"

John smiled, "you two are too cute"

"Agreed" Hallie said with a laugh, "So if this asshole is killing people who hurt you why did he kill Kaitlyn, she didn't hurt you did she?" blowing out a breath of frustration Molly said what she was thinking.

"I think he killed her because she was my first, my first crush, first kiss, maybe he was jealous that it wasn't him"

"I want you both to go to Dana's house, talk to her parents, Doc you go with them, if they have that gun test it and see if you can get DNA from the inside of the barrel, try and get prints too if you can, I'll send some of the uniforms to Tom and Phil's houses to speak to their parents, did you keep the clothes you were wearing when they raped you, maybe we could find DNA from them, I know you cant get justice for what they did but at least you can move forward knowing that the DNA proves what they did?"

"Yes, its in a plastic bag in the spare room closet, I kept it incase I ever decided to press charges" "I'll go Sweetheart, you go with Hallie and get that gun as evidence, talk to Dana Thompson's parents and find out if they knew their daughter was a child molester"
handing the keys to her they set off for the elevator with Hallie, who had her field kit with her.
Once they reached their respective cars Grace pulled Molly into her arms and kissed her passionately, arousal setting them both on fire.

"I'll get this bag to evidence as soon as I can then meet you at the Thompson's house, I Love You Baby"

"I Love You More"
with a final kiss they climbed into their cars and went to do their jobs.

Chapter 5.

Knocking on the door to the Thompson's house they waited for the door to open, it felt so strange to be seeing these people again, they wasn't the nicest of people by a long shot, the older couple praised the only child they had and painted her as a saint, they wouldn't like what they had to tell them.
The big antique doors opened and an older woman stood there with a cane, her husband just behind her.

"Yes?"

"Mr and Mrs Thompson i'm Detective Molly James, this is Doctor

Sanderson, i'm here about your'e daughter Dana"
the woman gave a sob and stood back to let them in, following them into a formal living room they all sat down on the hard couches.

"Please tell us you found our girl" the husband said as he gazed at the police Detective and Doctor in front of them.

"Your'e daughter's remains were discovered in Golden Gate Park

today along with two class mates who vanished when she did,"

"Oh My God, no! She cant be dead she can't be- it must be a mistake"

"her remains were identified by her dental records which you gave when she first went missing, Mr Thompson you have a Pistol registered under your name, a Glock, do you still have that gun- we believe your daughter was murdered for something she did to a student of hers, Dana was 24 when she went missing, the two she was buried with were

15 years old at that time"

"Yes, I have the gun it's in that cabinet there" Mr Thompson replied and got up to get it.

"What are you talking about? I know you don't I?"
the haggered woman asked with distain.

"Yes Ma,am you know me, I was in your daughter class, she was a teachers aid- your daughter and these two boys she was buried with

abducted me when I was 12 years old, they held me down for 8 hours and raped me repeatedly, your daughter raped me with the barrel of that gun"

Mrs Thompson jumped to her feet and snarled "Liar! My daughter would never do a thing like that, Harold put the gun away"

Harold handed the box to Molly with the gun inside, she opened it and a flash of fear shocked her at seeing the gun again after so many years, the painful memories almost chocking her.

Hallie snapped on some rubber gloves and tool out her swabs and got to work, she took the gun barrel off and swabbed the inside of it, she lifted her head and gave Molly a sympathetic smile.

"Evidence of Blood and Vaginal tissue, and what looks like dried semen, I think we can get a pretty good DNA match from this, we need to take the gun with us and log it into evidence"

"How dare you, get out of my house, NOW, you are not welcome here" Agatha Thompson shouted with hatred.

"Shut up Agatha, I knew something wasn't right with our daughter-she never had a boyfriend and she was constantly talking about you Molly, I wondered if she was sick or maybe she just felt pain for you losing your family, I never would've thought she had done something so disgusting, she was a very disturbed woman and I did worry about her working at the school, I spoke to the headmaster and he said she was doing fine, I honestly had no idea- i'm so sorry"

feeling brave, Molly stood and collected the gun in an evidence bag,

"You're daughter was a child rapist, so were the boys she was killed with, if she were still alive then she would be arrested for rape, abduction and fired from her job"

"I can't ever apologise for what she did, but can you tell me who killed my daughter?"

"She was killed by someone who is killing people who hurt me, we are trying to find this man before he hurts someone else," Molly replied and said goodbye, Hallie followed behind her with the DNA, Blood and

Semen samples taken from inside the gun.

   Grace pulled her car up outside of Molly's townhouse and pulled her keys from her pocket, she walked up the steps to the door and unlocked it, stepping inside she looked around and then made her way upstairs to the spare room closet, she pulled it open and saw at the back, a plastic bag with what looked like a bloody top, jeans and underwear, and a sweater covered in dirt and blood, she grabbed the bag and turned to walk to the door, when the sound of footsteps made her freeze, she dropped the bag and pulled out her gun, removing the safety she crept to the doorway, she checked the hall bathroom, then Molly's room, both were clear and she checked the hall closet to be sure.
Once she knew the upstairs was clear she headed downstairs and checked the living room, as she tiptoed to the kitchen something hit her from behind, knocking her to the floor, the gun hit the floor and scattered out of her reach, a swift kick landed in her gut and making her cry out in pain, she flipped onto her back and grabbed the nearest thing she could find, a baseball bat next to the kitchen door, she swung it and hit the man in the shoulders, he fought back and pinned her down on the floor, she lifted her knee and hit him in the groin, he reached back and punched her hard, sending blood all over the floor, he pulled her up and tried to throw her over his shoulder, she bit him on the neck and took a bite out of him, she spat it on the floor and pushed him off of her, she tried to run but he grabbed her and threw her into the glass coffee table, shards of glass shattered everywhere, blood seeped into the rug on the floor, Grace whimpered as she tried to pull her cell phone from her pocket, he stepped on her wrist and took the phone, he was about to stomp on it when it rang, he saw the name on the screen and growled. It was Molly. He let it go to voice mail, before he played the msg for Grace to hear.

   "My Darling Girl, we've finished at the Thompson's house, we are on our way back to the station, did you find the bag ok? Call me when you get this, I can't wait till we get home later, theres so much I want to do with you baby, I Love You so much, bye Beautiful"
the message made Grace cry with devastation, she tried to drag her battered body to the front door, she could hear the anger radiating out

of him as he grabbed her and beat her till she was unconscious, he dipped his fingers into her blood and wrote a message on the wall above the fire place, yes, this message would be loud and clear, Molly belonged to him, and he would kill anyone who tried to take her away.

Walking in to the Lieutenants office with a satisfied smirk on her face, Molly dropped the evidence bag containing the gun onto his desk, John smiled back as he sat back and folded his arms over his chest, Molly finally understood what he'd done, he'd made her go to the Thompson's residence to collect the gun as a way to face her demons, yes they had to inform the parents of their daughters death but he needed her to finally face what had happened to her, he was proud of her for that. Molly finally realised that John had been there all along.
She dropped into the seat and held her hands up in mock surrender.

"Ok Ok I should have come to you and told you what happened, John I was 12-years old and had just lost my family a few months before, I was alone and scared"
John walked around the desk and sat beside her, taking her hand in his.

"I understand that honey, I do, it was a very tough time for you, I wish I had known so I could have the pleasure of arresting those Fuckers"
Molly laughed at his remark, she actually laughed and John beamed at that, it had been years since she'd smiled, let alone laugh, her depression and sadness had shocked him to the core, he'd spent the last 6 years trying to get her to talk but her health gotten worse and then he'd noticed that she was losing weight, she wasn't sleeping and working double shifts to avoid going home, he'd become so concerned for her that the only way he could even try to help her was to turn to a woman who he hoped could help her, Grace Garrett was with the Missing Persons Unit, a great cop and an Amazing woman, he'd suspected that Molly was only interested in women and he knew Grace was too, he thought that maybe if Molly was attracted to someone she might open up finally, he could see the spark of attraction the moment they met, and Grace had admitted to him in his office she was falling in love with her, so when Molly finally gave in and kissed Grace in front of the whole squad room he was beyond thrilled.

"I'm so happy you found Grace, she is an amazing woman and she will love you unconditionally" John said as he gave her a nudge, the mention of her name made Molly blush like a lovestruck teenager, a full smile spreading across her face, *"I can see you blushing Molly, and I saw the Love Bite on Grace's neck, you two did more than sleep"*

She giggled with embarrassment as she covered her face, the memory of Grace's lips locked around her breasts as they made passionate love sent a twinge of arousal between her legs, she couldn't wait to go home with her later, she was planning a romantic dinner with candle light, soft music and a night of passion.

"You really are in love with her?" John asked, he hoped that she was.

"Yes, I'm in love with her, I'm so in love with her it hurts, I've never felt like this before John, I feel like I have found my other half, before I was empty, now I feel like I'm finally whole, when I'm with Grace I'm home" Molly smiled as she told him, happiness was radiating from her, the look of Love making her glow with beauty.

John squeezed her hands as he beamed, *"I'm so happy for you both, you're going to marry that woman, I just know it"*

Molly flushed with happiness at that suggestion, she loved the idea of marrying Grace, spending the rest of their lives together sounded good to her.

A knock sounded on the door, interrupting their conversation once more, his receptionist Jane walked in with a look of panic on her face, John got to his feet.

"Jane?"

"Molly, theres been a report of a disturbance at your house, two uniforms went over there, they found blood, a lot of blood"

Molly shot to her feet and pulled her phone out of her pocket.

"NO, Grace! Oh my god Grace"

running out of the office Molly tried to call her as she headed for the elevator, John was right behind her.

"Get in the car we can be there in 8 minutes" John said as he turned on

the lights and sirens and sped out of the parking garage.

"C, Mon Baby pick up, let me hear that beautiful voice" once again the

call went to voicemail. "Fuck!"

*tears were already running down her cheeks, fear evident on her pale
face.*

*Minutes later they pulled up to her house and she jumped out of the car
and raced inside.*

"Grace- Grace baby where are you?"

*she came to a halt when she saw the savage scene that had taken place,
her glass coffee table was shattered, a pool of blood in the centre, what
looked like drag marks on the foyer floor and blood all over the walls
and floors leading to the kitchen, a bloody handprint where Grace had
tried to reach the house phone.*

*A bloody baseball bat laid on the sofa with a DVD beside it, a note
saying PLAY ME, and a bloody message on the wall above the fire
place.*

> *You Betrayed Me,*
> *Let the Games Begin!*

"Oh my god, is that her blood?" Molly sobbed as she began to feel cold

*and lost. John snapped on some gloves and loaded the DVD into the
DVD Player, they weren't prepared for what they were going to see.*

*Grace appeared on the screen, she was restrained by her wrists,
handcuffed to a metal pipe overhead, she was stripped to her
underwear, covered in blood and her face stained with tears.*

"Oh God No- my poor baby, what is he doing to her?" Molly begged as

John place his hand on her shoulder trying to soothe her.

*A man came on screen wearing a mask, he was holding a leather belt,
which he proceeded to use as a whip as he lashed Grace Repeatedly on
the back, Grace screamed with every crack against her back, Molly was
sobbing as she watched her best friend and the love of her life being
savagely beaten.*

"You Betrayed me Molly, you belong to me, now your lover is paying the price, i'm going to kill her slowly, make her suffer the most"

"DON'T YOU FUCKING TOUCH HER YOU BASTARD" Molly raged as she burst into tears and collapsed to her knees, her heart breaking with the sound of her girls terrified screams.
Hallie burst through the front door and sucked in a breath of shock as she saw Molly in a heap on the floor and poor Grace being tortured on the tv, she bent down and pulled Molly into her arms and held her tight as she cried for Grace.

"We have to find her John, I can't lose her now I just found her, oh god please let her be ok"

"Hallie take her back to the station, don't let her out of your sight, get her the recliner chair from my office, if you have anything to help her sleep then do it"
Hallie nodded and helped her friend up from the floor, she guided her out of the house and to her car where she strapped her in and drove away as quickly as she could, Molly pulled out her phone and pulled up a photo of her and Grace laid in the big bed, Grace had asked her where her phone was after they made love, when Molly had told her it was in her room she had gone to retrieve it and climbed back in beside her, they had wrapped their arms around each other and taken a few photos together, Molly remembered what Grace had said as she sent them to her own phone.

"These pictures mean we belong together, your are so perfect My Darling and I need you by my side Always, "
Molly had kissed her then and snuggled into her warm body and had the best sleep in years.

Molly was still sobbing as she stared at the pictures and wished she could feel her girl's arms around her now, Hallie saw the picture as they pulled up outside the station, she wasn't bothering with the garage right now, she just wanted to get Molly inside and try to get her to sleep.

By now the whole squad was aware that Grace had been kidnapped and they all wanted to know how they could help. Hallie helped her friend out of the car and led her to the elevator in the main lobby.

"Where did you take that picture, its beautiful?" asked Hallie, she was trying to distract her as they rode up to The Homicide headquarters on the 5th floor.

"After we made love last night, Grace took the photo on my phone so I could carry her with me everywhere, she's not going to die is she Hallie?" Molly begged with frightened eyes.

"No, absolutely not- we will find her honey I promise you that" a fresh round of tears fell as she followed her.
Hallie got Molly settled in her desk chair for a few minutes and hurried down to her office in the basement, and returned a few minutes later.

"Officer Jackson can you bring the recliner from the Lieutenants office

please we need to get Molly settled as much as we can,"
Bill Jackson nodded and hurried to do as he was requested, he returned with the recliner and helped Hallie to move an exhausted and heartbroken Molly, he then disappeared for a few minutes and returned with a blanket from the room they had with beds in for those who were working night shifts.

"here honey, drink this and take these pills, they will help you sleep ok?"
Numbly Molly took the drink of water, downed the pills and turned away from her friend and the 20 other cops who were still in the squad room, soon enough her breathing turned heavy and she slipped into a deep and troubled sleep.

"Any sign of her?" Hallie asked as John walked into the bullpen after he had been back to the scene for the 5th time. he was beyond exhausted, and frustrated.
He shook his head and dropped into Molly's desk chair with a sigh.
"She's never going back to that house, not after what we found" he'd kept their findings from Molly, it would only scare her.
"What did you find?"

"All of her clothes were on her bed, there was semen all over it, semen on the couch and on her pillows, Grace's prints were on the bat so she tried to defend herself, he ambushed her Hallie, I hope he doesn't kill her, this will finish Molly off if she loses Grace now."

rubbing her tired eyes she looked at the sleeping Molly and hoped the same thing.

"how is she doing?" John asked.

Hallie picked up a photo she had printed off from Molly's phone, it was the picture of the two of them in bed, she handed it to John and he sighed when he saw the love and happiness on their faces, he hated that Molly had finally found her soulmate, if Grace was killed Molly wouldn't survive that loss, he had to find her before this fucker killed two people he loved with all his heart.

Chapter 6

2 Months Later

"*DNA from the victims lips matches the samples found at Molly's house, we have his DNA we just don't know who it belongs too, the answer is somewhere in that yearbook, he must have been in Molly's class or at least at her school- have we done a search of all the males at the school when Molly was there, any hits for drug arrests, indecent exposure, burglary anything for fuck sake,*"

John was talking to the room as everyone was crowded round the bullpen, he had called a meeting to crack this case, fast.

Officer Jackson stepped forward and held up his note pad, they had been working non stop since Grace was taken.

It had been 2 Months and Molly was a complete wreck, she was wearing a t-shirt and jeans, which now hung off her as she'd lost more weight, her hair was tied back in a messy ponytail and her eyes were red raw from crying, she was silent and shaking with fear.

"*I've ran a search on all the boys in Molly's class none of them have criminal records, one died after a car accident, there are several boys from the same school who were older than her who have criminal record, we are trying to locate them, but some of them don't have an updated address so they could be anywhere*"

"*Keep on it, we need to find all of them, I want alibi's, and a full house and property search for every single one of them,*"

Officer Jackson nodded and turned to Molly with a sad smile, "We'll find her Molls I promise we will find her"

Molly was holding onto the photo that Hallie had printed out for her, she gave a slight nod back, she hadn't said a word in 2 Months, they were all worried that Molly would give up if Grace died.

Pain tore through her body as she drifted in and out of consciousness, Grace tried to keep her eyes open but the exhaustion was making it difficult, she was laid in a small dark cage with barely any room to move, tears were still dropping onto her cheeks as she thought about Molly, her beautiful girl, she must be beside herself with fear and worry.

After the bastard had whipped her with a belt he had thrown her in a dark room, she'd been there till a few hours ago when he'd thrown her in here and chained the door shut, there were no windows so she couldn't see a way to escape, she didn't even know how long she had been here, she forced herself to sit up despite the pain in her body, she winced as she caught one of the lash marks, fire rippled down her back.

"Fuck" she hissed, when she finally got herself sat up she surveyed her surroundings and tried to see if there was anything she could use as a weapon, she'd lost her gun in the struggle at Molly's house, oh how she wished she had her gun!

Grace was feeling along the floor and felt something cold and hard, it was a metal pole, she picked it up and held it against her chest as she looked out of the metal cage surrounding her.

She gasped at what she saw, there were thousands of pictures of Molly all over the wall, pictures from when she was at school, a happy and beautiful child without a care in the world, to when she lost her family and lived with her Aunt, she'd become so depressed and withdrawn, she had the weight of the world on her shoulders, there were pictures of her at her school graduation, there were various snaps throughout her life, one of them was taken months ago of her and Molly at the crime scene, right before she had collapsed, he'd been watching the whole time.

Grace was looking at all the pictures on the wall when she noticed a picture that was bigger and more pronounced than the rest, it was a picture of the two of them making love in her bed, Molly was laid over her with her lips pressed to Graces neck, giving her a love bite as Grace's head was thrown back in ecstasy, Molly's hand was beneath the sheets as she touched Grace, the passion was written all over their faces, Grace had her hand thrust into Molly's hair her other hand was stroking her breast as they made love.

Oh God- he had been following them, he must have been on the fire escape outside her building, it's why he was enraged, he believed Molly was his, and seeing them making love deviated from that fantasy and made him angry.

Grace continued to search the photos on the wall, hoping to find some evidence of who this Fucker was.

Then suddenly it hit her, there was a school picture of the whole class,

Molly's head was surrounded by a heart, there was someone close by her who was circled, an arrow leading from him to her, now she got it, she understood why he was so obsessed with her, he'd been in love with her since she was a child, he'd been waiting for her to fall in love with him but it had never happened, and then he learned what had happened to her when she was 12, he killed the teachers aid and the two boys for what they had done to her- now he was killing everyone who was mean to her, thinking it was what she wanted, trying to please her so she would fall in love with him, so seeing Grace and Molly making love had tipped him over the edge, so he'd kidnapped Grace as revenge.

"You are one sick asshole," Grace whispered as she cast her eyes around the room, there were 6 metal cages all lined with dirt and hay, filthy rags and what looked like old blankets, a chill in the air made her shiver, she rubbed her exposed skin trying in vain to warm herself.

"Pssst"

Grace jumped at the sound and looked around trying to find where it came from.

"Look to the right honey" came a voice

Grace saw a woman in the cell beside her, she was passing something under the fence.

"Take these blankets honey your gonna need them, get wrapped up"

Grace took the blankets gratefully and wrapped herself up.

"Who are you, what are you doing here?" Grace asked softly, the woman smiled sadly and rested her head on the metal.

"my name is Tessa Wilcox, i've been here a long time, I don't know how long, what month is it? what year?"

"Its 2018, I don't know what Month or date though"

the woman sighed and shook her head, she looked defeated.

"I've been here two years, I was taken in 2016,"

Grace was determined to find out who this man was, she had to find a way out of here and get home to Molly, she missed her already.

"Who is this man Tessa? Why did he take you?"

"I saw something I wasn't supposed too! I was running through the park

when I saw a man carrying a body- a dead body, he spotted me and ran after me, he knocked me out and I woke up here, i've been here ever since, what's your name, why was you taken?" Tessa asked.

"My name is Grace Garrett,This sicko is obsessed with a woman I work with, he's dreamed up this fantasy that he's in a relationship with Molly and he's killing people who have hurt her or stands in his way of being with her"

"Does this Molly love him?"

Grace shook her head as she growled, "No, Molly is my Woman, she's not interested in men, especially not killers" Grace shouted to make sure that he heard her, she was staking her claim once and for all, he needed to know that Molly didn't want him.

"You two are a couple?" Tessa said with a smile, Grace nodded, Tessa smiled back, "You must love each other so much, how long have you worked together?"

"I was transferred over from Missing Persons Unit to Homicide, I fell in love the minute I saw her- she did too, I won't let this sick fuck anywhere near her, I promised her i'd protect her, thats what i'm going to do, i'm going to find a way out of here and go home to the woman I love"

"Tell me about Molly"
Grace smiled as she thought about her only love, she couldn't wait to put her arms around her and just hold her.

"Molly is the most beautiful wonderful woman i've ever met, she's loving and sexy and the most passionate lover, she's my soul mate and I want to marry her when I get out of here"

"I wish I had your ambitions,"
Grace pulled herself up more and looked around, she was determined to get out of here, the dim light in the cellar gave hardly enough light to see anything, but there was illumination coming from a bank of computer screens, it was CCTV footage of Molly's house, and outside of

her loft, she could clearly see the view of her bedroom, the camera was trained onto the bed, so that's how he got the picture of them making love!

The fact he had a camera in Molly's house and aimed into her bedroom at the loft infuriated her, she grabbed the metal pole and began hitting the gate to her cage, pain radiating through her body slowed her down, but she persisted, Tessa winced as she watched Grace hammering at the door to get it open, she saw blood seeping from the lash marks on her back.

"Be careful, don't hurt yourself" Tessa pleaded.

Grace heaved the metal pipe against the gate and she didn't stop until the gate swung open, she looked around to make sure that the man wasn't there, Phew, he wasn't there right now, and hopefully he wouldn't be there anytime soon, Grace stepped out of the cage and searched for a way out, but there several doors throughout the room, all leading to different areas, Shit!

Grace moved in front of the cage and heaved the pipe to smash open Tessa's gate, after several minutes the gate swung open and Tessa sighed with relief.

"Let's find a way out of here" Tessa followed as Grace searched all the doors and rooms, finally she saw a door that led to a staircase going up, a staircase was to the right going down further underground, a cough made Grace freeze, Fuck! He was here after all, but he hadn't heard Grace swinging the pipe to free herself and Tessa.

Grace hurried back to the wall where all the photos were and grabbed the one of Her and Molly in bed, she handed it to Tessa along with what looked like a dvd and a memory card inside a memory card reader.

"Take these and run! Get to the San Francisco Police Department, Homicide on the 5th floor and ask for Detective Molly James, give these to her and no one else"

Tessa took the evidence and began to worry.

"what about you? Aren't you coming?"

"I will be right behind you hun, don't worry, I can't move well right now, but I need to do something before I leave, can you give Molly as message for me?"

Tessa nodded, "Of course I can"

"Molly I Love You and I'm fighting to get home to you, to your arms, I want to spend the rest of my life with you, your my soulmate" tears rolled down Grace's face, Tessa patted her hand kindly, "I'll tell her don't worry"

"Go, before he comes back up"

she watched as Tessa crept up the staircase and pushed open the door to freedom, she breathed a sigh of relief, then walked over to the computers, she worked quickly to set up a link to the computer at the SFPD, she was connecting them so they could try to trace the location without him knowing, she'd also opened up his webcam so they could see what was happening in this room, she just hoped he hadn't used a Proxy Server to bounce his IP Address all over the world.

Once she had done that and made sure that none of it showed on his computer by deleting the history, she made her way toward the room with the staircase out of here, she was about to walk to freedom when he came up from the basement stairs, he saw her and snarled, "Fuck" she said and tried to run, he caught her and hauled her back into the cellar, he grabbed her wrists as she tried to fight him, and he soon had her handcuffed to the pipes above her, Again.

He back handed her hard and she cried out at the pain.

Screams echoed in the dark dank cellar as The Kiss Me Killer picked up his knife and smiled at his next victim- Grace Garrett felt the fear in the pit of her stomach and prayed that her partner and best friend would find her soon, The Kiss Me Killer was angry and she knew he was ready to kill her any second.

"Please don't do this, if you let me go they will stop hunting you I swear it, just please let me go" Grace begged, he sneered and laughed at her request, it was an angry laugh, he was pissed, at her- and at her partner, but she didn't know why.

Tears rolled down her cheeks as she closed her eyes and thought of the one she loved so much, the memory of the day they met fresh in her mind, the bittersweet memory now like a lead weight in her stomach as she realised that they might not find her in time to stop him.

"You think I'm going to let you go? After what you did I don't think so- you are going to pay for what I saw you do" he snapped, as he thrust his face into hers, rage and hatred evident in his eyes.

"I don't know what you mean, you can't get away with this" she sobbed as her body began to sag with exhaustion and fear.

"Liar" he screamed and dragged the knife across her skin in a jagged X over her left breast.

"Aggghhhh, please stop" she screamed in tears, he laughed at her cries of pain.

"What the Fuck do you want from us? Why are you doing this?" she begged, once again she was rewarded with the knife cutting another jagged X on her right breast.

"You know why- she belongs to me and you took her from me, for that i'm going to make you suffer the worst fate, Say Goodnight Grace, you will never see her again, now she's all mine Bitch" he lunged at her with the knife and she screamed with all the strength she had left as she pulled against the restraints that held her tethered to the metal pipes, she thought of Molly and her beautiful smile, and how much she loved her, and how she would be devastated when they finally found her body on the side of the road.

Grace closed her eyes, Conjuring up the image of Molly and their last night together, their laughter, echoing in the bedroom as they made love for the first and last time, the feel her fingertips still tracing her skin.

"I Love You Molly, Forgive Me" Grace whispered as the knife cut deeper with each jagged X.

"Bitch, she's mine" he snapped and struck her hard around the face, her eyes rolled back into her head, and darkness took her under.
Silence filled the room.

"Molly please eat something, you have to keep your strength up," Hallie said as she handed her friend a bag of Taco Bell, she was still withdrawn and more fragile than she was before, her eyes were glassy with unshed tears, her skin was pale and she was extremely thin, she had hardly eaten, a sandwich here and there, but Hallie and John were trying to get food into her.

Molly pushed the bag away and laid her head onto her folded arms, she was tired, scared and missing her best friend, her lover, her soul mate. John had been working the case trying, and they still had no idea who this fucker was, or where he was hiding.

"You will get sick if you don't eat honey, Grace needs you to be strong for her, when she comes home she will need your help, she's going to need a lot of help to heal, please eat the Taco Bell"

Molly grabbed the bag and opened it up, she reached inside for the food and ate it slowly until it was all gone, she then folded her arms and looked at the framed picture of her and Grace, her heart ached, her head constantly pounding with a headache that wouldn't leave.

"Detective James?"

Molly, Hallie and John looked up to see Rissa from the front Desk stood there, she had a disheveled woman with her wearing tatty clothes, she was filthy.

"This woman has asked to speak to you, and you alone, she says its about Grace"

Molly jumped up and went to her, hope in her heart.

"My Grace, where is she?" Molly begged.

John led the woman to a chair and sat her down, he draped a blanket over her.

"Grace saved my life, she was kept in a different room till today, she found a metal pipe and began hitting the cage door until it broke open, she then did the same to my door, we found some stairs and she told me to run, she gave me these to give to you Molly, she asked me to give you a message" Tessa handed the items to Molly, she looked at what she was now holding and frowned at the DVD and the Memory card reader, with a memory card in.

"What was the message, please I have to know if she's ok, where she *is?"*

"Molly I Love You and I'm fighting to get home to you, to your arms, I want to spend the rest of my life with you, your my soulmate"
Molly burst into tears as John embraced her and tried to soothe her broken heart, "She's alive, where is she? Can you take me to her?"

Molly asked, the woman shook her head sadly, "I don't know where I was, I was running through the woods for hours, I have no idea where I came out I just ran-she said she was right behind me but she couldn't move well because of the wounds to her back, they started bleeding again after she hacked her way out of the cage, she said she had something to do before she escaped, I think it was something to do with the computer, here, she asked me to give you this too" the woman handed Molly a photograph, Molly gasped when she saw the picture of her and Grace making love, he'd been watching them at their most intimate moment, the picture was clear and bright, Grace's head thrown back as Molly gave her a love bite, her hands beneath the sheets as she touched her lover, stroking her with passion- her fingers deep inside her, Grace had one hand in her hair, the other covering her breast.

"Oh my god, he's been watching us this whole time, that means he has pictures of me from before Grace was my partner, he's not going to stop, he's going to kill her" Molly whispered as it suddenly dawned on her, Grace was running out of time, they had to find her, before it was too late.

Chapter 7.

Receiving that photo had shaken Molly but it had pulled her out of her silence, Molly left the woman with Hallie so she could have a shower, get some clean clothes and a hot meal, they learned that she had been taken in 2016 after a night time jog in the park had resulted in her witnessing The Kiss Me Killer carrying a dead body, he had gave chase and taken her back to his hiding place.

"Tessa said that Grace was right behind her, but she had something to do, something about his computers? I don't get it- what was she talking about John?" Molly asked with confusion, John huffed as he tried to figure it out, he was watching Molly as she went through her computer, she checked her email, but there was nothing, then she checked her instant message board that was on all the computers, it was designed so the cops could keep in contact with the crime lab and the M.E's office. A link popped up from an unknown server, she and John frowned at each other wondering what it is.

"What do I do?" Molly asked with uncertainty, John took a gamble, reached over for the mouse and clicked the link, a browser opened and a webcam was activated, it was a dark room with poor lighting, it was the same room from in the DVD of Grace being tortured.

Molly gasped as she saw Grace hanging by her wrists from the same pipe as last time, she was unconscious and had blood on the side of her face.

"Oh my darling, what has he done to you baby?" Molly whispered, her face was a mask of pain and desperation. John picked up the phone and called the tech department,

"Anna, this is Lieutenant John Owens from Homicide, I need you down her now, we need you to work your magic and trace an IP Address for me"

"I'll be right down," Anna replied and hung up, he waited for Anna to join them with her computer and everything she needed to track an IP Address, she breezed into the squad room with a smile as she placed her laptop next to Molly's computer and remotely connected to the

system, she copied the link and ran a trace, "Huh"

"what is it?" Molly asked as she watched what Anna was doing, Anna frowned as she tapped a few keys on the keyboard.

"I Can't trace it- he's using a proxy server to bounce across the world, this is going to take weeks to isolate, I have to get through the firewalls this guy has on his computer to isolate where the IP Address is coming from, all of this is encrypted that's why its going to take weeks maybe months to get through." Anna informed them,

Molly pointed to the video on the screen with Grace hanging from the roof of a cellar.

"Grace doesn't have weeks, or months, The Kiss Me Killer is going to strangle the woman I love if we don't find her, soon. Please I'm begging you find out where this Fucking Asshole is so I can shove my fucking Gun in his mouth and blow his brains out!" Molly snapped, Anna gave a frustrated moan and huffed, "I'll do what I can but I cant promise I will find them in less than a week, it's going to take some time" Anna warned, John stepped forward, "Then get to it, whatever you find that can locate Grace we'll take it"

"Ok, I'll call you when I know something"

Anna went back to her floor and got to work, John hoped that she can trace this IP Address, it was their only shot at finding Grace and bringing her home and locking this maniac up for good.

Molly headed down to the autopsy suite where Hallie was going over the bodies once more, hoping that the killer had left a clue.

"Hallie- did Tessa say anything more about Grace?" Molly asked quietly as she watched what her friend was doing.

Hallie smiled at Molly and removed her surgical gloves, she walked over to her and held her by the shoulders.

"Grace said that when she gets out of there she's going to Marry you *and she couldn't wait to make you her wife"*

"I want nothing more than to Marry My Best Friend, My Soul Mate, My Destiny" Molly wiped away the tears, it seemed all she did these last two months is cry, she was desperate to bring her home and find out who this killer was.

"Please tell me you found something?" she asked hopefully, Hallie put on a clean pair of gloves and passed some to Molly, who did the same. They were standing over the body of Kaitlyn Downs, the last victim, whom Molly had a romantic relationship when they were teenagers.

"Put your hand in here and tell me what you feel"

Molly slipped her hand inside the body of Kaitlyn, she felt around until she felt something strange in her stomach.

"She was pregnant?" Molly declared with shock.

Hallie nodded and folded her arms triumphantly.

"All the women were pregnant at the time they were killed, all in different stages of decomposition due to being killed at different times, but they were all pregnant, and they had all been in captivity for some time before death, each woman was held prisoner for at least two months before they were all killed"

"Fuck, how the hell did he know?"

Hallie frowned at that statement.

"You were Pregnant, after them boys raped you you fell pregnant didn't you?" Molly nodded.

"I was about 2 months when I lost the baby, no one knew, even my Aunt Jackie didn't know, I wrote in my diary but that's- oh Fuck, he's been in my house more than once, he's been reading my diary Hallie, thats how he knew everything that happened to me, he has been reading my diary, I have to go, I need to talk to John, thank you Hallie"

Molly called as she ran for the stairs, she felt her heart beating wildly. Running into the bullpen Molly headed straight for her boss, he saw the determination on her face.

"Molly what is it?"

"I know how he knew what happened to me, he knows every aspect of my life since before my parents and sister were killed, my diary, John he's been in my house more than once, he's been reading my diary every time he came into my home. Every one of his female victims were 2 months pregnant at the time of death, after those boys raped me I fell pregnant, I lost the baby at 2 months, no one knew about any of this- he's been stalking me since I was a child, he's broken into my home god knows how many times and read my diary, the last two times he took things from me that mean the world to me, he took my picture of my parents, me and my sister and the yearbook, i'm guessing because he's in it somewhere. And he took Grace, he took her John, but he's not going to kill her, not yet-"

John frowned at that, "How do you know that?" John asked with doubt.

"Because she's a part of me, my soul mate, the last thing we did together-" Molly picked up the picture that Grace sent her from this sickos hideout.

"-This is the last thing we did together, we made passionate love, it's what he craves more than anything, he wants me and Grace has a part of me in her heart, in her soul, if we can figure out who this fucker is from the yearbook you found online then we have a shot at actually stopping him, he's in that yearbook i'm telling you" She said with more clarity than she'd ever felt.

John was shocked by this as he finally realised that Molly was right,

"Print off the entire yearbook Molly, Officer Jackson Put on a pot of coffee, Jane order two large Pepperoni Pizza's, Detective Sanchez And Detective Ortiz can you give us a hand to go through this yearbook"

They got stuck in and kept at it all night and into the next day, they were searching for everyone who was in the year book, one of them was The Kiss Me Killer, they just had to find out which one.

At 9;47am the next morning a call came in that gave them all a sense of dread, a woman's body had been found in Golden Gate Park, near where the others were found, Molly drove there with John, the press were already there shouting questions, John ignored them as he drove through the barricade.

He could see that Molly was shaking with fear, she was afraid that he'd killed Grace.

Walking over to the crime scene tent that surrounded the dead body, Molly felt short of breath and seriously close to tears.

As soon as they stepped inside Hallie walked to them with a reassuring smile, "It's not her," she whispered, Molly let out a breath of relief as the tears began to fall.

Jeez, she needed to get a grip on her emotions, she couldn't find Grace if she was a basket case.

"This one has already been identified, her mother reported her missing 8 Hours Ago, she was meeting with a friend for a double date, only she never showed, her name is Nicole Bradshaw, another student who was in same school, only this one wasn't part of the in crowd"

"I remember her, she was unpopular like me, quiet and had little to no friends, why did he kill her? She never hurt or humiliated me, she was a sweet girl who kept to herself" Molly stated.

"Maybe it has something to do with this" Hallie said as she lifted the woman's shirt, a message had been carved into her stomach.

Be Mine and your Lover will Live!!

Holy Fuck, he wanted to trade her life for Grace's life.
He would let her go if Molly took her place, but if Molly took her place then she couldn't Marry her, but she wasn't about to leave her Beautiful girl in the clutches of a madman, she was going to save Grace no matter what it took. She knew John would never agree to her trading places, so she had to do it on her own terms.

Molly returned to the station and went straight to her computer to see if the webcam was still active, she hoped Grace was alive, her heart was racing as she sat down,

Grace was still handcuffed to the pipes above, she was barely conscious, her head hanging to the side, Molly reached out and placed her hand on the screen, she stroked her fingertips over the image of her love.

"I'm going to find you Baby, I promise. I'm going to get you out of

there" Molly whispered as she felt her heart break all over again.

Molly turned to the pictures of all the victims and tried to figure out who The Kiss Me Killer was, she looked through the list of suspects that they couldn't locate, and something hit her, she jumped up from her seat and ran to John's office where he was talking to the Chief of Detectives, he was asking for more man power in the search for Grace.

"John, I think I know who this guy is, I have to go to my house, Now!" John promised to call the Chief back and hung up.

"I'll drive"

Anger coursed through Molly's veins as she threw open her front door and stormed up the stairs, John was right behind her, following as she pulled down the hatch for the attic, the ladder dropped down and she climbed up into the dark space, John flipped on the light switch.

"Molly what are you looking for?"

Molly grabbed a step and reached up to the top shelf of an old bookcase, she pulled a big box down and took the lid off, she dug through the pile of paperwork and pulled out a stack of letters, and a school photograph, she handed the photograph and letters to John, she was seething.

"Ethan Hackett, he was in my class until he stopped coming to school, he was a very strange boy, had no friends and was obsessed with death, he kept writing me love letters about how when we die our souls can lie together forever, he was always waiting for me outside my house, after the fire he started following me back to my Aunt Jackie's house, Ethan

Hackett is The Kiss Me Killer"

"Grab Everything, let's go, we need to find Ethan Hackett"

"You won't find him, he wants me John, he will let Grace go if I trade places with her, I have to take her place or he will kill her, I can't let

him hurt the woman I love,"

John stared at her as though she had lost her mind, "Hell No, we will find Grace, and we will find Ethan Hackett, but i'm not going to let you offer yourself up as bait to a serial killer Molly, not a chance in hell!"

"We may not have another choice, he's been one step ahead the whole time, he's not going to screw up now-" Molly snapped as she headed for the ladder, she left the attic leaving John shaking his head in frustration.

Chapter 8.

 Back at the station Molly was sat at her desk watching the webcam as John held a meeting in the bullpen, everyone was silent as he explained the new information.

"This man is Ethan Hackett, he was in Molly's class until he stopped going to school, he was obsessed with death, and he's obsessed with Molly, he wrote her disturbing love letters, he was stalking her from a young age, and we believe he has continued to to stalk her. Ethan Michael Hackett is The Kiss Me Killer, find him, search his home, his car his place of work, I want to know what this guy has been doing with his life, how he has made his living- find his parents talk to them and find out if this bastard has any skeletons in his closet, I want this Fucker in custody yesterday, get to it everyone, Grace is Family lets bring her home before he kills her"

The room divided into teams quickly as they all headed out to find the man responsible for all this, John was working on getting warrants for his home, car workplace and any other place he might own, finally, they were one step closer to closing this case and saving Grace's life.
Molly was teamed up with Officer Lucy Grant, a woman who was openly gay and made her attractions obvious, she kept sneaking glances at Molly as they headed to Ethan Hackett's parents house before they searched his house.

Molly walked up to the front door of an old run down clapboard house, the house hadn't seen a lick of paint in years, and the sound of someone shuffling to the front door meant someone was home.

"Can I help you?" a frail man asked as he took in the uniformed Officer and the woman by her side.
Molly held up her badge and introduced herself.

"Mr Hackett i'm Detective Molly James, i'm here about your son Ethan,

may we come in?"

"Of Course" he stepped back and let them inside, despite the rundown appearance of the outside the inside was well cared for, and had a few bright cheerful colours.

"What has that screw up done this time?" Mr Hackett asked as he struggled to sit on the chair in his kitchen, he looked frail and out of breath, Molly suspected he had cancer from years of smoking.

"Mr Hackett your son is a suspect in 8 murders, dating back to when he was at school, I was in your sons class, he was obsessed with me and started to follow me home, I believe he started killing people who hurt me as a way to get close to me,"

the man looked stunned but not surprised by this news, he nodded and sat back.

"I remember you Miss James, I'm sorry for what happened to your family, your baby sister- it never should have happened, your parents were a wonderful couple,"

Molly smiled sadly, "Thank you for that, it means the world that someone remembers them for who they were, Mr Hackett Ethan Killed a teachers aid and two 15 year old boys when we were in school for a sexual assault they carried out on me, their bodies were found 2 months ago in Golden Gate Park, 5 more bodies have been left in the park with the same wounds, his DNA was on all the victims, but his DNA isn't in the database and he has no criminal record, we have to find him before he hurts someone else, Ethan Abducted a Police Detective and he's holding her hostage now, he's torturing her and we need to get to him before he kills her"

Mr Hackett hung his head and gave a sigh of sadness, the news that his only son was murdering people was weighing on his heart heavily. "I haven't seen Ethan in 10 years, not since his mother passed away- he was a difficult and disturbed child, he had an obsession with you and that was bad enough, you were just a child and so was he, but his love of fire took over his life, he was hiding boxes and boxes of matches in his room, when I found out I took them and threw them in the sewer so he couldn't get them, he was violent and very smart, I always suspected he had something to do with the fire at your house, but I had no proof it was him,"

Molly felt her heart tighten with pain, Ethan had killed her parents and baby sister, this hurt her more than she ever though possible.

"Can we see Ethan's room? " Molly asked quietly,

"I packed his room up 10 years ago, it's all there by the wall. everything he owned is in them boxes, take them and do what you can to find him "

"Thank you, Sir " Molly stood up and headed for the boxes, she picked two up so did Officer Grant.

"Miss James, this woman he abducted, she's someone special isn't she? "

Molly nodded. "Yes Sir, she's the love of my life " Standing up and walking over to a kitchen drawer he retrieved a black velvet bag and took it to her.
He placed it in her jacket pocked because she had her hands full.

"Take this, its something that Ethan wanted but I always refused to hand over, he doesn't deserve it, but you do, take it with you and know that your future isn't over, Find Ethan and stop him from hurting people, if you cant stop him, then kill him. I must rest now, I need my Oxygen "he walked away as they were leaving the house through the kitchen door at the side of the house, after loading the boxes into the back of the car they headed to Ethan's apartment in a bad part of town.

As they parked their car around the corner from Ethan Hackett's Apartment Molly turned to Officer Grant and gave her a subtle warning.

"I don't know if he's even going to be here, be on guard and have your weapon ready in case he tries to shoot, don't let him get away and if you don't have a clear shot aim for his leg, he can't run with a bullet in his leg, got it! " the uniformed Officer nodded and pulled her weapon, removing the safety, Molly already had hers at her side as they climbed the stairs to his apartment on the 3rd floor.

Molly banged on the door and called out "Ethan Hackett- San Francisco Police Department Open the Door "
they waited but heard nothing, she knocked again, still nothing.
The sound of footsteps made them turn, John appeared holding a piece of paper.

"here's the warrant for his apartment, what did the parents say?"

"Mother died 10 years ago, father hasn't seen him since, he suspects that Ethan was responsible for the fire that killed my family, right now i'm thinking he may be right, we need to buildings super to open the door,"

John held up a set of keys, "The Super is in a wheelchair, knee surgery so he can't walk right now, I showed him the warrant and he said to go in a do what we need to do"

Molly took the keys and managed to get the right key on the fourth try.

"Ethan Hackett, SFPD," she called out again, they all entered and stopped dead when they saw the floor to ceiling picture spread of Molly through out the room, every piece of the walls were covered in images of her from being a small child, to when she lost her family, to her out working crime scenes at different locations across San Francisco, he had been following her everywhere, he even had pictures of her wearing nothing but a towel, or a silk nightie as she laid on the sofa watching a film, the various images of her in different parts of her house gave her chills, from the angles it looked like he had taken them from inside the house, then it dawned on her, cameras, he had cameras in her house somewhere, that was the only explanation she had for how he had pictures of her in the shower, there were no windows to see through in her bathroom, the glass was frosted so he couldn't get pictures from through there.

"This is Fucking creepy, he's had cameras in my house the whole time"

"You are not living in that house anymore Molly"

"Agreed!"

they searched the place and tried to find a clue as to where he was hiding.

"Well we definitely have the right suspect, now we just need to find out where he's hiding"

Molly was searching through paperwork when her cell phone beeped, she saw a txt from an unknown number, so she opened it to see who it was, it was a picture of Grace, she was tied to a table and had multiple cuts to her body, she was wearing nothing but her underwear, her face showing pain and fear, a txt followed.

Unknown Number: Don't say a word, I'm Watching You, follow the GPS Coordinates i've sent you, come to me and she lives! Tell anyone I will kill her and you wont see her again

Looking over her shoulder she saw that her boss and the rookie were deep into the search.

Molly: Ethan, I can help you, let Grace go and I will come to you please just don't hurt her.

Unknown Number: Come to me first, I may let you say goodbye before I release her

Molly: Ok! I'm on my way

"I'm just going to get some air for a few minutes, be right back"
John nodded as she left the apartment.

   Walking out of the apartment building, Molly climbed into her car and entered the GPS Co-ordinates into the Sat Nav, she set off and hoped he kept his word and let Grace go.
An hour later she pulled up outside the entrance to Golden Gate Park, her phone beeped as a new txt msg came through.

Unknown Number: Leave the car, keep walking until you reach the Willow Tree, by the Lake, then turn your phone off and take the blindfold off of the tree branch and put it on!

Molly: I need your word that you will Let Grace go, and that you will let me have some time with her to say goodbye?

Unknown Number: You have my word!

Molly walked through the park until she reached the Willow tree, the lake close by gave a picture perfect view, Molly turned off her phone and picked up the blindfold as instructed and put it on, she wasn't sure how long she was waiting when a hand landed on her shoulder.

"Walk, I'll guide you, hand over your phone" Ethan said, Molly handed over her phone, he took it and threw it onto the grass, he guided her towards the trees and into the thick dense forest that led to a shaded path, hidden deep behind the green expanse of trees.

Molly stayed silent as she was taken to his secret place, the sound of a heavy wooden door opening was making her feel nervous, she was guided down a staircase and into a room that smelled musty and damp, he pushed her into a metal cage and chained the door behind her, walking away in silence and leaving her blindfolded.

She waited for Ethan to speak as she waited in the darkness but no sound came, she was starting to get worried when the sound of someone moving in front of her startled her, she was about to ask who was there when small delicate hands cupped her face and stroked her tenderly, happiness surged through her as she ripped the blindfold off and gazed into the deep ocean blue eyes that belonged to Grace.

"Grace, oh my sweet darling girl, I've missed you so much baby" Molly threw her arms around her and held her tight, Grace was clinging tightly as Molly ran her hands over her body, checking for injuries, Grace was wearing nothing but her underwear, she was filthy and cold, and had dried blood on the side of her face, her back was covered in belt marks that was still healing, Molly hated this fucker for what he'd done to her, Molly reached for her hip and was relieved to still feel her gun there, she removed it and hid it under a pile of rags in the corner of the cage, she removed her jacket and sweater and draped them over her, she was determined to get her warm, she pulled her bruised face into her and kissed her passionately, Grace climbed into her lap and wrapped her arms around her lover, she buried her face into her neck and breathed her in.

"I Love You So Much Molly Rose James, Will You Marry Me, Be Mine, Forever-Always" Grace said as she held her lips over hers, Molly smiled as she placed her hand over Grace's heart.

"I Want Nothing More Than To Marry You, I Love You So Much Grace Alora Garrett, I'm Marrying you and i'm going to give you all that I am, all that I feel and we are going to spend the rest of our lives together, *laughing, Making Love, having a family together."*

Grace reached down to Molly's Jeans and unzipped them, she slipped her hand inside of her panties and stroked her deeply, Molly gasped as she felt the woman she loved touching her intimately, Molly did the same as she took Grace's lips in a kiss so deep and passionate that tears fell from their eyes, it had been two months since they made love for the first time, Molly had been lost and aching with out her by her side, Grace didn't know that Molly was here to take her place, it would break her heart once she knew that, Molly made love to her with as much love and urgency as she could, their bodies began to shake as they caressed one another, taking their love to heights they had never felt before.

"I Love You, I Love You, I Love You" Molly Breathed as they climaxed together and wrapped themselves around each other and held on tight.

"Times up!"

Grace's head shot up, they had fallen asleep moments after they made love, "What? No, Molly no you cant take my place, I won't let you"

Grace sobbed as she held onto her, the cage opened and Graces clothes were thrown in.

"Get Dressed, Now!"

Molly grabbed the clothes and dressed her quickly as Grace finally realised why she was here.

"Molly Please No, you can't do this. I Love Her Please Don't Take Her From Me"

Molly grabbed her hands and pulled her close, she kissed her and whispered against her lips, "I'll Always Love You Grace, I'm with you wherever you go, Goodbye my Beautiful Girl" Tears were streaming down their faces as he reached in a grabbed Grace, he placed a blindfold over hey eyes and dragged her away, Molly sobbed as she heard Grace crying out for her.

The sound of John shouting through the squad room echoed as everyone sat stunned into silence, Molly had been Missing for 12 hours, she'd left Ethan Hackett's apartment to get some air, or so she said, but she never came back, her cell phone was switched off and they couldn't track her, her signal had faded once she reached Golden Gate Park, two uniforms where there now searching for her phone and hopefully they could find out where he was holding them.

"What the Fuck was she thinking, someone- anyone tell me where the fuck she was when the signal went dead, how did he lure her out of the apartment?"

Anna from the tech department walked into the room, she held up some papers and gave them to John.

"He txt her from a burner phone, sent her messages with Co-Ordinates that led to the park, he told her to meet him at the Willow Tree by the Lake, she had to wait for him there, i'm guessing he led her from there to where ever he is hiding, I think they are in the park somewhere"

Hallie stepped forward, "That would explain how he's dumping bodies and getting out without being seen, he must have a house or shed or something in the park where he can hide his victims and have complete privacy"

John looked at the white board and realised that she was right, he would need complete privacy and enough space to hold his victims until he was finished with them.

"Pull all the plans for Golden gate park, I want to know every square inch of that place, I want to know if theres any tunnels, basements, storm drains- this asshole has my two best detectives, he's killed 8 people and he could kill more, this ends, NOW!"

As John was dividing up sections of the Park to his entire squad room ready for a grid search he became aware of the elevator doors opening, he turned and gasped when he saw Grace fall forward and collapse to the floor, she was badly beaten, thin and filthy, her eyes were glassy as she tried to force herself to her feet, Hallie ran to her and checked her over, "Call an Ambulance now, she's been drugged" John picked up the phone and called for help, then ran to Grace as she began to cry with sadness.

"Grace, Honey it's ok your safe now, did you see Molly?" Grace nodded and sobbed harder.

"My Molly- My Beautiful Girl, He took her, he traded my place with

Molly, he wont let her go, I want her back! please help her" Hallie held her as she cried, until she passed out from whatever Ethan had drugged her with.

With the whole department out searching every square inch of The Park, the press camped outside the Hospital and his best Detective in the hands of a mad man, Grace drugged and traumatized John had never felt so useless.

Grace was starting to come round from the drugs she been given, her whole body was twitching and the sound of her cries in her sleep broke his heart, she was constantly calling out for Molly, he reached for her hand and held it gently.

Chapter 9

"Molly, Let her go please" Grace whispered frantically in her sleep,
she was still twitching badly, shaking as though someone was still
attacking her.
She'd been in the hospital for 4 days, heavily sedated and on a host of
Anti- Biotics after the wounds became badly infected.
Grace's eyelids fluttered open open as she finally came too, she
grabbed John's hand with urgency and stared him directly in the eyes.

"Where is she? Where's Molly? Find her John- Don't you Dare Leave
Her Out There With Him, Get Her Out Of There, I Want My Fiancee
Back" Grace Begged as she gritted her teeth through the pain, Grace
was very weak and slightly malnourished after 2 months in captivity.
John flinched when he heard Grace refer to Molly as her Fiancee, now
more than ever he had to find Molly and bring her home.

"We are doing everything we can to find her Grace, I promise, please
just rest your extremely weak" "Fuck That!"
Grace pushed the covers back and climbed out of the hospital bed, John
tried to stop her but she pushed him away, she screamed at the pain in
her back. there were some clean clothes on a chair with her sneakers
underneath, she walked into the bathroom to dress.

"Grace get back into bed, your not strong enough to be up yet" Grace
ignored him as she quickly washed her hair, then braided it over her
shoulder.

"where's my cell phone?" John reached into his jacket and pulled her
phone out, she took it and turned it on, she breathed a sigh of relief as
she saw the photos were still there, the pictures she'd taken after they
made love for the first time meant everything to her, she held the phone
to her chest and made a silent vow, she was on the hunt now, she was
going to search the whole city until she found Molly.
Dr Henry walked in and thrust his hands on his hips.

"What are you doing Ms Garrett?"

"A Killer has the woman I Love, I'm going after this asshole once and
for all, get me the release papers and any medication I need, I'm outta

here"

Dr Henry shook his head and went to get her the papers, he returned 10 minutes later with the papers, which she dutifully signed, he passed her a package of medications, which she took with a sad smile, "Thank you

Dr Henry, I just can't sit here while a serial killer is hurting my Love" he nodded his understanding with sympathy.

"I understand, I hope you can find her before he kills her, take it easy and take them pills twice a day till the course if finished, I added painkillers too, use them"

with a grateful hand to his shoulder, she thanked him again and walked away.

"Take me to Golden Gate Park" Grace asked as she climbed carefully into the car, "Grace" John said as she watched her hissing through the pain, she pulled out the painkillers and took one before they set off, he handed her a bottle of water which she drained quickly.

"Molly traded her life for mine, I'm going out there and i'm going to find her, Drive" she snapped as she latched her seatbelt.

Once they reached the park Grace headed for where Molly's cell phone was located by the lake.

Hallie frowned when she saw Grace heading for her with a determined look on her face.

"Grace you need to be in the hospital honey" Hallie said with concern.

"No Fucking Way, I'm Bringing Molly Home"

Hallie looked to John who shrugged his shoulders back at her.

"What do we have?"

"Molly's cell phone was found here, we are trying to figure out where he could have taken her from here, there no houses, sheds, tunnels or storm drains, none that we have found anyway, I'm starting to think maybe he stashed her somewhere else, use the park as a cover then take her somewhere else that we haven't found yet"

Grace shook her head as she looked around.

"No, he's here somewhere, where are you, you Son of a Bitch" Grace walked toward the trees that lay at the edge of the forest, John and Hallie were right behind her.

As she walked in deeper she saw Molly's jacket on the floor, Molly had wrapped her in it to keep her warm, she had kept it when he led her from his hideout, but she dropped it as she was guided through the woods.

Grace reached into the pocket and found a black velvet bag with a box inside, she pulled it out and opened it, inside was a beautiful gold Necklace, the light blue diamonds sparkling in her grasp, tears fell from her eyes as she closed the box and slipped the bag back into the pocket, and put the jacket on.

"I'm coming Molly, I'm coming baby"

Grace took off into the woods, she searched every clearing, every area with disturbed ground, she was certain that she was underground while in captivity, the pain in her back was getting worse, her head was pounding, her scars were burning.

Hours passed and exhaustion was making her feel dizzy, but she refused to give up the search, a light rain started to fall as they went deeper into the woods, they soon found a dirt path that led to a hill side- in the side of the hill Grace saw a door hidden by tree branches and leaves.

"John, Hallie, I found it!" Grace called, she pushed all the debris aside and pulled the door open.

Grace hurried inside and down the stairs to a dark room, John was there with her, he handed her her gun and a flashlight, he pulled his gun and turned on his flashlight.

"Ethan Hackett, SFPD" John called, Grace ran over to the cages and pulled open the doors, the cages were empty, Molly was gone.

"Molly, Molly can you hear me" Grace shouted as loud as she could, she raced through the cellar, room by room as she searched for Molly and the Serial Killer who murdered 8 people.

"Fuck!" Grace snapped as she slammed the door to the cage, "We're too late, he's taken her"

John turned to Hallie and gave her a pointed look, "Get CSU down here, I want this whole place lit up and dusted for prints, hair fibres

DNA I want to know where this bastard was and where he is going"

Grace walked over to the wall of pictures she's seen before Molly traded places with her, she looked at the wall of pictures, she noticed something different, a new picture that was added recently, a picture of Molly wearing a filthy yellow dress, her hair was in pigtails, she was covered in dirt and her face was bruised and swollen on the left side, she also had bruises all over her body, he'd beaten her violently, the sight of bruises on her body made Grace see red, she ripped the picture off the wall and stormed out of the cellar, ignoring the pain in her back she made her way back to the willow tree where her cell was left.

"Officer Grant, you were the one who took Molly to the fathers house?"

she asked, Officer Grant looked up and nodded, "Yes Detective," she said sweetly.

"Take me there, NOW"

Officer Grant led her to her squad car and drove her to a house 6 miles away, she kept glancing at Grace and giving her a seductive smile, "I'm so glad your ok Grace, we have all been so worried about you"
Grace rolled her eyes as she ignored the comment, the young Officer was flirting with her.

"Just Drive, I don't know how much time Molly has left" Grace answered coldly. She noticed that the Officer frowned at her reply,

"She's probably already dead" Officer Grant muttered under her breath,

Grace shot her a dark look, "Keep your mouth shut!! I don't appreciate your assumptions Officer Grant, Molly James is a Detective with the SFPD, she's a fantastic Detective, and a wonderful woman, she's beautiful and loving, she's my Fiancee and i'm going to find her, now drive to Hackett's fathers house" Grace said sternly, biting her tongue the young Officer said

"Yes Detective Garrett"

Grace knocked on the door to Ethan Hackett's father house, the man opened the door a few minutes later, he looked tired and out of breath.

"Mr Hackett, I'm Detective Grace Garrett, SFPD, I need to speak to you about your son"

Edward Hackett let them in, he glance at the Officer and scowled at her.

"Is he dead yet? Miss James came to me and told me what he'd done, I hate that boy for what he's done-"

Grace stepped up to him and looked him in the eye.

"Mr Hackett, 2 months ago your son kidnapped me, Molly James came to you for help in finding him, Molly traded herself for me so he would let me go, "Grace handed him the photo of Molly in the dress and beaten black and blue.

"This is what he's doing to her, the cellar he was using is empty, he's taken Molly and we don't know where they are, we need your help sir, does he have any other hiding places? is there a place he used to go as a child that he could be keeping her? Please Mr Hackett I know he's your son but he's killed 8 people because he is obsessed with Molly, he has her now and he's hurting her"

Tears rolled down his face as he looked at the photo with disgust, he sat down heavily and sighed as he rubbed his tired face.

"He and his sister used to play in an old cave in the woods, but i'm not sure if its still there, it may have caved in, he had a thing for hiding in dark places"

Grace's eyes opened wide. "He had a sister? Where is the sister now?"

"Kristin died, a long time ago she was as disturbed as he was, they were both violent, and they both love guns"

"Do you have a picture of them both?"

he pointed to a picture on the table in the living room, Grace picked it up and gasped when she saw a familiar face, she turned to Mr Hackett and looked around, Officer Grant was gone.
She pulled out her cell and called John.

"John, Officer Grant is Ethan Hackett's sister, she's his partner in this, she's been helping him"

"Tell me your Fucking Kidding?" John shouted down the phone.

"Put out and APB on Officer Lucy Grant, I want her brought in for questioning"

Grace looked the father in the eyes and snarled at him as he stood there with a smile on his face.

"You sick Son of a Bitch, you lied to Molly, and your lying to me now, Where the Fuck is Ethan Hiding her, Tell Me Now or so help me god I will put this gun in your mouth and pull the Fucking trigger, now tell me where he is"

Mr Hackett laughed as she stood there, he was finding this all very amusing.

"You won't find them" he sneered evilly as she picked up a picture of his wife and her ashes, it was obvious that he adored his wife, "Don't you touch that!" he snapped at her, Grace held the box of ashes up and gave him a level stare.

"Where are they?"

"Fuck You" he seethed.

Grace grabbed him by the collar and led him into the kitchen, John burst in through the front door and walked over to them.

"Where are they?" she shouted

"FUCK YOU" he spat. John saw what Grace had in her hands, he raised his eyebrows in surprise.

"Last chance asshole, tell me where your son and daughter are hiding" he said nothing, but he tried to grab the box of his wife's ashes, John held him back, Grace turned on the water and went to pour the ashes down the sink.

"Bitch"

Grace moved in real close to him and got in his face, she gave him the most hateful look as she told him what he was about to experience.

"you are going to jail, and your going to spend the next 20-years on your hands and knees being fucked by every man in there, who's the bitch now, Take Him Away"
his face went pale as he realised that she was right , he was going to jail and he couldn't do anything to stop that.

Feeling Numb and cold in the darkness Molly curled up into a ball and tried to get warm, she shivered as she pulled the blankets around her battered body, the small yellow sun dress doing nothing to cover her almost bare skin as the dress only just covered her butt.
Sadness filled her heart as she clung to the memory of Grace Loving her, touching her, asking Molly to Marry her, she cherished that memory, Molly was chained up in a small dog cage in what looked like an underground cave, it was freezing cold and the only light came from Lanterns hung on the stone walls, Molly was frozen to the bone as she watched what Ethan was doing at his work table in the corner, he was clipping photos he had printed out before they had to leave the cellar, his phone beeped in his pocket.

Lucy: They are onto us!

Ethan: Fuck, What Happened?

Lucy: That Bitch Figured it Out, Dad Arrested! Police Looking For Me!

Ethan: So you Fucked Up! I've spent Years planning this so I can finally be with Molly, and you Fuck it up! Where are you?

Lucy: In hiding, theres a warrant out for my arrest, i'll come to you as soon as I can. What are you going to do with your girlfriend?

Ethan: She stays with me, keep your head down and get here safely!

Lucy: You Got it Big Brother.

Placing his phone on his desk Ethan turned to Molly and walked over to the cage and unlocked the door.

"Do you think we can try this again? After all a Husband and Wife need to Consummate their marriage, and we were so rudely interrupted before we got a chance to make love"
Molly snorted with disgust.
"It's not Love Asshole, It's Rape! And if I find out you touched Grace in any way I will kill you!" she said hatefully, he reached into the cage and pulled her out after removing her shackles, he dragged her to a box spring bed with a filthy and mouldy mattress on top, Ethan back handed her, Hard and she landed on the bed with a groan, the taste of blood in her mouth made her gag.
"That's no way to talk to your husband" he snarled at her, Molly looked him dead in the eye.
"I'm not your wife- I will never be your wife, I'm Marrying Grace the woman I love, so you can get Fucked, because you will never have me!" Molly told him Defiantly, she stood inches from him as she stood up to him, she could see that he hated that, so he pushed her backwards onto the mattress. "You belong to me Bitch, your mine"
he started to pull her dress off but she fought him as much as she could,
"Your mine, I wont let you near that Bitch again" he shouted at her, she bit his arm hard and he howled with pain. "Fuck You Dick Head" she yelled at him and brought her knee up into his groin, he doubled over with pain as he grabbed his crown jewels, Molly pushed him off and she leapt to her feet, she grabbed a piece if wood off the floor and hit him in the head, knocking him out cold.
Molly bolted for the only entrance she could see and ran through the tunnels until she saw light ahead, it was her way to freedom, she left the dark tunnels and found herself running through the trees that led into the park, she glanced over her shoulders to make sure he wasn't following her, he wasn't. She carried on running and passed a few Joggers and people taking their dogs for a walk in the rain.
As she ran through the park and onto the street she breathed a sigh of

relief when she spotted a police car.

She made a Beeline for it and the Officer saw her running and climbed out of his cruiser.

"Miss, are you hurt?" he asked with concern, Molly tried to catch her breath as she reached out for him, he retrieved a blanket from the trunk of his car and wrapped it around her.

"I'm Detective Molly James, Homicide, I was being held by a serial killer we were hunting, I need you to get me back to my squad room, Now" she begged, his eyes widened as he realised who she was, he'd heard that she was missing and that every cop was looking for her.

"Get in Detective, I'll drive you back right now" he answered, he reached for his radio to let them know she had been found, but she stopped him.

"Please don't, he's been watching me for years, he might be listening too" she said with fear, he nodded and drove to the station as quickly as he could.

"Thank you for taking me back,"

Officer Daniels smiled at her, "You don't need to thank me Detective, I'm happy to have been able to help, do you have someone waiting for you at the station, family? Husband?"

Molly smiled as she thought about who was waiting for her.

"My Fiancee, Grace, she's my best friend, my soul mate"

Officer Daniels smiled at her again. "Lucky Woman, let's get you Home then shall we, we're almost there"

Chapter 10

It was 1:45pm and Grace was back at her desk and going through Officer Grant's Jacket and the files they had obtained from the Psychiatrist that had seen Kristin Hackett from age 2 until she was 13 when she had supposedly died in a drowning accident while camping with family and friends.
Once Dr Merrill had the warrant in his hand he happily handed over the files and all information regarding Kristin's case.

"So from what i'm reading of Dr Merrill's notes he suspected that Kristin was being sexually abused by not just the father but the big brother as well, Young Ethan had his fingers in a lot of pies, it says here that she was referred at age 2 for aggressive sexual behaviour, and the Dr worked with her until she died at age 13 after a drowning accident while camping with friends and family. After the funeral he never heard from the family again and their phone was cut off"
Grace handed over a picture that Kristin had drawn when she was 5, the sexual content of the picture made John feel sick as he turned the picture over so he didn't have to look at it again.

"How anyone can do this to a child is beyond me, ok so Kristin died at 13 years old from a drowning accident, so how did Kristin change her name and live her life from age 13, then get onto the police force?"
Grace asked as they went through the paperwork.

"Obviously she lied on all the tests, we need to find out where she lives and go over her place top to bottom, she has to be keeping in contact with Ethan somehow, get a warrant for her cell phone and her home and car,"John replied, Grace nodded as she reached for the picture of her and Molly, she traced her fingertips over the image of Molly's smile and felt her heart break, she was starting to lose hope of ever finding her, she was aching so badly to have her in her arms,she missed the sound of Molly's voice, her smile that lit up the room when she was in there, the gentle cries of pleasure as they made love, Grace wiped away a stray tear as she pulled the picture close against her chest and sighed with sadness, she wanted nothing more than to have her back, to feel her soft skin against hers and the feel of her lips as they kissed

she missed her so much. *"How you doing Kiddo?"* John asked softly, Grace shrugged with sadness.

"I want her Back!" she said as tears fell down her cheeks.

"We'll find her Honey" he soothed as she cried quietly.

Suddenly her heart began to pound, her skin was tingling, she only felt like this when Molly was near, it was as though she could feel her at all times, it was an intoxicating feeling, Grace began to feel as though Molly was there with her.

"John, there's someone here for Grace" Jane the receptionist called out with a smile, he frowned at her when he saw the smile. the room went deadly silent as the doors opened, Grace turned and gasped when she saw Molly stood there, with an Officer by her side.

"MOLLY! MY BABY, OH DARLING, MY BEAUTIFUL GIRL"

Grace cried as she shot out of her seat and ran to her, Molly met her half way across the squad room and they threw their arms around each other, Grace thrust her hands into her hair as she kissed her with all the passion she felt for her, her hands then travelled down her body to her ass and she hauled Molly into her arms, wrapping her legs around her as Molly let her tongue stroke Grace's, she kept her hands in Grace's hair as she tried to get closer, Molly was soaked through but Grace didn't care, her baby was home, the whole room erupted in applause as their kiss turned erotic, and they had an audience, but they didn't care. *"I Love You, I Love You, I Love You So Fucking Much My Beautiful Baby"*

"I Love You Grace, Marry Me, I Can't Wait to Make You My Wife" Molly breathed against her lips, Grace smiled as she licked her lips seductively, she knew it turned Molly on when she did that.

"I'm Marrying You Today, I Can't Wait Either, We're Getting Married Now" she breathed back and took her lips in a toe tingling kiss.

"Jane, get a Marriage Licence, Hallie your on wedding bands, we need flowers and cake, and a reception area" John called out to the room, Officer Daniels stepped forward.

"Sir, my father owns a bar, my sister has a wedding company, come with me and I can get it all sorted for this afternoon," John looked at the young Officer and smiled great fully.

"Done, Officer Jackson can you get a Minister sorted for 4pm please" he nodded and hurried out of the room.

"OK People, we have a wedding to pull together, let's get cracking, you two love birds, wedding dresses, and no peeking at what each other is wearing, its bad luck!" Molly laughed as she snuggled into Grace's arms, John kissed her on the head, and then he kissed Grace on the cheek.

He followed Officer Daniels to his car outside, and they set off for his sisters wedding company two blocks away, the bar was across the street from the company.

Jane left seconds later to get a Marriage Licence as quickly as possible, Hallie was fast on her heels as she headed out to get wedding bands for her friends.

Grace finally put Molly on her feet and brushed her lips tenderly, "Go to the Locker Rooms and take a shower, I have some clean clothes on my locker, get dressed then we can go and get our wedding dresses, after today your all mine" Grace whispered, "Oh Baby, I was yours the moment I saw you" Molly told her and kissed her gently, then she walked away towards the locker rooms, to get cleaned up.

A half hour later Molly was dressed in a pair of thick jeans, and a sweater, and wearing Grace's boots as they left the station via the garage and drove to a Wedding Dress Shop not far away, Grace turned up the heat to get her warm, but Molly preferred to snuggle up against her body and take in her heat instead, Molly was still shivering as she wrapped her hands around Grace's arm as she drove, Grace kept leaning down to kiss her, and as they pulled up outside Wedding Boutique Molly couldn't wait any longer, she crawled out of her seat and took Grace's mouth in a kiss so urgent and deep.

"Let's go inside and find our dresses" Grace breathed with heat, she was desperate for her, her body almost shaking with the urge to bury her fingers deep inside her lover.

As Grace climbed out of the car Molly was still in her arms, kissing her and making those small moans that turned her on, Grace hated to put her down but they didn't have long to get their dresses.

"Good Afternoon Ladies, How May we Help You Today at Wedding Boutique"

"We are getting Married Today, and we need dresses, I know its last minute but we don't have a lot of time"

Grace said as kindly as possible.

"Come with me my love we will get you the best dresses you could find, Elizabeth is my assistant, she will assist you girl in her choice of dresses, Elizabeth dear, take this lovely lady to suite 1 and get a rack of dresses lined up, we will be in suite 2"

Elizabeth nodded and led Molly away to a different section, not before they shared another kiss, the two women smiled sweetly at them.

"That's just too beautiful"

Molly Followed Elizabeth into a changing suite and waited as she measured her for the perfect dress, "I think I have the perfect dress for you" she smiled as she hurried out, then returned with a a rack of 10 dresses for her to try on.

Molly undressed and pulled the first dress off the hanger, but it wasn't right for her, she looked through the dresses but none of them were her style, but then she saw the dress on a mannequin to the side, her mouth dropped open as she got closer to it, it was a beautiful Stella York Dress that was satin with lace over the bodice, and a simple waistline that would fit her perfectly.

"I Don't Care How Much, This is the Dress" Molly said as she turned to Elizabeth, the woman beamed and gave her a wink, "You have impeccable taste, let's try it on to make sure it fits"

Molly helped her remove it from the mannequin and take it to the changing stall, when she came out a few minutes later wearing the stunning dress, the look on her face made it clear that this is the dress.

"This is the one, I'll take it" Molly said with happiness, Elizabeth nodded with pride.

"Lets get this stunning dress into a garment bag, we can't have your wife seeing it before the wedding" she laughed.

Molly rolled her eyes and quickly got back into her clothes, she wondered how Grace was getting on.

Grace was undressing in the second Suite as Louise, the woman who had greeted them, brought in a rack of dresses, she searched through them and found one that she loved on first sight, it was a Sophia Tolli Dress, it was white with one shoulder and a beautiful flower design winding down from the shoulder to the toes and a sash on the waist, it was the most beautiful dress she'd ever seen, she pulled it out and tried it on, it fit perfect, "This one, This is my dress" Grace gushed as she looked in the mirror.

"You Look stunning, she's a very lucky woman to have you, lets get it into a garment bag," Louise said happily, Grace dressed and hurried out of the suite, Molly was waiting for her on a bench by the cash register.

"We have thrown in a few free gifts with your dresses, what size shoes do you need"

"I'm a size 6" Molly said, Grace smiled.

"Same" she said as she reached for her hand.

Elizabeth walked away and returned a few minutes later with two shoe boxes, she showed them the shoes and they both gasped.

"They are beautiful"

"Excellent, thats everything, it's all been paid for"

Grace was shocked by this. "it has?"

"Yes, Officer Daniels called in while you were trying on dresses, Maggie at the till took the payment in full"

"Oh wow, that's incredible" Grace said as she reached for the garment bags, Molly picked up the shoes and the extra gift bags that they had been given free, the with a thank you they left.

"Ok, we have the Marriage licence, the wedding bands, and John says the minister is on his way to the Wedding company, they have a beautiful indoor Garden you can use, and the bar is being decorated with flowers and food for the reception, the cake is on its way to the bar." Hallie said as she saw Grace and Molly walking into the squad room, she turned them round and herded them back to the elevator and to her car instead of theirs.

"Get in, I have my friend waiting with her make-up kit to get you all glammed up for the best day your lives"
they both giggled as they were driven to a Wedding Company not far away.

When they arrived at I Do, Wedding Boutique, they both gasped once they saw the indoor Garden being prepared for their wedding, Molly pulled Grace into her arms and kissed her deeply, pure joy on both their faces.

"Break it up you two, its time to go into different room to get ready for your wedding, make up and hairstylists are waiting, we have an hour before the wedding" John called, Molly flashed him a seductive smile, "I can't wait to see what she has under her dress" "Oh Behave woman, go get ready" he said with a fake scowl, she laughed as Grace pinched her ass as she walked away.

"Am I going to regret setting you two up?" John asked with a grin, Grace shook her head, she looked at him with pure love.

"Never, i'd die for her" Grace declared as she headed into a room opposite where Molly was getting ready.

Hallie stood in the room with Molly and stared at her with astonishment, the dress fit like a glove, and she looked so damn beautiful in it, her long brown hair was curled and styled so it hung over her shoulder, there were sprigs of Baby's Breath in her hair, she *had a beautiful veil that was attached to a tiara, and a bouquet of Purple Orchids in her hands, radiance shone from her as she waited for the cue that it was time to meet her soul mate at the alter.*

"Oh Grace" John was holding his hand over his mouth as he looked at her in her dress, her hair was braided down her back with satin ribbons intertwined in the braid, the tiara she wore was fitted with diamonds and a beautiful veil that was flowing down her back like water, she looked gorgeous as she held a bouquet of Purple Orchids.

The sound of the music signalled that it was time, the beautiful Melodic sound of Creed Don't Stop Dancing filled the room.

"It's time, are you ready to meet your soul mate at the alter?" John asked.

"I am, take me to my baby" she whispered softly, he held out his arm, and he led her to the doors, Molly would be waiting at the Alter for her. As the doors opened, the whole room filled with friends from the station, Grace gasped when she saw her Mama and 3 sisters and Niece waiting for her, her brother-in law was overseas in Iraq. What Grace didn't see was her sister snapping photos on her SLR Camera as they all beamed with pride.

John led her down the Aisle as Molly waited, with Hallie at her side, smiling proudly, Grace finally reached the alter, and Molly reached for her hands, the minister smiled at them both.

"We are gathered here today to witness the Marriage of Grace Alora Garrett and Molly Rose James, do you have your vows?" they both nodded, he held out his hands to Grace, so she could say her vows.

"Molly, the day I met you I fell head over heels in love with you, with your beauty, your grace, your heart, and your soul, I finally found my missing piece, you made my soul come alive, when i'm with you I feel whole, when you touch me my heart bursts with love, when you kiss me I know i'm home, I Love You With All My Heart Darling, your my

forever, My Destiny" tears were falling down Grace's cheeks as Molly reached out to brush them away.

"Grace, the moment I laid eyes on you I knew i'd found my destiny, I tried so hard to deny myself the love I felt for you, no matter how hard I pulled away, you pulled me back from darkness and shone your beautiful bright light into my soul, you gave me the love and happiness I never thought I deserved, you made me a woman again, you held on tight and you didn't let me go, I won't ever let you go sweetheart, your my one true love, my light in the dark, my best friend, my wife, and my soul mate, our forever starts here, now. I Love You With All My Heart body and soul"

Grace reached for her face and stroked her tears away as the minister asked for the rings, Hallie handed a ring to him, so did John. Grace picked up the ring and placed it on Molly's finger.

"I Give you this ring as a sign of my love and faithfulness, as I place it on your finger, I commit my heart and soul to you, I ask you to wear this ring as a reminder of the vows we have spoken today"

Molly picked up her ring and slipped it onto Grace's finger with a loving smile.

"I Give you this ring as a sign of my love and faithfulness, as I place it on your finger, I commit my heart and soul to you, I ask you to wear this ring as a reminder of the vows we have spoken here today"

"I now Pronounce you Wife & Wife, you may kiss your bride" The Minister said with a wink, and a smile.

Grace reached for her wife and kissed her more deeply that she'd ever kissed her before, the whole room erupted into applause as they finally wrapped their arms around one another, they had done it, they were married and Molly couldn't believe her eyes, Grace was the most beautiful woman she'd ever seen, and she loved her so much it hurt.

"I Love You Molly Rose Garrett" Grace said as she used Molly's new name, Molly smiled with love as she kissed her again and again

"I Love You Too Grace, With All That I Am, You Look So Sexy in this

Dress"

Grace leaned into her and whispered in her ear, "Wait to you see what I have under it, I'm going to give you a night to remember baby,"

Molly's eyes filled with heat, her skin flushed with arousal as she took Grace's neck between her teeth and bit her like she did before, Grace moaned as the pleasure bloomed in her belly, making her ready to combust, Molly was giving her another love bite.

"Grace" the sound of someone calling her name pulled them both out of their bubble, Molly smiled at her with a seductive lick to her lips, "I can't wait to finish this later" Molly whispered, Grace growled and pulled her into her embrace and devoured her lips, taking her mouth in a blatant display of sexual desire, despite the fact all the guests and her family were stood right there beside them waiting to meet Molly and congratulate them.

When they finally pulled apart Grace's family were beaming with pride at them, Molly was slightly embarrassed but they quickly put her at ease.

"Hi Mama" Grace said as she hugged her mother, tears were rolling down Isabelle Garrett's face as she embraced her daughter, followed by her sisters Evie, Hannah, Brooke, then picked up her sisters baby girl.Brooke's Husband was in Iraq and had been for 2 months, he'd be home in December.

"Mama this is Molly, my whole world, Baby this is my Mom Isabelle, my sisters Evie, Hannah and Brooke, this is Brooke's baby girl Summer who is 4 months old"

Isabelle pulled Molly into her arms and held her tight, Molly felt scared at first, but as her Mother In-Law held her she finally began to relax and held her just as tight, Molly had missed being able to hug her mom, so this meant the world to her.

"Welcome to our family baby girl, call me Mama ok?"

Molly nodded as she clung to her. "Thank you" Molly whispered.

"No, Thank you! You have made my daughter shine like she's supposed

to, you really are her destiny, and we love you for making her so happy"

"Grace makes me happy too, I'd die for her" Molly told Isabelle as they
finally pulled apart, Isabelle kissed her cheek and stepped aside for her
other daughters to welcome her.
First Evie gave her a big hug, thanking her for loving her sister, then
Hannah hugged her, and as she did Molly realised that Hannah was
pregnant, so there would be another baby joining the family soon.
Brooke stepped up next and hugged her tight.

"welcome to the family honey, it's about time someone picked her up

and got a ring on her finger,"

Molly looked at Grace who was cradling Baby Summer in her arms,
seeing Grace with a baby in her arms made Molly yearn for a family,
she wanted a baby with Grace, to watch as Grace nursed their child at
her breast.
Pulling her wife into her arms, baby and all she embraced her and laid
her head on her shoulder, watching as the baby slept against her
breasts, warm and surrounded by love, Grace kissed the babies soft
curls and breathed in the baby scent she loved, Molly could smell it too,
she had the look of a mother in her eyes.

"I want to have a baby with you" Molly said as she stroked the babies

soft cheeks, Grace lifted her eyes to meet Molly's, Grace kissed her
happily.

"I want to have a baby with you too,"

Isabelle smiled at their exchange, she was so proud to see her daughter
married, and happy.

"It's time for the reception everyone, would you like to make your way

to the bar across the street, its all ready for the newly weds to join in a

few minutes" John called as everyone made their way to the doors.
Officer Daniels and his sister Lexi walked up to them after everyone
was gone.

"Congratulations to you both, you look absolutely breathtaking in those *dresses"*

"Thank you so much for throwing a wedding together so quickly, I know
it must have been difficult on such short notice,"
Lexi smiled at them and gave them both a hug.

"You are so very welcome, it was a beautiful wedding, and the vows
were perfect, and not a problem at all to be honest, I had a cancellation
this morning so it worked out perfectly,"she laughed.
Molly swatted her brother on the arm playfully.

"And you paying for our dresses, you didn't have to do that, I was going
to buy them both myself"
he chuckled at her and shrugged.

"I wanted to do something nice for you both so I followed you to the
bridal store, when I saw you go into the changing rooms I ran in and
paid for them, your boss told me what's been happening and I didn't
want that sicko to ruin a beautiful love like this, so your welcome"Lexi
turned to her brother with a smile.

"Gabe that's so sweet"she gushed as she nudged him, he blushed
slightly.

"You're a great Friend Gabe, I owe you big time, now keep in touch, I
still need to repay you for saving my life today"
Grace looked between Molly and Gabe.

"He saved your life?"she gasped, Molly nodded.

"After I knocked The Kiss Me Killer Unconscious I ran, he found me on
the street, wet cold and wearing that hideous dress, he drove me back to
the station, to you"
Grace threw her arms around his neck and kissed his cheek, she held
him for a few minutes, then turned back to Molly.

"Thank you, Thank you, Thank you"she said as she smiled at Molly.

"It was my Pleasure Detectives, and yes I will keep in touch, I want to
see Honeymoon Pictures,"they all laughed at that.

"Are you ready to go over for the reception baby?" Molly said she stroked the wedding band on her finger, Grace hummed with happiness. She nodded.

"Join us for the reception, please it's the least we can do"

"we'd love to" Lexi said, she handed the reins over to her assistant, and they both headed over to the bar with her and Molly.
As Grace and Molly walked into the bar, the whole room erupted in applause and cheers as confetti reined down on them, Molly pulled her in for a kiss as the music started, the night passed with lots of drinks, great food, dancing and laughter as Molly was welcomed into Grace's family with open arms and given so much love that she didn't realise she had been missing.

"John has booked us into a hotel and spa for 3 days, the Honeymoon suite, so we can be alone, I saved us some cake. And a bottle of champagne" Grace whispered as Molly was rocking baby Summer in her arms.

"That sounds wonderful," Molly said happily.

"People are starting to leave, want to come say goodbye before we go?"
Molly nodded and carefully got to her feet, she followed Grace to the door and handed Summer back to her Mommy.
They said goodbye to their collogues and friends, then to Grace's Family, promising to come and see them soon.
John walked up to them with a smile and embraced them both.

"I'm so proud of you two, Congratulations kids, love you both now clear off to the Spa your bags are waiting at reception" he pushed them out the door with a wave.

They Both gasped when they saw Hallie's Husband Chris stood outside with a Limousine, he was holding two glasses of Champagne and a bowl of Chocolate Covered Strawberries.

"Good Evening Molly, Grace, Your Limo will take you to The Huntington" he smiled,

"Thank you Chris" Molly said as they both climbed inside with their Champagne and Strawberries, Grace leaned over and kissed her passionately as they set off for their Honeymoon and 3 whole days to make up for lost time and.They arrived at their destination 20 minutes later, Chris helped them both out of the Limo with a wink and waved as they walked inside the Beautiful Hotel to check in.

"Welcome to The Huntington, How may I help you?" a cheerful woman asked as they walked over to the desk.

"we are checking in, Molly and Grace Garrett for the honeymoon suite" the woman smiled at them and handed over the key cards.

"Your Bags are right here, there is a bottle of Champagne on Ice in your room and candles are lit, we hope you enjoy your stay at The Huntington, and Congratulations on your Wedding"

"Thank you" Grace said as they followed a young man who was pushing the baggage trolley into the elevator that led only to the honeymoon suite.
Once the man had stashed their bags in the closet he walked to them with a smile.

"A Wedding Gift was left for you both, a gift from The Manager and staff here at The Huntington. they are on the bed waiting for you, have a wonderful time" he said and left them alone.

Grace plugged her phone into the sound system on the desk and selected a song and put it on repeat, the beautiful sound of Miley Cyrus, When I Look at You filled the room, Molly wrapped her arms around Grace and looked into her eyes.

"Dance with me"

Grace wrapped her arms around her neck and they stepped closer as they danced slowly to the music, they kissed softly at first, but as they danced their kiss became more passionate, Molly ran her fingertips over her Wife's soft skin, making her shiver with arousal, Grace ran her lips down Molly's neck and reached behind to unzip her dress, the dress fell to the floor and Grace bent down to pick it up and remove Molly's shoes, she laid it over the sofa, she then removed her dress and kicked off her shoes, she led Molly to the bedroom, the candlelight in the dark room set a romantic tone as the scent of Jasmine essential oil filled the room.

Grace's eyes filled with desire as she looked at Molly in her Pink lace Panties and matching Bra, her mouth watered at the sight as she hungered for her, Molly was shaking with anticipation as she looked at Grace in her Lavender Silk Panties and Bra, Grace pulled her into her arms and bit into her neck with desire, the sound of Molly moaning with pleasure made her heated core flush, her lips moved lower as she trailed kisses down her body to her full breasts and took the tight nipple into her mouth, Molly cried out as she thrust her hands into her hair. Grace laid her on the bed and went back to her breast as she teased the tip with her tongue and teeth while she reached down to the edge of her panties and eased them off of her hips, once she had teased the tip she moved to the other side and gave it the same treatment, Molly was writhing in her arms as she gasped and moaned with what little breath she could muster, Grace then licked her way down her abdomen to the apex of her thighs, she eased her legs open gently and ran her tongue over her core, the scent of their combined arousal heavy in the air, Molly was panting with desperation as Grace finally slipped her tongue inside and lapped up her juices, moaning wildly Molly fisted the sheets to keep herself tethered to the bed, she'd never felt this much pleasure before, and when Grace touched the tip of her tongue to her clitoris and sank two fingers deep inside to stroke her sensitive walls, Molly screamed as she exploded into an Orgasm so strong her body shook with tremors, Grace reached up with one hand and their fingers linked as they held hands, Grace thrust her fingers in and out as she lapped up every drop of her release, she stroked her through her Orgasm until the shaking had almost stopped, Molly's eyes were dark and filled with hunger as she reached for Grace and pulled her up into her arms, she kissed her and tasted herself on Grace's lips, it was an Erotic feeling as Molly took her nipple into her mouth and grazed her teeth against the tight bud, she laved it with her saliva and blew on it, making Grace cry out at the feel of her breath on her, she then trailed her tongue down the tight stomach she loved and found her apex waiting for her, Molly shivered at the scent of Grace's arousal, she was desperate for a taste, so she clung to the back of her thighs and laid her mouth over her centre and finally took what Grace was offering her, the tip of her tongue delved inside as she placed her thumb over her Clit and stroked her with swift circles, Grace began to shake as her orgasm loomed close.

But Molly wasn't done with her, removing her tongue from her heated sex, she surged up and over Grace as she sank her fingers deep inside and continued her ministrations on her clit, she took Grace's lips in hers and they shared the most Erotic kiss they had ever felt, Grace reached down and inserted her fingers inside her as she wrapped her legs around her, their bodies were damp with sweat as they made love, their bodies rocking into one another as they rolled on the bed and Grace came up over her, she pulled her lips away and bit down on her neck once more, their breathing heavy and filling the room around them, Grace gasped as she felt Molly's core tightening around her fingers, the sound of her cries making her own muscles tighten with pleasure.

"Come Molly, Come for me, with me" Grace breathed against her Breast, Molly screamed and Grace cried out as they both climaxed, their bodies shaking together as their Orgasm rocked through them. Breathing deeply they wrapped their arms around one another as the sheets tangled up in their limbs, but they didn't care as they held each other close and kissed as their bodies came down from the most powerful Orgasm either of them had ever felt.

"How did I ever get so Lucky to have you in my arms?" Molly asked as she snuggled close, Grace was stroking her hand through her hair as she embraced her.

"You can thank your boss for that one" Grace giggled.

Molly lifted her head and rested her chin on Grace's stomach with a smile.

"John, Why?" she asked innocently, Grace ran her fingers over her lips softly.

"John came to me for help, he knew I was into women, and he'd figure out you were too, but he wanted you to come to him when you were ready, but that never happened, he was getting really worried about you- you were unhappy and your health was getting worse because you weren't sleeping and doing double shifts, he was so scared for you Molly he ended up crying at my loft one night"

Molly was shocked by this. "He did?" Grace nodded.

"I worked for The Missing Persons Unit, he'd been trying to get me to to leave there and transfer to Homicide for years, he wanted me to be your partner, what John told me about you broke my heart, I wanted to help you and I hadn't even met you yet- then John gave me a picture of you taken at his birthday party last year, the minute I saw that picture I fell in love with you, that night I called John and told him I wanted to transfer over, I met you a week later in his office and I knew you were mine"

"You did that for me! You left your unit and moved to Homicide for me and I pushed you away" Molly whispered with sadness, Grace reached for her and pulled her tight against her body, their foreheads resting together.

"Molly Look at me, look into my eyes Baby, you were in pain and you felt that you didn't deserve happiness, but you do, I Love You So Fucking Much My Heart is Burning, its Burning for you and I hate that you were hurt so badly, we will stop this son of a bitch once and for all and then we can move on with our lives and have a baby together, we can buy a house and make a home for us and live the rest of our lives loving one another, we can make love and laugh and be happy, that's what our future holds my darling, you and me"

Grace place her hand over her heart, Molly did the same.

"I Love You, I Love You, I Love You" Grace whispered to her, Molly took her lips and lost herself in her love.

They made love all over again, and continued to make love all night, and into the early morning sunrise as they finally fell asleep about 5;45am, wrapped around one other and safe in each others arms.

The sound of talking woke Grace up from a deep and restful sleep, they had both been through so much since they had met and to finally have her soul mate by her side made her tingly and ready to face the whole world.

She looked at the clock and saw it was 9:56am, she climbed out of bed and grabbed a satin robe and nightgown off of the ottoman at the end *of the bed, a wedding gift from The Huntington, they both had one in purple and one in a soft Mint colour, which was Molly's.*

She walked out of the bedroom and found Molly sat on the sofa with a hot Latte and whipped cream. She felt her tummy tighten at the sight of her in her sexy nightie and robe, her feet pulled up under her as she talked on the phone to someone, she smiled when she saw Grace stood there watching her, Grace joined her on the sofa and she handed her sleepy wife her Latte, the moaning sound she made had her ready to explode.

"John can I call you back? My Wife just woke up and I think round 15 is starting" Molly said with a sexy smirk, Grace chocked on her drink and the sound of John laughing down the phone made Molly giggle.

"If you two are going to Fuck Like Rabbits then don't call me back, now go and spend time with Grace" he replied, Grace could hear what he was saying and she smiled seductively.

"I'd love nothing more than to drag Molly back to bed right now, but I'm starving,"

Molly chuckled, "Actually so am I, breakfast calls" Molly said as she stroked Grace's face, "Have fun you two, enjoy your stay"

"We will, thanks John, bye" "Bye"

They both hung up and Grace leaned over and kissed her.

"Good Morning My Darling" Molly said with love, Grace licked her lips and snuggled in close.

"Good Morning Beautiful" she said happily.

They shared the Latte as they cuddle on the sofa looking out over the beautiful view of San Francisco in the morning.

"How did you sleep?" Grace asked as they entwined their hands and looked into each others eyes.

"I slept deep, same as you,"

Molly thought of the deep scars on her back that looked like they were just about healed, it pained her to think that she had them because of her, what made it worse were the jagged X's on her chest that Ethan had put there as revenge for falling in love with Molly.

Even though they weren't nearly as bad as the belt marks it still upset her that she had been tortured because someone was jealous over their relationship.

Seeing the pain in her eyes Grace put the cup down and climbed onto her lap, straddling her and holding her face in her hands.

"I'm So Sorry Grace" Molly cried as tears slipped down her cheeks, Grace felt her heart break a little, Molly was blaming herself for what happened.

"Baby don't, it wasn't your fault, I don't blame you for what he did, I blame him- but more than that I blame the fuckers who held you down and raped you, he wouldn't be doing this if they hadn't done that to you, please Molly don't cry, it breaks my heart to see you cry"

"I Love You" she whispered, Grace kissed her eyelids, then her lips.

"I Love You Too, now feed me I'm hungry"

Molly laughed as Grace kissed away her tears. They had a luxurious shower where they made love again beneath the spray then walked back into the bedroom to dress.

Molly put on a long dress in pale blue with butterflies on it, Grace wore a blue skirt and a white camisole top, they headed down to the restaurant to have breakfast.

As the doors to the elevator opened at the main lobby, they continued to kiss and caress as they walked to a table and sat down to order, Grace ordered the pancakes, bacon and a fruit platter, Molly had Pancakes, bacon, syrup and some toast, both ordered a hot Latte and orange juice, they noticed a few people staring at them as they held hands and kissed while giggling at the table.

A woman walked up to them with a smile, her badge said Manager.

"Mrs Grace Garrett, Mrs Molly Garrett, I'm Gina Ford, the Manager, Congratulations on your Wedding and Welcome to The Huntington, we have the spa booked for you today at 12pm, followed by lunch by the pool, tonight we have booked you into the restaurant at 6pm for a romantic meal in our private room with music and Champagne and dancing, feel free to use the pool when ever you like, and don't feel embarrassed about who you are, we are proud to have you both here"

Gina cast her eyes at the people who were staring at the newly weds, they quickly looked away, ashamed to be caught staring.

"Thank you so much, we appreciate it very much, we are looking forward to staying here and finally getting some time to be alone" Gina smiled at that and gave them a wink.

"I've been married to my wife Bethany for 3 years now, light of my life even after 15 years together before we got married," Grace beamed,

"Congratulations, it's the best feeling in the world to have Molly right here in my arms, there's nothing I wouldn't do for her"

"That's what I like to hear, enjoy your stay and if there's anything I can do give me or my staff a call they will be happy to help you" Gina walked away with a wave and they relaxed into each other as they kissed once more, Molly didn't care that they were being watched. no one else mattered but Grace.

Chapter 11

   Ethan paced as he held an ice pack to his head, he was seething with anger, Molly had escaped and now he had to find her and get her back before she made it back to the bitch.

Lucy was sat on the mouldy bed rolling her eyes and casually filing her nails, she really didn't care if he got Molly back, because she wanted Molly for herself, ever since she joined the force and this fucking plan had been set, she had developed a huge crush on Molly, and hoped she could entice Molly away from Ethan when he wasn't expecting it, she'd helped her big brother because she wanted Molly, and he'd made it clear that if she didn't he would ruin her life, but her life had been ruined anyway, Grace had put it all together to quickly, and forced Lucy to retreat earlier than she anticipated, a warrant was issued for her arrest, the whole fucking police force was looking for her, their father was arrested and her brother had fucked up and let Molly escape, now they were going to have to go through all this again to get her back, all in all this was a major fuck up- god her head hurt, she downed a bottle of vodka as she listened to her asshole brother curse over Molly escaping.

"I can't believe she got away, after all I've done for her, this is how she repays me? How dare she do this to me! I've done all this for her, to make her happy, I thought letting that Bitch go would show that she could trust me, and love me" he raged as he continued to pace up and down the cave.

Lucy huffed and rolled her eyes again, she shot her brother a look that told him to simmer the Fuck down.

"Calm The Fuck Down Ethan, you should have been smarter and handcuffed her to the posts before you tried to Fuck her!"

"I don't appreciate that tone Sis, "

Lucy snorted and got to her feet, she looked him in the eye.

"You Fucked up Ethan, you killed 8 people, kidnapped a cop and tortured her on camera, then traded her life with another cop, who you let escape when your Dick got over excited, now we are back to square one and have half the fucking police force hunting us down. They have

our names, our address, they have arrested our father, and they have your cellar being torn apart by the CSU Team, we are reduced to hiding in a cold damp and mouldy cave and I haven't eaten in over 24 hours, what the Fuck do you think is going to happen now big brother, because we can't exactly go about our business and killing and

dumping dead bodies in the park to get the message across"

"I hate Sarcasm" he snapped at her.

"It's not sarcasm, its the truth, what exactly do we do now? We have no

where to go"

Ethan sighed as he kept pacing, his head was pounding, and his balls hurt from where she brought her knee up into his groin, Bitch, how dare she do this to him after all he'd done for her.

Her parents hated him, so he'd took care of them, and her baby sister, once the kid was gone he'd thought her attention would be on him, but no, she'd shut herself off from everyone, school was the only place he'd been able to see her, and he wanted her desperately so he'd started following her home to her Aunt's house, he'd kept a discreet distance and hope that she would finally realise that she was in love with him, then he could have her all to himself, but then that Teachers Aid had lured her into the school gym after school when everyone had gone home and held her down as them boys raped her for 8 hours, she then took out her fathers gun and raped her repeatedly with the barrel. the Aunt was at work so she didn't even know what had happened, but he knew, he could see it on her face the next day, but what no one knew he'd been outside the gym, looking through the windows, he watched her being raped and he hated them for what they had done, he was jealous, it should be him who got to feel her like this, not those cowards who thought they had the right to touch his girlfriend.

Be cause that's what she was, she was his girlfriend, she belonged to him, and him alone, he'd taken care of her parents, he'd killed the 3 who hurt her, and he'd been killing all the girls who were mean to Molly, including Kaitlyn Downs, even though she hadn't been mean to her, they had fallen for each other and started dating when they were teenagers, they were dating for 4 months, until Angela got jealous and forced them to split up, he was glad when they split up, I mean, she belonged to him, so she had no right to put her lips on any one else, did she?

Fuck! How was he going to get her back now? Lucy was right, they were in a predicament, how could he possibly get Molly back now that the police knew who they were and were hunting the city for them. Ethan hoped that their asshole father kept his mouth shut!, if he didn't he would tell them where the cave was and lead the police right to them, and they had no where to go, the cave tunnels only went so far before they led off into the sewer system beneath the city. They could hide under the city but they needed food, water, supplied, and a shit load of blankets to keep them warm, plus they needed somewhere to sleep so they could remain focused and work on getting Molly back with out attracting too much attention, Molly was probably in the hospital right now, he wondered if Grace was in the hospital too, he hoped so, he could sneak in at night and go into Graces room and overdose her on enough Morphine to kill her, then he could inject a sedative into Molly's IV Bag and let her drift off into a deep slumber, then he could carry her down to the basement and into the sewer system and disappear without a trace, yeah, he thought with a smile, he could do that, he could kill the lover, and sedate Molly and run away together where no one can ever find them, he started to hatch a plan in his head, he wouldn't say anything to Lucy, not yet! She had a tendency to Fuck up his plans, so he kept his mouth shut until he had it all worked out first, excitement trickled down his spine at the thought of having his girl back in his arms, he reached for his sisters bottle of vodka and took a swig, his dick was getting hard thinking about Molly and how he was going to tie her to the bed and Fuck her hard and fast for their first time, once she'd felt him inside her she would love him the way he loved her, then it would all make sense, the things he'd done, killing all those people and sleeping with his sister to get his rocks off while thinking about Molly, yes it would all make sense, and soon, very very soon he would have her back and then she would appreciate all he'd done for her, he grabbed his sisters head and unzipped his fly, he could feel her shaking as he pulled her close to his waiting erection, tears streamed down her face, she was scared of him, but he didn't know that, he assumed the tears were because she loved him and wanted him, he forced his dick inside her mouth and took what he wanted before pushing her away after he achieved his release, she pulled away from him and ran into one of the tunnels, where she threw up and rid herself of his seed that he'd spurted down her throat, she cried quietly as he went back to preparing to get Molly back.

Molly Glided through the crystal clear water of the swimming pool and surfaced in front of Grace, who was sat on the steps drinking a rose wine and watching her intently, she bit her lip as she watched Molly come up and over her and took her lips deeply, there were couples all around and in the pool drinking and having fun, they were watching them with interest and talking about them, but they didn't care one bit as they kissed.

Grace placed her glass on the side of the pool and reached for her baby, she laughed as Molly pushed her back onto the steps so she was leaning over her.

Molly deepened the kiss and slipped her arms around her back and Grace thrust her hands into Molly's hair, Molly moaned into her mouth then took Grace's lip between her teeth and bit it with a grin.

Grace moaned back and slipped her leg around Molly's and pushed her to the side, so she ended up and over her.

"Do you know how much I Love You Grace?" Molly asked as she caressed her.

"Yes I do. I Love You Too, and tonight I will show you how much I love you," they kissed tenderly as their hands roamed all over each other.

"Let's go and get ready for dinner, I want a hot shower, and then i'm going to devour you, every inch of you" Molly said as she licked her lips, which made Grace growl with desire.

They climbed out of the pool and headed for the sun longer where their bags were with their towels, a flash of desire turned Grace's eyes smoky at the sight of Molly in a two piece swim suit, she hadn't cared about showing off her scars that marred her skin all over her chest and stomach, and Grace was proud of her for that.

As Grace bent to pick up her towel and bag, she saw a flash of pain flit across Molly's face.

"What's wrong sweetheart?" she asked as she reached out and held her by the hips, Molly winced as she dropped on to the sun lounger, she grabbed her stomach as the pain intensified. "Molly? What is it baby tell me what's wrong"

"It's the scar tissue, I need my meds" she winced, Grace grabbed her bag and pulled out a bottle of medication, she opened the lid and tipped one into her hand, then passed her a bottle of water, Molly took her pain meds and drained the water, she could see people watching her with concern. Grace reached out and caressed her face gently as she watched her breathing slowly, then laid her hands delicately over her scarred stomach, she stroked her soft skin and leaned over to kiss her.

"Are you ok Sweet Girl?" she asked softly, Molly nodded and reached for her hands, "I'm ok baby, I'm so sorry Grace," Grace pulled Molly into her lap and held her against her, she kissed her softly.

"Don't you ever apologise to me Molly, you never have to apologise for being in pain, I Love You just the way you are, scars and all, if the scar tissue is hurting you then we can ask the doctors if they can remove it, ok? just take a deep breath and know that i've got you baby, I will always have you safe in my arms" Molly breathed deep and then relaxed.

"The pain has gone, lets go upstairs baby, I just want to have a shower and hold you in my arms and make love to you" they gathered their belongings and walked into their hotel and over to the elevator that goes to the Honeymoon Suite, once they entered the bathroom Grace turned on the shower and poured some Jasmine essential oil into the glass shower stall, the scent filled the room as Grace peeled the wet swim suit off her body carefully, then removed her own swim suit, they walked into the shower stall and let the hot water cover them as they wrapped their arms around each other and kissed with urgency, Molly trailed her lips down her neck till she reached her breasts and took her sensitive tip into her mouth and grazed her teeth over it, Grace gasped as she reached for Molly.

"I Love You Molly" Molly then brought her lips back to hers and they devoured each other as they made love beneath the spray of the shower, feeling satisfied after their lovemaking, they washed their hair and then got out so they could dress ready for dinner.

"How are you feeling Sweetheart" Grace asked as she ran her hands

gently over her belly as they waited in the hallway for the elevator to take them to the lobby, so they could go to the private dinning room for their romantic meal.

Molly smiled at her as she ran her fingertips over her wife's cheek with all the love she felt for her.

"I'm ok baby, the pain passed quickly, I'm sorry you had to see that, and

I'm sorry if I scared you" she whispered, Grace pulled her into her arms and held her firmly against her body, she kissed her tenderly.

"Hey, I told you don't ever apologise to me baby, we will get through

this together, you and me"

Molly smiled happily and reminded herself to thank John for his matchmaking skills, the doors opened and they stepped in as a couple came out of the Honeymoon suite next door, they were arguing and looked like they were ready to throw a few punches, Grace held the door for them as they stepped in, as the man thanked her, his wife shot her a dirty look, then scowled at her husband, things were not too good between them from the looks of it, the woman looked at Grace and gave her another dirty look, taking a defensive stand in front of her man, thinking she would flirt with him.

Molly was annoyed at the woman for staring at Grace, so she reached for her love and placed her lips over hers and took her in a deep and erotic kiss, the woman's mouth dropped open as she realised her husband was safe, he on the other hand looked like he was enjoying the show, maybe a bit too much.

Grace thrust her hands into Molly's hair and returned the kiss with urgency, moaning with arousal as she ran one hand down the pale blue silk dress that looked stunning on Molly's beautiful body, to grab her ass and pull her firmly against her, she pressed Molly up against the wall of the elevator.

"I can't wait to have a repeat of last night!" Grace said against her lips, smiling sexily, Molly darted her tongue out and licked her neck.

"I think I can manage that, I may take it up a notch-you up for a

challenge My Darling?" Molly asked with a smile, Grace grinned back and laughed.

"You bet I am"

Molly cast a quick glance at the couple by the elevator doors as they descended down to the lobby.

"Good, because i'm going to make you scream as i-" Heat filled Grace's eyes as she cut Molly off and took her mouth in a kiss just as deep as the last one.

The doors opened and they walked out leaving the couple in complete shock after hearing their conversation, they giggled as they headed to the private dinning room and took their seats at the table, they shared a bottle of Rose Wine and ordered their meals, Grace went for steak dinner, Molly chose Chicken in white wine sauce and creamed vegetables.

As they waited for their meals they cuddled up in the booth and just held each other.

"Molly, are you going to tell me what happened to you in that place?" Grace asked quietly as she held her close, she could feel Molly's heart beat racing, she tightened her arms around her and kissed her tenderly.

"It's ok Honey, I'm here and you're safe now"

Molly began to shake when a flash back hit her, tears pooled in her eyes as she climbed into Grace's lap and straddled her, holding on tight.

Grace soothed her as she stroked her hair and her back.

"He tried to rape me" Molly said through tight lips, suddenly the dam broke and she finally burst into tears and cried against her shoulder, Grace gasped as she clung to her, heartbroken for her beautiful girl who was almost brutalized again at the hands of a madman.

"I'm going to kill him, I'll kill him with my bare hands" she said angrily, Molly shook her head and looked into her eyes.

"No, baby please he's not worth it, just hold me and never let go" she said, Grace cupped her face and leaned in to kiss her.

"Always and Forever My Sweet Girl"

Walking up to the back door and turning the handle, the door opened into a huge kitchen, he smiled with victory, the stupid Fuckers had left the door unlocked, all the better for him, he didn't need to break in after *all.*

Ethan crept into the house and made his way toward the stairs, he stopped when he heard snoring coming from the study, he peered inside and found the old man passed out cold on the sofa, with an empty glass of wine in his hand.

Hatred for this man surged through him as he pulled out his knife and held his other hand tightly over his mouth, he pulled the knife swiftly across his throat and watched as his blood poured down his front, turning his white shirt into a dark red, he watched as the life drained from his eyes and his body went still.

Ethan quickly left the study and hurried up the stairs to Agatha's room, where she was sleeping in a single bed. He snarled at the sight of the bitch, he couldn't wait to watch the life leave her eyes, god he loathed the whore, putting his gloves on he leaned over her disgusting form and wrapped his hands around her neck, and squeezed, her eyes shot open as she struggled to breath.

She clawed at his arms as she tried to fight him off, but her was too strong for her elderly and frail hands.

He squeezed harder as her gasps grew weaker. He bent closer and whispered into her ears.

"I killed your daughter"

her eyes widened with fear.

"I killed your husband, Now, I kill you Bitch!"

Taking a final breath Agatha went still, her face screwed up in fear, even in death.

He retrieved his knife and ripped her nightgown off, then proceeded to carve a message into her chest and stomach, before dragging her from her bed by her arms, and down into the study.

He laid her on the sofa next to her lifeless husband and smirked at his masterpiece! Yeah this would get the message across nicely.

It had been over a day since Molly had escaped and he was desperate to get her back so she was safe in his arms.

But before he got her back, he had no choice but to kill that Bitch who had taken her from him, there was no way in hell that his girl would be marrying anyone but him, once that Cop Bitch was dead then she would come home to him, and they could run away together and be happy.

He felt his Dick grow hard as he thought about her, he placed his hand over the bulge in his jeans wanting nothing more than to ram his hardness into her tight heat, NO! He couldn't do this unless he was with her. He wanted to feel the pleasure once he was inside her, thrusting home hard and fast, he knew she would like that too, so he removed his hand and got back to work, he needed to get this done before someone found them and called the cops, he walked to the front door and opened it so they would be discovered quickly, he then went back to the study and turned on the stereo system full blast, so the neighbours would hear it, then he walked swiftly to the back door and out into the garden, he smiled as he thought about his girl coming to this crime scene and seeing his handiwork, it would make her so proud to know that he had killed Dana Thompson's parents for raising a child abuser. He walked away from the house and quietly faded into the night.

Later that night Grace pushed the button for the elevator that took them to the Honeymoon Suite, Molly was snuggled into her arms, after a great evening with a romantic meal for two in the private dining room, they were ready to go back to their room and fall into bed.
Molly saw the same couple from earlier walk over to them and wait for the elevator too, they were still arguing and snapping at each other, which made Molly great full that she had Grace in her arms.
The doors opened and they all stepped inside.

"I can't wait to get you out of this dress," Molly breathed into her neck as she traced her lips over her skin, Grace shivered in her arms, her breathing grew heavy as she pulled her tight against her.

"I think you will like the surprise I have for you" Grace said as she stroked her tongue against her shoulder, she smiled as Molly groaned in her arms.
The couple at the side of them were trying not to make it obvious that they were staring at them, but Grace was all too aware that the husband was turned on by watching them, the wife on the other hand looked pissed at her husbands reaction.
The doors opened and they all walked out and to their own Suite's, Molly grabbed Grace and lifted her into her arms as they approached their door and unlocked it.
Once they were in their bedroom Molly stopped at the foot of the bed and put Grace down, she reached behind her and unzipped the dress, when she saw the sexy underwear that Grace was wearing for her, her

eyes filled with hunger, she growled with desire as she roamed her hands all over her body, the deep red satin Bra and Matching Panties were driving her crazy as she leaned forward and kissed her nipple through the fabric.

She unclipped the bra and then helped her out of her heels.

"Lay down baby" Molly whispered. Grace climbed onto the bed and laid down to wait for her, she watched as Molly removed her heels and then removed her dress, she gasped as she saw Molly wearing the lavender lace set that she'd fantasized over so many times, she looked delicious in that set, and her mouth hungered to taste her, she reached out for her and Molly smiled as she lit a few candles then climbed in beside her after removing her underwear.

They kissed for a few minutes.

"Touch yourself baby, I want to see you Come while you touch yourself," Molly breathed into her mouth.

She watched as Grace's hands started at her neck, then travelled down to her perfect full breasts, she teased her nipples, making them tighten into tight little buds, Molly was breathing heavily as she watched her caressing her body, the way she would.

Then one hand slowly travelled down to the edge of her panties, slipping her hand inside them she caressed her fingertips over her flushed core and groaned with desire, feeling her body responding she added two fingers inside her core and gasped with pleasure, she opened her eyes and looked at Molly, what she saw was deep and primal desire, Molly was caressing herself as she watched.

"When I saw you touching yourself in your room, it was the most erotic thing i'd ever seen, I tried to walk away, but when you moaned my name, I couldn't walk away, I needed you so badly, I craved you Grace, I was on fire every time I thought about you,"

Grace groaned as she stroked her sensitive flesh, but the desire to have Molly's hands on her body, inside her was so strong.

"Touch me Molly, I want your hands on me, inside me, I want you to make me Come, please I love it when you touch me" Grace begged as she reached for her.

Molly slowly removed her panties and reached for her.

"Turn on your side, face me sweetheart"

turning to face her, Grace shivered as Molly brought her leg up to rest over her hips, then slipped one arm beneath her shoulders and cradled her head, their bodies as close as they could be.

"I'm going to start slow, then when I feel you getting close i'm going to take you hard and fast, Ok?" Molly asked, Grace nodded as she trembled with anticipation.

Molly slipped her hand between them and began to stroke her sex with firm fingers, gasping with pleasure Grace bit her lip and moaned, wrapping her arms around her wife she held on tight.

Their breathing grew heavy as the strokes grew more urgent, Molly watched her as she fell apart in her arms, crying out in bliss, her body shaking as the pleasure rippled through her now damp skin, Molly could feel her body tightening as she grew close to her release, so she slipped three fingers inside and added her thumb to her clit and began a deep and hard thrust, her thumb rubbed her with firm strokes, Grace cried out as the pleasure made her blood boil, her body trembling, Molly leaned down and took a nipple into her mouth and grazed her teeth over it, the sensation caused Grace to scream as fireworks burst behind her eyes as she exploded with a mind blowing Orgasm, Molly continued to thrust in and out of her, stroking her through her release, it took a while for Grace to open her eyes and look at her, her body was sated, her limbs felt like jelly as she came round. Her breathing still heavy as her heart pounded.

"Did you like that baby?" Molly whispered as she kissed her, Grace nodded and smiled.

"That was incredible, I Love You" Grace replied.

"I Love You"

"I'm so sleepy," Grace said as she yawned.
Molly stroked her face gently, and kissed her softly.

"Sleep baby, you need to rest" Grace frowned as she looked at her, "But what about you? You didn't get to Come"

"Don't worry about me, tonight was about you honey, now sleep, your

exhausted"

Molly blew out the candles and then climbed back in next to her, she wrapped the comforter over them both and pulled her soft and sated body into her arms, they kissed for a while until Molly felt her grow heavy with sleep, she smiled at her and held her close.

"I Love You Grace" she whispered in the dark, then drifted off into the land of sleep.

 John walked into the house with a troubled frown, they had got a call about a double homicide at 6:38am, Hallie was already there and the forensic team were busy doing their jobs, but it was clear that this was meant for Molly.

Harold and Agatha Thompson had been murdered in their home and the stereo system turned on to wake the neighbours.

He sighed as he looked at the grotesque scene in the study, the husband was laid on the sofa in his shirt and black slacks, the white shirt now stained deep red.

Agatha was naked and spread out beside him, a message carved into her chest and stomach, now The Kiss Me Killer was playing games with them, they had somehow managed to stay hidden despite a city wide man hunt for him and his sister. No one knew where they were, and they hadn't been back to their apartments, the cellar was still being processed and the cave that the father mentioned had caved in some years ago, so they couldn't be in there, so they had to have another hideout somewhere.

"Jesus Fucking Christ, please tell me that message doesn't mean what I think it means?" John asked with disgust, Hallie just nodded as she photographed the bodies and the scene, the tension in this house was very heavy, they could see that Ethan Hackett was losing it.

"He's made this message very clear, Molly escaped and it's pissed him off, I think he's working on his end game" Hallie said as she scowled at the two dead bodies in front of her.

"He killed the Thompson's because he can't get to Molly, his end game includes Molly, getting her back is what he wants, but if he has to kill her to keep her with him he will,"

"Hell no- that asshole isn't getting near either of them," Hallie said with anger.

John rubbed his tired eyes, and turned to the bodies.

He pulled out his cell phone and did something he didn't want to do, he called his two best detectives and interrupted their Honeymoon.

"Grace it's John, I'm sorry to wake you up so early, I need you and Molly too come to a crime scene"

the sound of the phone buzzing on the nightstand woke Grace from a deep sleep, she reached for the offending item with a grumble and answered it with a sleepy yawn.

"Hello"

"Grace it's John, I'm sorry to wake you so early, I need you and Molly to come to a crime scene"

Grace sat up in bed and turned to Molly, thinking she was dreaming, but the frown on her face made it clear that she was having a bad dream as she reached for her.

"Ok send me the address, we'll be there soon" Grace said, then hung up, a txt came through a minute later.
It was Dana Thompson's parents house, this didn't look good.
Grace wrapped her arms around her love and kissed her shoulders,

"Molly, honey"

Molly tensed in her sleep, her face radiated pain as she began to shake with fear.

"Molly, wake up baby, it's just a bad dream, it's ok"

Molly shot up in bed and screamed, her eyes streaming with tears. "Grace, don't touch her- let her go" she cried with terror.

Grace hauled her off the mattress and into her lap, she wrapped her in her love and kissed her skin until she opened her eyes and looked at her with fear, her body trembling as the nightmare slowly receded.

"I'm here darling, your ok, I wont let him hurt you honey, I promise I will keep you safe." she waited as Molly cried softly, and then she lifted her chin and looked into her eyes deeply.

"Are you ok?" she asked.

Molly nodded sadly.

"John called, he needs us at a crime scene, we have to go"

They dressed quickly and then headed to the elevator, Grace rolled her eyes when they saw the same couple waiting to go down, probably to the dining room, that was open for breakfast.

"Morning" the man said with a smile, his wife thumped him on the arm with annoyance, they had heard them making love earlier and he'd enjoyed the show while he sat on his balcony next door, his wife was laid on the bed sulking because he had gotten his pleasure earlier when they made love, but she hadn't, she was less than thrilled with their sex life.

Grace gave a nod, then watched as Molly put on her Jacket and zipped it up, it was cold outside now.

She reached inside her bag and pulled out Molly's badge and gun.

The couple were wide eyed when they saw them.

"Your badge was in the jacket you gave me, CSU found your gun in the cage, they tested it and found no prints but yours, John had it re-issued so you can carry again,"

"thank you honey" Molly said as she clipped her gun and holster to her waist, then added her badge to her other side. She pulled a hair tie off her wrist and tried to tie her hair back, but her hands were shaking. Grace took the tie and swept her hair back and braided it so it was out the way, Molly was impressed by the style, she'd never had her hair done like this, she usually had it down or just in a messy pony tail.

"So where is the crime scene?" Molly asked, Grace sighed.

"The Thompson's house"

"You have got to be Fucking kidding me! Ethan killed them didn't he?

He left another message" Molly spluttered.

"Maybe" Grace replied.

"Maybe my Ass, John wouldn't call us at almost 7am unless it had to do with The Kiss Me Killer, Ethan killed them and left a message for me- I cant wait to put a bullet between his eyes"

"After what that Fucker did to you I may beat you too it" Grace muttered angrily.

"How long have you been having Nightmares Molly?" Grace asked.

"The Nightmares started when he kidnapped you"
Grace closed her eyes and sighed with sadness.

"Fuck, i'm so sorry baby, I didn't know"

"It's not your fault, lets go and catch this Fucker and put him away for good"

"sounds good to me" the doors opened at the lobby and they walked out and toward the front entrance, Molly's car was there waiting for them.

John was pacing the room as he waited for them to arrive, he was getting frustrated when he say them walk into the study, he saw them holding hands and thought it was sweet, but then he saw that Molly was shaking, her eyes guarded as they walked around the sofa and stood in front of the fire place to get a good look at the message that was left for her.
Tears filled Grace's eyes as she read the message, she felt her heart break for Molly as her wife went still and silent, he face began to quiver as she realised what he'd left her.

I Killed Your Family,
Your Girlfriend Will Be Next!
Come Back To Me!

"He did kill them, he killed my parents, he killed LilyAna" Molly tried to walk away from the scene, but her legs gave way, she collapsed and Grace caught her, she sank to the floor and held her in her arms as she sobbed with devastation, Grace rocked her gently, sobbing with her, Molly was grieving for them all over again.
Hallie was stood there with a devastated look on her face, she hated that her friend was being hurt like this.
John was seething as he sat on the window sill smoking a cigarette.

"Oh Honey, I'm so so sorry," Grace cried as she held her.

"Why is he doing this?"

"Because he thinks you belong to him, and he thinks you want him to do these things" Hallie said.

"I hate him, I want him dead" Grace said against her neck.

"He's killed 11 people so far and we can't find him, it's time this stops" Molly said as she finally pulled herself up and out of her arms, she pulled Grace with her and held her firmly against her.

"I agree, I have a plan, it could be dangerous though" Grace said as she looked John in the eyes.

"What kind of plan?" he asked with concern.

"Let's head back to the hotel, we can talk there," Grace said, Molly curled into her arms as they walked back to the car and John followed, Hallie turned the bodies over to her assistants, who bagged them up, she followed them to the car and climbed into the back, John called The Chief and asked him to meet them at The Huntington Hotel, if this plan had any hope of working, they needed his ok to pull it off.

*It was 8:15am and they were all sat in the dining room eating breakfast, The Chief was there, so was John and Hallie.
The room was filled with diners eating with their friends enjoying their breakfasts.*

"Ok Grace, what is this plan that you have to catch The Kiss Me Killer?" Chief Haddon asked as he sipped his black coffee, he ignored the dozens of people watching them, listening to their conversation.

"Ok this might sound insane, but what if we trap him, Ethan Hackett has no idea that Molly and I got married, the message he carved on the Thompson Woman's body said Girlfriend, not Wife, set up a venue ready for a wedding, take a picture of us and announce our Wedding in the papers, if he see it he might just be enraged enough to come out of hiding and try to sabotage our wedding, but we will all be ready and armed to take him out"

Molly stared at her with shock.

"Are you Fucking Crazy? No absolutely not, no way! Grace i'm not putting you in danger- he took you from me once, i'm not going to let

you stand in the same room as him, he's a killer, forget it, i'm not going to risk losing you again"

"Molly, this may be our only shot at capturing him" Chief Haddon said to her, tears rolled down her cheeks as she sat back in the booth, feeling exhausted and emotionally spent, she noticed the couple from the Honeymoon Suite next door was looking at them again. She stood up, put her hands on her hips, showing her gun and badge, the Chief looked over his shoulder.

"Yes? You have a Fucking Problem?" she asked the couple who quickly turned away, Grace smirked at that, then reached out for Molly, who sank back into her seat and wrapped her arms around her waist.

"This plan will work, announce our wedding in the papers and make a big deal out of it and give the name of the venue, have a cake and decorations set up, make it look like a real wedding, but have the room filled with cops who are armed and ready to party, I know he will show up, he wont be able to resist the temptation of taking out as many cops as possible and getting Molly back, only this time he's the one who will end up in a cage"

"I gotta say Grace, that's pretty Fucking smart, we need a place thats not used much and wont put innocent people in danger, we can't risk more blood shed, any ideas as to where we can pull this off?" John wondered out loud.

"I think I know somewhere, there's a place in Sausalito, a Barn that host Weddings and Parties, I know the owner and he will rent the place to us, any damage I can pay for, that's not a problem, let me give him a call and see what we can come up with, I know it means travelling but this might just be the only way to get him out in the open, but away from innocent bystanders" Hallie said with hope.

"Do it" Grace said to Hallie, she pulled out her cell and called him, he answered on the second ring and Hallie put it on loud speaker. Sal had known her Molly since she was a kid, he missed her parents like crazy, and he missed Molly, but she just hadn't had the drive to see anyone from her past, it was too painful, she'd not spoken to her Aunt since she left her house at 18, she was 29 now. Hallie had met Sal about 5 years ago through a case that Molly had been working and she'd been trying to get her to call him or go and see him.

"Sal, hey it's me, I have a business proposal for you" she said with a smirk.

"Go On" he said down the phone with a deep voice.

"We need to rent out your barn, to trap a serial killer, we need to set up a fake wedding, announcement in the papers here In San Francisco, the whole nine yards,"

"Awe shit, when?"

"When can you have it all ready?"

"Give me 3 days, I can have it all done in 3 days, get the announcement in the paper, and make sure you send me the info for the newlyweds so it all look legit, is there anything I should know before we do this?"

"No one there but the people we bring, keep innocent bystanders away at all costs, this trap has to be air tight, I mean it Sal- this man has murdered 11 people, he's trying to get to Molly"
that got his attention, he knew Molly well and he knew how important she was to Hallie.

"Give me everything you have Hallie, I mean everything, I'll have this place tighter than a nuns ass"
Grace choked on her drink, Molly smirked at Sal's wicked sense of humour, Chief Haddon laughed, and John felt his face turn red with embarrassment, as people all around the room heard the exchange.

"I didn't know you were into religion Sal" Molly said down the line, Sal chuckled and gave an amused sigh,

"If it isn't my little songbird, how you doing beautiful?" he said back, using her nickname.

"I'm doing better than I was, I'm married now"
he chuckled again.

"You don't say? So who is the lucky woman who captured your heart?"

Molly slammed her glass down on the table "Oh come on, you knew

too?" she screeched at him, Grace laughed as she leaned over and

kissed her cheek.

"Everyone knew baby, that's how much your friends love you, hey Sal,

I'm Grace Molly's wife,"

"Hey Grace, looking forward to meeting you, did you know your wife

can sing, I mean really sing"

Grace looked at her with a smile, "She can? Honey you didn't tell me

you can sing" "I haven't sang for so long, not since my sister died"

"Sing for us Molly, show your wife what you can do" Sal encouraged
her, looking at the expectant faces around the table she took a deep
breath to steady her nerves, the last time she sang was to her baby
sister, LilyAna loved it when she sang, she would climb onto her lap
and ask her Sissy to sing to her, it was the only thing that soothed her to
sleep at night, Molly would spend hours laid on her sisters bed singing
to her as her tiny hands curled around her hair and fell asleep snuggled
against her, she missed her sister so much and wished she was here to
meet Grace, she was such a sweet little thing with a small round face,
blonde curly hair that reached the middle of her back by the age of 3,
her laughter would light up the whole room, and Molly had missed that
sound, she wished she could turn back time and be able to save her
sister, and her parents.

Molly took one final breath before she began to sing to Grace, a song
that meant so much to them both, the song that they made love to on
their wedding night, a song that would forever be in their hearts and on
repeat when they made love.

Everybody Needs Inspiration
Everybody needs a song
A Beautiful Melody
When the nights are long

Cause there is no guarantee

That this life is easy

Yeah When my world is falling apart
When there's no light
to break up the dark
that's when I, I
I look at you

Grace was in tears as she sat there looking at the woman she loved, who was singing to her in a dining room full of people, he friends, her boss and the Chief of Police.
The room erupted as everyone cheered her, Grace was kissing her as she held her.

"I told you she could sing" Sal said as he laughed down the phone.

"Shut up Sal or I wont bake your favourite cake" Molly said as she looked at the phone in Hallie's hand.

"Shutting up now, Hallie call me tonight and we can get all this worked

out" "Will do" they hung up and Hallie gave an innocent smile.

"You set that one up nicely Hallie, you knew he'd get me to sing"

"Sal adores your voice Molly, you know he was your biggest fan when you were little, besides me, your parents, and LilyAna, he was crazy for your singing voice,"

"It's been so long I didn't realise how much I missed it, I guess I should thank him for that one, and I need to thank you too John, You had Grace transfer in hoping we would fall for each other, you were right, I fell for her, I found my best friend"

"You are so welcome" he said with a smile, then they got back to business, they needed to get this plan in place, if they were going to trap Ethan and his sister they needed this plan to go as smooth as possible.

Keeping her head down Lucy Grant was walking down a back street in The Tenderloin District, she was freezing cold and hungry, she was looking for somewhere she could steal some food, she had dyed her hair black, changed into some baggy sweats and a sweater, she had a thick jacket on to keep warm in the early evening chill, as she walked down the street she say a headline in the front of the papers outside a corner shop, she grabbed one and hurried inside to pay for the paper, then she ran down a dark alley into a parking lot.

She opened the paper and read the article, her blood boiling as she looked at the pictures, how dare she!

They can't do this.

Happiness for Homicide Detectives

Homicide Detectives Grace Garrett and Molly James are tying the knot at a beautiful Beach side Barn in Sausalito in 3 days time, the two became partners at work not long ago, but sparks flew and they are happy to announce that they are getting married and are ready to settle down into family life, a close friend of the pair has said that they are talking about buying a house and having children. They posed for photos earlier at a private celebration at an undisclosed location and have given us a few of their happy snaps to announce their wedding, we wish this lovely pair a happy wedding day and all the best for the future, we wonder where the honeymoon will be?

Rage coursed through her veins as she headed back to the hideout where her brother was busy making a stronger cage for his "Girlfriend" he was gonna spiv when he read this, how the fuck was she going to get Molly for herself now, if she marries that bitch then it would be near impossible to get to her, she would be living with another cop, Ethan wasn't going to take this one well, he was almost excited when he came back from killing the pathetic parents of Dana Thompson, he was sure that he could get Molly back when she came to the crime scene, he'd kept watch, waiting for the right time to grab her, but she was tightly surrounded by the bitch and her friends, he was angry by that, very angry. So now he was making a cage to keep her locked up until he broke her.

"Ethan, you might want to read this" Lucy said as she walked to him in the cave and held out the paper.

"I'm too busy right now Lucy" he snapped, she hit him with the paper,

"It's about Molly" she said, he spun round and snatched the paper from her.

She could see the white hot rage burning down his body, he was livid, he grabbed the sledgehammer and began hitting the box spring bed, he smashed it to bits in a rage, Lucy knew he was ready to blow, Molly had just made the worst mistake of her life, he was going to kill Grace, any anyone else who got in his way, he'd kill them all and drag Molly back here so he could fuck her into submission, he would brutalize her until she broke, then she would be his slave, just like she herself had been his slave since she was a small child, this wasn't going to end well for anyone, it would end with dead bodies and Molly bound and shackled to the cage as he beat her savagely and raped her violently, if he got her back, then she had no hope of enticing her away from him, she needed a new plan, and quickly.

"Fucking Bitch, how dare she do this to me, after all i've done, Bitch, Fucking Whore, i'm going to Kill her girlfriend, then i'm going to kill everyone else for good measure, no one does this to me, i'm going to make her fucking life a living hell for this" he snarled.

Lucy stepped back as he raged, she took the paper and walked to one of the other tunnels to sit alone, she left him to it as she looked at the picture of the woman she loved and prayed she could get her away from her Psycho brother.

Chapter 13.

  Grace was sat on the bed in their Suite taking off her boots with a yawn, Molly was in the bathroom, she'd been in there for 30 minutes.

"Molly, Sweetheart"

she could hear the sound of the shower, but then she heard the sound of her girl sobbing, her heart was pounding as she jumped up from the bed and ran into the bathroom, Molly was stood in the hot shower, her arms braced against the wall as she sobbed uncontrollably, Grace pulled the door open to the shower stall and dragged Molly into her embrace, she didn't care that she was still wearing her clothes, she held the one she loved and rocked her in her arms as she cried.

"Molly, Oh Molly honey what is it? Talk to me baby" Grace soothed, but Molly just sobbed harder into her neck, Grace shut off the shower and walked over to the cabinet and grabbed a fluffy towel and wrapped her in it, she then swept her up into her arms and carried her to their big bed, she laid her down and stripped off her wet clothes and crawled in bedside her, Molly removed the towel and moved over her.
Grace cradled her as she sobbed, and eventually the sobs died down to a whimper, as she fell asleep.

"My Grace," she mumbled in sleep, Grace stroked her hair gently.

"That's right Baby, i'm yours, I will always be yours, I Love You so much" she soothed softly.

5 hours later Molly opened her eyes and saw that she was curled up beside Grace, who was typing on her Apple MacBook, Grace wrapped her arms around her and pulled her in for a kiss.

"There's my Beautiful Baby, come here sweetheart, Look in my eyes"
she looked up into her eyes and she could see all they love they felt for each other, her heart was bursting with so much emotion.

  "Molly I'm so in love with you, I wont ever leave you, where ever you are, is where I will be, right by your side my darling is where I belong, you're holding so much fear inside and it's hurting you"

"Grace, promise me you wont get hurt, please, I'd die if I lost you" she

whispered as she moved in for a deep and passionate kiss.

"I Promise you honey" she replied. "I Think I have found us a house, it has 7 bedrooms, all with En Suites, large kitchen, living room, library, study, walk in wardrobes- massive garden and a 4 car garage, floor to ceiling windows, private balcony in the master bedroom, and a

fireplace in there too,and it has a swimming pool"

Molly pulled the laptop over to her knee so she could have a look at the pictures, she loved it the moment she saw it.

"We need to check out today so we can get back to the station and go

over the plan with Hallie, I have to go to the bathroom, be right back" she said and hopped out of bed and shut the bathroom door.
Molly grabbed her purse and took out her bank card, she quickly entered her details, and bought the house online, she then e-mailed the agent and said she would pick up the keys once they had approved the sale, she was going to keep this a secret from Grace, she wanted to surprise her once all this with Ethan was over with.
She shut the computer down as Grace came out of the bathroom.

"What do you think to the house?"

"It's beautiful, let's hope its still there once this nightmare is over" she said
Grace kissed her softly and pinched her bare ass, making Molly squeal

with laughter, "Ooh you devil woman, if we didn't have to leave I'd drag

you back to bed and devour you"

"I'll hold you to that"

Molly just smiled at her sexily as she pulled her into her arms, kissed her and proceeded to blow her mind.

They both looked at each other in shock as they stepped off the elevator in the squad room, their desks had been rearranged to an l shape so they were right next to each other, there were photos of them at their wedding framed and sitting on their desks , they had no idea that anyone had taken pictures that day. A bouquet of Orchids and

Calla Lillie's were between there computers, and a mountain of wedding gifts and cards were stacked in the corner by John's office.

"Wow, look at all this, the pictures, the wedding gifts this is incredible" John was stood just outside his office smiling at them as they took in all the love from their co-workers and friends.

"Can I have your Attention Please everyone" John called out to everyone in the squad room, the buzz died down as John stepped forward.

"I'd like to Introduce Mrs Molly and Grace Garrett" everyone clapped as they came forward and offered their congratulations and gave them both hugs, John walked over to them and gave them both a kiss on the cheek.

"Welcome back to my two favourite Girls, How was the Honeymoon Suite?" he asked them, Molly raised her eyebrows as Grace tried her hardest to stifle her laughter, "Want Details Boss?" Molly said with a wicked grin, John gave her a fake scowl as he shook his head.

"Very funny smart ass, ok we have the venue booked, everything is in place, we have a team set who will be in that room dressed up as guests as the two of you say your vows, I need you armed and ready, we have 2 days until we pull this off, I need you rested and alert, we can't risk anything going wrong, i'm afraid you girls are going to have to sleep at my house until this is over- just in case he decides to strike early and try to get into your home Grace"

They both agreed and the realisation that this was really happening was setting in, Grace prayed it would work.

Going over the plans for the fake wedding Grace could see that Molly was tense, it was almost 5pm and everyone was getting ready to leave for the night, John was ready and leaving his office as they turned off their computers, "Are you ready honey?" Grace asked as she laid her hands on her shoulders, "Yep" she said as she got to her feet, she stroked her hair and gave her a soft kiss, then wrapped her arm around *her waist as they followed John to the elevator, "Have you met John's*

little girl, Alexa?" Molly asked her, Grace smiled at him, then nudged
him playfully.

"No! You never told me you had a daughter John"
he smiled brightly at the mention of his little girl.

"She's 8, Alexa was born deaf and has nerve damage down her right

side, she can't walk"

"Poor baby, I can't wait to meet her"
they walked out of the elevator and went to their cars.

"Just follow me"
John called out to them as he passed their car, they followed him all the
way to his house.

"Honey I'm Home" John called as he walked through the front door of
his house, His wife Deanna walked out of the kitchen wiping her hands
on a cloth, she beamed when she saw Molly stood there with her arms
around Grace.

"Oh my goodness, Molly you look radiant my girl, it's been so long
since you came over for dinner, i'm so glad you will be staying with us,
and you must be Grace, I can't thank you enough for finally making this

woman happy- we've been worried sick for so long"

"What can I say, I fell in love the moment I saw her"

Deanna smiled proudly, "Come in, I made the guest bedroom up for you

both, come and meet Alexa, she's in a very good mood today"
they followed them into the big kitchen where Alexa was sat in her
wheelchair at the table painting pictures, her face lit up when she saw
Molly walking over to her, she held her arms out for her and gave her a
big hug.

Molly stroked Alexa's cheek as Grace watched her with the beautiful
child, Molly turned to her after talking to her in sign language, she

smiled as she said "Alexa likes you, she says your pretty"

Grace leaned forward and kissed the child's button nose, which made her giggle with delight.

"I'll take out things upstairs baby" Molly said as she brushed a kiss over her lips, Grace caressed her eyes softly before she walked upstairs, then got to her feet as she walked over to the Kitchen island where Deanna was cooking dinner, she checked the potatoes and then got a Beef Joint out of the oven, she added some herbs to the top and put it back in the oven, it smelled delicious.

"Ok, Molly is upstairs, out with it, I've known you long enough to know when something is bugging you"

Grace took off her jacket and laid it over a chair and faced John and his wife.

"Molly is having nightmares, her anxiety is through the roof, I found her sobbing in the shower this morning- it took me an hour to get her to sleep, John, Ethan tried to rape her" her eyes were swimming with tears as she told them this, Deanna gasped.

"Fucking Asshole" John raged.

"If we get a shot at taking him out, I want to be the one to do it, I want to be the one to bullet between his eyes" Grace said firmly

"Grace, honey I don't think that's a good idea"

Grace turned and pulled up her top, showing them the scars from the belt he'd used on her, then she showed them the Jagged X's on her chest, Deanna began to cry softly when she saw them, her heart hurting for them, after all they had been through.

"Look at what he did to me, John, He did this to me, he beat me for 2 months, he held me in chains and did things to me, he took Molly and he hurt her," she said as she fought back the tears.

"Did that son of a bitch rape you?" Molly said from the doorway, they hadn't realised she was there.

"Molly!"

"Did he rape you Grace?" Molly asked with tears falling onto her cheeks, barely restrained anger was coursing through her, Grace went to her and cupped her damp face in her hands, she kissed her softly.

"No, he didn't rape me, but he assaulted me" she breathed against her cheeks, the feel of tears breaking her heart.
Molly pulled out of her arms and walked out of the house, Grace followed her, but she began to panic when Molly climbed into the car and sped off.

"Molly wait, come back please" she cried after her.

Deanna wrapped an arm around her shoulders as she sobbed, John pulled out his cell phone and tried to call her, but the call went to voicemail, he tried again 4 more times but again, it went to voicemail,

"Where is she going, it's not safe out there for her" Grace cried, John kissed her on the cheek as he hurried over to the car.

"I'm going to look for her, go inside and wait for me to call" Deanna nodded and led her inside and shut the door behind them.

"Here sweetie, drink this" Deanna said as she handed Grace a glass of Whiskey, which she downed in one and laid down on the sofa, clutching one of Molly's sweaters that she had left on the bed.
The phone rang at 7:30 and Deanna jumped up to answer it, hoping John had found her.

"Have you found her?"

"No, I've looked everywhere, Hallie hasn't seen her, she's not at the loft, or her town house, she's not at the station and i'm getting scared, how is Grace doing?"

Deanna cast her eyes over to her new friend who was sobbing on the sofa.

"she's falling to pieces, I just gave her a glass of Whiskey, where else could Molly be?"

"Your guess is as good as mine hun, I have to go, I'll let you know if I find her" he said, Deanna sighed with worry.

"Just bring her home to her wife, she's devastated" she said with sadness.

They hung up and she went to sit beside her, patting her knee gently.

"Molly isn't coming back is she? She's left me because of what he did" Grace said as she breathed in her scent, more tears fell as she began to feel numb.

"Why don't you go and lie down honey, I'll come and get you once he finds her"

Grace shook her head as she looked at the wedding band on her finger, feeling heavy and lost she buried her face into the sweater.

"I can't live without her,"

John came home an hour later looking worried, he kept trying her cell phone, but she didn't pick up, Grace was becoming hysterical by then, she refused another glass of Whiskey, she just sat on the sofa watching the window to see if she came back home, Deanna dished up dinner in a bid to keep her hands busy now that Alexa was in bed asleep, Grace ate the food but didn't really taste it, she was numb and slipping into depression, she wanted Molly back home, by 10pm Grace was curled up on the sofa with her arms wrapped around her legs, rocking as she cried, eventually she began to drift off into a tearful sleep.

John's phone beeped with a message from Molly at 10:45pm, he took his phone into the kitchen and shut the door, he called her.

"Where the Fuck are you Molly, Grace has been sobbing since you walked out, where are you?"

The sound of Molly crying took him by surprise.

"I'm so sorry, I never meant to hurt her- I love her so much, he hurt her because of me! She's never going to forgive me for what he did"

John grabbed his keys and headed out the front door and got into his car.

"Grace loves you so damn much Molly, she's your wife, she thinks you have left her, now where are you, I'm coming to get you"

"My car went off the road, I hit my head, I think my wrist is broken" she said into the phone. "I'm near Golden Gate Bridge,"

"I'm on my way, don't move" he said as he set off to find her. He was cursing as he drove to where she was.

John saw Molly sat on the side of the road half a mile from the Entrance to Golden Gate Bridge, her car was smashed up at the front, luckily her dash cam was intact, John noted as he ran passed the car as he headed straight for her, her head was bleeding and she looked shook up and beyond tired.

"Molly! Jesus are you alright, my god your head is bleeding" he said as he dropped to his knees in front of her, she looked at him with fear.

"Is Grace ok?" she asked sadly, he shook his head as he inspected her wrist, she winced in pain, he moved her wrist and it didn't feel broken, John looked at her and saw tears in her eyes.

"Grace thinks you have left her Molly, because of what he did to her,"

"What!? No I haven't left her, I'd never leave her, I Love Her John, she's my entire world"

John went to her car, grabbed her bag, jacket and anything else that belonged to her, then checked to make sure nothing else was in there, he locked the doors and called a friend who could come and collect the car for them and tow it to a garage, then he helped Molly to her feet and got her in his car, "I'm taking you for a CT Scan, you might have concussion or internal injuries, and you need that wrist looked at" he said as he buckled up and headed for the hospital.

After an hour wait Molly was taken to a room and had her wrist X-Rayed, and then a CT Scan, all came back clear, just a mild concussion, her wrist turned out to be Fractured in two places, she had it set in a cast 15 minutes later, and a package of painkillers.
John drove home, it was almost midnight by then, and Deanna was waiting at the front door for them as they pulled into the drive way, she gasped when she saw the blood on her face and the cast on her arm.
Molly excepted the hugs Deanna gave her, then walked into the house, she gasped when she saw Grace asleep on the sofa, her legs tucked up

in front of her, her arms wrapped around them, she was crying in her sleep, Molly dropped to her knees in front of her and stroked her tears away, hating herself for hurting her so badly.

"Oh Baby, I'm so sorry" she whispered as she touched her gently, Grace opened her eyes and gasped as she saw Molly in front of her, she reached for her and kissed her deeply, "Molly, Honey what happened?" Grace asked as she took in the blood on her head, and the cast on her wrist.

"Mild concussion, Fractured wrist in two places, my car came off the road" Molly said as she pulled Grace into her arms.

"I'm ok sweetheart, I'm so sorry for walking away like that, I shouldn't have done that, I hurt you and I hate myself for that"

Grace shook her head as she climbed off the sofa and into Molly's arms, wrapping her body around her,

"I love you Molly, more than anything, take me to bed- I need you to hold me" Grace said as she kissed her lips softly, Molly kept her in her arms as she carried her upstairs and into their guest bedroom.

John sighed with relief as Deanna locked the house up tight and set the alarm, he turned off the lights and they walked upstairs to their bedroom next to the guest bedroom, they could here them talking.

"I'm so glad she's home safe, now can you explain what the hell has been going on at work, John why didn't you tell me that Grace had been kidnapped by a serial killer, and what the Fuck happened to Molly!

Don't you dare leave anything out" Deanna said as she thrust her hands on her hips, John sank on to the bed and groaned.

"This serial killer is after Molly, he's obsessed with her, he's the one who killed her family hun, he set the house on fire because her parents didn't like him following their daughter around, he's killed 11 people so far and he's not done, he's invented this fantasy where they are madly in love and he's killing anyone who has ever hurt Molly in anyway, including a female teachers aid and two 15-year old boys who held her down and raped her when she was 12-years old" "Oh my god"

"I asked Grace to transfer to Homicide in the hope that Molly would open up to her and maybe they could fall in love, I wanted Molly to be happy, and she wasn't happy was she?"

Deanna shook her head at that.

"well Grace eventually came to me and said she wanted to help, so she transferred and the minute they laid eyes on one another there was a huge spark, love at first sight, Grace didn't give up trying to get through to her,"

John got to his feet and undressed and climbed into the bed before he continued his explanation of what had been happening.

"Grace really stepped up when Molly needed someone, she surrounded her with love and showed her it was ok to tell the world that they loved one another, that's why Grace was kidnapped, tortured, beaten for 2 months and sexually assaulted by a maniac, because she fell in love with Molly, eventually Molly was contacted by this bastard and offered to exchange Grace for her, Molly took the trade to save the woman she loved, we were searching for days for Molly trying to locate her, we found the cellar where he had kept his victims, but he'd cleared out and took Molly with him, she got away and found a cop on the street who drove her back to the station and reunited her with Grace"

Deanna sat on the bed beside him, taking his hands in hers.

"Are you setting a trap for him?"

he nodded at that question, then sighed.

"I just hope it works"

Molly laid Grace on the bed and walked over to the dresser, she removed her badge and gun, then opened the package of painkillers, she opened a bottle of water that was on the bedside cabinet and took one to help with the pain in her head and wrist, she then took a nightgown out of their bags and handed one to Grace, they both undressed silently, Grace watched her with worry as she stood by the windows and looked out over the dark city, lost in her own thoughts.

Grace went to her and wrapped her arms around her from behind, she caressed her body as she slowly kissed the tender skin of her neck, she knew that kissing her neck would turn her on, the resulting shiver made her smile.

"He's out there Grace, Ethan is out there and he wont stop until he has me, I hate him for what he's done to you, I want to kill him for touching you-"

Molly turned in her arms and wrapped her arms around her as she kissed her.

"He won't ever hurt you again, I swear I will keep you safe baby, I Love You so much Grace,"

caressing Molly's head where she hit it she leaned forward and kissed the swollen and tender wound.

"I thought i'd lost you tonight,"

"Grace, never- you will never lose me sweetheart, you're mine baby, and I'm yours"

Grace held her close as they clung to one another.

"I can't wait until this case is over, we can finally get a real honeymoon, settle down into Married life with the woman I love, we can find a house and turn it into a home" Grace said as she stroked her face gently,

Molly turned and pulled something out of her bag, she led Grace to the bed and sat her down, she handed her the envelope, Grace opened it with a frown, she gasped at what she saw in her hands.

"Molly?"

"I bought us that house baby, all we have to do is sign the papers and then it's ours,"

"Oh my god, oh Molly my darling, we have a house, somewhere we can make memories, make love and raise a family"

"I love you my beautiful girl" Molly whispered as she kissed her softly,

"I love you too sweetheart"

they signed the papers then and climbed into bed so they could make love and fall asleep in each others arms.

Chapter 14

Hiding in the dark as the venue was prepared for the wedding of San Francisco's two best Detectives, Ethan could feel the hatred coursing through his veins, he couldn't wait to kill that bitch and watch her bleed, the thought of killing her excited him, almost as much as the thought of taking Molly hard and fast for their first time. The ever present erection made it uncomfortable for him to hide in this tight spot, he'd been there for 9 hours already, just hiding in the dark cellar that was barely big enough to fit two people, the wedding would begin in just under 1 hour, the buzz of activity was loud and irritating as he waited for the first sign that his girl was here, he'd feel her the minute she walked in, he could here the voices in the barn calling out orders to the staff, he could smell the flowers that had been placed around the room, the scent of Jasmine was strong, it was her favourite scent, he'd missed that scent since she had escaped, he needed to get her back so he could Fuck her finally, he was as hard as a rock and it was damn uncomfortable.
The sound of a voice calling out to everyone in the room, it got his attention.
"Ok people, everything is set, let's clear out and let them get this show

on the road, thank you for helping to organise this event,"
the staff nodded with gratitude and cleared out seconds later, leaving Molly's boss and a woman with a clip board there with the owner of the building.
"Is everything in place? This need to go as smoothly as possible, we

can't fuck up on this" John said as he stared at the owner, he replied with a sigh.
"Yep, everything you asked for is here, there will be no innocent

bystanders within a mile radius, are you sure he's going to show?"
The Lieutenant nodded at the owner with a scowl.
"He'll show, there no way he can resist the opportunity of a lifetime, kill

as many cops as possible and get Molly back, it's what he lives for, he's

been planning this since he killed her parents, He will be here"
Fuck! This was a trap, they had set this up as a way to catch him, Now he was Fucking mad.

"So this asshole doesn't know that Molly and Grace are already married, what will he do when he finds out that little surprise?" the owner asked, he could feel his blood boil with anger, Molly had married that Bitch! How dare she do that, he was seething with rage as he fought the urge to burst out of his hiding place and kill them all.

"I don't give a shit what he thinks, let's go and check on the girls and make sure they have everything they need to pull this off"

the boss and the owner left, leaving the woman with the clipboard on her own to give the room a final once over, she had headphones in her ears, he could just hear the faint sound of music as she went about her business, he crept out of his hiding spot and stalked up behind her, his knife at the ready as he wrapped his hand over her mouth and quickly ran the blade over her skin, leaving a Jagged cut to her throat, he then carved Jagged X's on her chest, then he headed for a door that led to the beach, no one was on that side but people who were sun bathing and having fun with their families, he blended in with them as he shed his dark clothes and walked away wearing bright coloured shorts and a t-shirt.

"Are you girls ready?" John asked them as they looked at each other in the hideous wedding dresses that they had bought for this occasion, Grace let out a sigh as she reached for Molly who was less than thrilled with this plan, "I don't know, I just want it to be over so Molly can stop stressing out, she's been wound tight all day"

Molly gave her a pointed look, "Can you blame me? I don't want you in the same room as that Fucking maniac, he's a god dammed serial killer and I don't want my wife anywhere near him" Grace smiled at her protective streak as she kissed her softly. "I love you, but stop worrying"

"Not happening, when it comes to you my protective side goes nuts, so shut the fuck up and don't get shot!"

Grace tapped the kevlar vest under her dress, with a smile.

"I'm wearing my vest Honey"

"He could still shoot you in the head Grace, I'm not losing you, the

minute he starts shooting I'm taking him out"
John decided to change the subject.

"It's almost time, let me see if the co-ordinator is ready"
as he said that a scream from inside the barn made them all turn, they
pulled out their guns and ran in the direction of the screams, they found
a woman screaming hysterically at the body on the floor by the altar, a
clip board still clutched in her hand.

"It's the Fucking Wedding Co-Ordinator, he cut her throat, Jagged X's

on her breasts"
they all looked around the room at the growing crowd who came
running at the sounds of screaming.

"He was here, he killed her before the ceremony! He could still be here"
Molly said as she searched the crowd for him.

"Then where the Fuck is he? And why did he kill this woman?" John
whispered harshly, his eyes blazing with anger.

"He figured out it was a trap! It's the only explanation why he would
kill this poor woman, he wanted us to know that he was here and that

we can't catch him" Grace said, Molly rolled her eyes as she felt a
Migraine setting in, she felt more tense than before, he'd gotten away,
Again.

"Son of a Bitch" Molly snapped as she punched a wooden beam with

her good hand, Grace ran to her and took her hand in hers, "Molly don't,

you already have your wrist in a cast, please honey don't hurt yourself"

"How is this Fucker always one step ahead of us?" she raged as she
looked at the poor woman who had been killed for no reason, other than
she was in the room when a maniac snapped. Molly wanted this Fucker
in a body bag, she wouldn't settle for any less.

It was just after 1am as Ethan opened the window to the loft where

Grace lived, they hadn't slept here for a while, they only came to pick up some clothes, he had no idea where they were staying, Molly's townhouse was up for sale, which angered him, but what angered him more was the news that they had gotten married, his blood boiled at that, now he was out for revenge, he just knew that the bitch had made her do it, she couldn't possibly be happy with that whore, no! He wasn't going to let that bitch take his woman from him.

He slipped through the window and stood in Grace's bedroom, where they had first made love, he could almost feel Molly here, writhing in pleasure as he Fucked her hard, that's how he'd take her when he finally had her back.

He walked over to the bed and noticed something different, all the framed photos were gone, the things that belonged to Grace were missing, the pictures of her family, all her little nick knacks and personal items were gone, the closet was almost empty, so were her dresser drawers, he walked into the guest bedroom and saw that the suitcase that Molly brought here was gone, leaving the bedrooms he went to the living room and found that the only things there were a coffee table and an old sofa, the carpets were gone and so were the framed pictures that were on the walls, he began to lose it as he realised that Grace had given up her loft, now he had no idea where they were living, and that made him see red, he took out a canister of lighter fluid and poured it all over Grace's bed then lit a match that he had brought with him, he threw it on the bed and watched as it caught fire, he slipped out of the window he came in through and walked off into the dark, he made his way to the building where they worked and crept into the parking garage round the back, he watched as they got out of their car and headed to the elevators and waited for the doors to open, he felt his anger flare when Molly took the bitch into her arms and kissed her deeply, their kiss turned into something more as Grace pulled her into the elevator car and pushed her up against the wall, they both laughed as Grace slipped her hand down to touch her in the way he wanted to touch her, he had to stop himself from storming over there and killing the bitch, he wanted to grab her and drag her hands off of his woman and then slit her throat, once he was sure that no one was around he walked over to the car and smashed the window, he poured lighter fluid inside and threw another match inside, two fires in one night, he smirked when he thought of Grace finding out that her loft and her car had gone up in flames within hours of each other, he slipped back to his hiding spot and waited for the fire alarms to sound, excitement raged through him, his dick was hard as a rock as he waited for chaos to ensue, time to play Bitch.

Molly dropped into the chair at her desk and groaned with delight, Grace had just made love to her in the elevator on the way up, she remembered the feel of her fingers inside her, the toe curling pleasure that had made her explode with love, Molly felt sated and happy despite the tragedy that had befell an innocent Wedding Co-Ordinator today, John was still on his way back from Sausalito and he wasn't happy at what had happened, what pissed them all off was the fact that Ethan was already there, and no one had seen him come in, or leave the scene.

"Feel better?" Grace asked with a sexy smile, Molly licked her lips and nodded, she reached for Grace's hands and pulled her close, Grace kissed the bruised knuckles of her hand where she punched the wooden beam, she was lucky it wasn't broken.

"I'm sorry the plan didn't work, I really wanted it to work, just so I could put a bullet in his brain"

Grace left her seat and climbed into her lap, straddling her and wrapping her arms around her neck.

"we'll get him Honey, I promise we will get him, but i'm not going to let him ruin our lives, we have a house to decorate, and a lot of rooms to christen" she said as she wiggled her eyebrows at her seductively, Molly laughed as she pulled her in for a cuddle.

"God you are so good for me, I'm the luckiest woman in the world to have you right here in my arms,"

"We have each other and that's all that matters,"

the fire alarms went off and made them both jump up out of the chair.

"What the Fuck" Grace said as she looked around, the night shift guys were running for the stairs, Molly grabbed her hand and led her toward the stairs, when John stepped off the elevator with a grim expression on his face.

"You two better come with me, Now!" he said with an agitated growl,

Grace looked at Molly and they both groaned with dread.

The followed him into the elevator and waited as the car descended to the Parking garage, when the doors opened Grace gasped when she saw the burnt out shell of her car.

"You have to be Fucking kidding me, how the hell did he get in here, it's a secured parking garage he shouldn't be able to get in here" Molly shouted as she watched the fire crew putting out the flames, John pulled them both to his car across from where Grace parked.

"It's worse than that, Grace I'm sorry, but your loft was set on fire tonight too"

"I'm going to kill this Fucker" she said as she climbed into the car and laid her head back onto the seat, exhaustion weighing her down. Molly climbed in beside her and pulled her into her arms, soothing her as she stroked her hair.

The next day they were all sat around the boards that had all the info on The Kiss Me Killer, the room was now packed with cops from 3 different stations weighing in to search for the two suspects, tension was high, and now the FBI was involved.

"Ok People, The Kiss Me Killer has taken his pursuit of Molly to the next level, he set Grace's Loft on fire, then torched her car in the parking garage out back, can someone explain to me how this Asshole has managed to get into a secure garage and set her car on fire without anyone seeing it, this maniac has killed 12 people now- and he's getting closer to his intended target, I want this case closed, yesterday! Now what the fuck do we have that can nail this guy to the wall?" John shouted

"His apartment has remained empty, he hasn't been home, neither has Officer Lucy Grant, they are off the grid, we have their pictures posted on the SFPD website and a news crew is coming in this afternoon to do a piece on this, we can get their pictures out to the media and make the news at 10pm, the more we get their faces out there the more people will be looking for them"

"Good, get it set up, I want their ugly mugs all over the Fucking papers, tv and internet, someone has to have seen them" John said as he slapped the desk with a loud thud,

"Molly, Grace, I want you two on the streets, canvass all the local stores, diners, knock on fucking doors if you have to, find any relatives or friends that they had and shake their Fucking Monkey Tree,"
they both nodded and got to their feet, after grabbing their guns from the desk drawer, they left the squad room to get out there and find them. They had been out there for almost 5 hours when they walked into a diner and sat down at a booth, a waitress came over and poured two cups of coffee with a smile.

"What can I get you two ladies?" she asked as she pulled out a notepad.

"Burger and fries for me, what do you want baby?" Molly asked as she reached for her coffee cup and took a long sip, she moaned in delight,

"can I have spaghetti carbonara plz" Grace said as she pulled out two pictures to show the waitress.

"Have you see either of these two in here lately?"
the waitress took the photos and looked at them, she handed them back a second later.

"Him I've seen, a weird guy with an obsession about someone called Molly, claimed she's his girlfriend and that they are going to run away together and live happily ever after, if you ask me, Molly doesn't know he even exists, her i've never seen but if I do I can call you"

Molly handed the woman a card with her name and number on it, although she had scratched out her last name and replaced it with her married name, the woman took the card and looked at the name, her eyes widened as she realised who she was talking to.

"It's you, he's talking about you isn't he?" she asked, Grace nodded as she reached for the woman's arm with a cautious frown.

"If you see him then call us, I mean it, he's extremely dangerous, he's hurt a lot of people- Do Not Approach Him under any circumstances, he's hurting people because he want's Molly, we have been hunting him for months, he's killed 12 people"

"I'll keep an eye out" the woman said as she walked away to get their meals.
Molly laid her head on Grace's shoulder and watched as she sketched on a drawing pad, it was a big heart with Lily flowers around it and their names were written inside the heart in a calligraphy script, it was stunning.

"That's beautiful Sweetheart, I didn't know you could draw like that"
Molly said as she wrapped her arms around her waist and breathed her in with happiness, Grace kissed her head with tenderness as she smiled at her with amusement.

"You never told me you could sing"
Molly rolled her eyes as their meals arrived and Grace put away her sketch and dove into her food with hunger, after they had finished their meals they headed out so they could continue the search.

"Ok we have two more doors to knock on, An Aunt from his mothers side over on Beacon Hill, and a cousin on the fathers side in The Tenderloin District"
they climbed into the rental car that John had arranged for them and headed to The Tenderloin District, the cousin may have information and they hoped a location for where he was hiding.

"I hate this Fucking car, smells like cigarettes" Grace said as she opened the window.

"Don't worry baby, we can buy a better car once the insurance company deal with the claim for the car and the loft"

"I'm just glad we packed our stuff and left when we did, it still hurts that the loft was destroyed though, it's where we made love for the first time, it meant something to me" Molly took her injured hand off the steering wheel and held her hand, Grace stroked her fingers with love.

"I know Honey, it hurts me too, but we can move into our house, we can make love on our new big king size bed and make all new memories right there in each others arms,"

Grace groaned at that, she crossed her legs to ward off the desire that was coursing through her veins. Thinking about Molly writhing in her arms as they made love was turning her on, she was feeling flushed and groaned as she wished Molly's fingers were inside her right now, stroking her to a magnificent release, she could feel that her panties were very damp, her breathing became deep and breathy as she felt Molly's hand caressing hers.

"Mmm, I want you so badly Molly,"

Molly looked over at Grace and saw the flushed look of arousal in her cheeks, she was biting her lip with need. Seeing her clutching her legs closed as she gasped with need, she felt a surge of sexual desire shoot to her core.

"Fuck"

she reached over and slipped her hand between her legs to touch her through her jeans, she could feel that Grace was wet and ready for her, she groaned as she caught the scent of her arousal, god she wanted to stop the car and take her right there. Grace gasped with pleasure and moaned as her fingers pressed against her heated centre and massaged her, Grace was trembling as she clutched the seat, it was dark out now, and Molly was searching for somewhere to pull over that was deserted, she saw a dark alley between a row of deserted stores that had been vacant for almost 5 years, Molly pulled in and drove round the back, it was pitch black and there was no one around, thank god.
She locked the doors to the car and turned off the engine, Grace threw off the seat belt and climbed into Molly's lap, Grace crushed her mouth to Molly's as Molly reached inside her panties and stroked her with desperate fingers, their breathing was heavy as Grace slipped her hand into Molly's jeans and touched her too, Molly moaned as Grace writhed in her arms, thrusting her hips into Molly's talented hands.

"Oh God, Molly!"

"Come for me baby, I can feel your close, I am too"
Molly said as she felt her muscles tightening around her fingers, she could feel her own sex clenching as Grace stroked her fiercely, "Come with me " Molly whispered into her mouth, they both cried out as they came together, shaking as they held one another.
Grace dropped her head to her Wife's shoulders as she tried to catch her

breath, her trembling body was sated and buzzing from an amazing Orgasm, Molly slowly withdrew her hand and did something that Blew Graces mind, she put her fingers in her mouth and sucked her juices off her fingers, she moaned with hunger.

"Yummy, I love the taste of you,"

"That's so Fucking Hot" Grace said as she took her fingers and had a taste, she too moaned before she leaned forward and kissed her passionately.
After they had righted themselves they got back onto the road and headed for Ethan Hackett's cousin's place, they just hoped he was willing to help.

Knocking on the door to Danny Hackett's apartment, they had their guns unclipped ready in case Ethan or Lucy was here and ready to party, Party meaning shoot their way out- or go down trying.
The door opened and a girl stood there with a baby in her arms, she looked to be about 17 years old, and she had a black eye and split lip, Grace felt her anger spike at the sight of the young girl, who looked terrified when she saw the badges on their hips.

"Can I help you?" she asked meekly, the baby began to fuss, the little girl looked to be around 2 weeks old wearing a pink onesie wrapped in a pale purple blanket.

"I'm Detective Grace Garrett, this is Detective Molly Garrett, we are looking for Danny Hackett, is he home?"
the girl looked at them, and noticed the wedding rings on their fingers.

"He's in the bedroom, asleep,"
the girl said as she stepped back to let them in, Molly handed her a card with her number on it.

"How old are you Honey?"
the girl bit her lip with worry.

"I'm 14"

"Where are your parents? Do they know that you are living with a 45 year old man?"

she shook her head and began to cry with fear.

"Do you want to be here?"

again she shook her head as she clung to her baby, she tried to keep her daughter quiet before she woke her father up.

"There's a black car down stairs, go and get inside, we can take you home if you want to go"

"Thank you" she said as she grabbed a few things she needed from the living room, things for her daughter, she left all her belongings.
Once she had left the apartment, they took out their guns and walked to the bedroom, and opened the door, they found Danny Hackett laid on the bed with another girl, who looked to be at least 13 years old.
As they approached the bed they could see that the girl wad dead, a bottle of pills in her hand and a bottle of vodka on the floor beside the bed, she's committed suicide
rather than live this hell for the rest of her life.

"Dammit, she's dead," Grace said with anger.

Molly shook her head as she felt for a pulse on the man beside her, he was snoring heavily as he turned over.
Grace kicked the bed hard enough to wake him, he shot up in bed with a growl, the stench of alcohol permeating off him made them gag.

"Who the Fuck are you?" he slurred as he glared at them with an unfocused gaze.

"SFPD, Detectives Grace and Molly Garrett, we're here about your cousins Ethan Hackett, and Lucy Grant, Formally known Kristin Hackett"

"Where is Eliza, and Paige?" he slurred again as he rubbed his sore head and got to his feet, stark naked and showing off his erection to the two women in his bedroom, he snorted when he saw the girl dead on his bed, disgusted that she'd chosen a cowards way out.
Molly threw clothes at him and turned away from him, trying not to throw up at the disgusting sight of him.

"What's wrong Sugar tits, you fancy a taste of this candy pop?" he said with a smirk, as he reached round and placed one meaty hand on her breast, the other he place between her legs, and dug his fingers in.

Grace walked to him and twisted his hand back behind him, making him howl in pain, Molly moved away as she felt a flash of panic inside her stomach.

"Danny Hackett, your under arrest for the sexual assault of a police officer, the rape of this child here, and the one who opened the door, you have the right to remain silent, anything you say can and will be used against you in a court of law, you have the right to an attorney. If you cannot afford an attorney , one will be provided for you, do you understand the rights as I have read them to you?"

"Yes" he snapped as he dressed quickly, she then cuffed him and made him sit on the floor, while she called it in to dispatch, "Are you ok Honey?" Grace asked as Molly got her breathing under control, her anxiety was through the roof because of that sick bastards cocky move.

"I'll be ok, just scared me a little" Molly replied as she kissed her forehead with gratitude.

Grace turned to the man with a disgusted look.

"I can see where Ethan gets his evil streak from, it runs in the family, so is this the family business, child sex ring and murder?"

"Fuck You"

Grace smiled with a hint of amusement at his words.

"That's exactly what your uncle said as I poured his wife's ashes down the sink,"

he tried to get to his feet as he spat his anger at them, "Now, where are your lovely cousins hiding? We need to find them before they hurt someone else?"

"I'm not supposed to talk, unless the woman he's dating comes looking for him!"

"What woman?" Grace asked as she stepped in front of him.

"Molly James! He's been dating her since high school, he's obsessed with her- they are getting married next month" he said.

"I'm Molly, and i'm not marrying this Fucker, he's been stalking me since I was a child, he's killed 12 people.
And just for the record, i'm already married, I married my best friend, now what are you supposed to tell me?"

Danny looked at her with a scowl, "In the top drawer over there, there's a big brown envelope with your name on it"
Grace pulled out a pair of latex crime scene gloves and snapped them on, she opened the drawer and pulled the envelope out, it was heavy and thick.
"We better wait for crime scene techs to get here, do this by the book baby" Molly said as she looked at the object in her wife's hands, Grace nodded and placed it back in the drawer, she looked over at the man sat at the end of the bed, he was staring at Molly with eyes filled with lust, he was checking her out, and that pissed her off.
"do you fancy a night with a real man sexy? I bet I can blow your mind" he said as he licked his lips with hunger.
Grace stood in front of Molly protectively, she looked the creep in the eyes and gave him a cocky smile.
"Sorry asshole, but she's mine, I'll be the one blowing her mind, not you"
Molly wrapped her arms around her from behind and kissed her neck.
"And I blew her mind earlier," Molly said with a smirk, then they turned away from him as John walked in with Hallie and the crime scene techs.
He saw the child on the bed with a bottle of pills and huffed with anger, he swore as he looked at the man cuffed on the floor.
"Is this the cousin?"

"Yep, we found him passed out on the bed next to the little girl, she's been dead a few hours, she's cold, id say she's 13 maybe 14 years old, too young to be in this situation, she killed herself rather than go through this nightmare for the rest of her life, a young girl answered the door, she's 14 and has a baby, he's been keeping her here against her will, she said she wants to go home so we told her to get in our car and wait" Molly said as she ran her hand through her hair, feeling tired and ready for a long hot bath, and sleep.

"I had one of the uniforms take her home, the baby was getting cold so I didn't want her sat in the car any longer than she needed to be, so what's this sicko's story?"

"This sicko Sexually Assaulted Molly" Grace said with anger, John Glared at him as he cowered on the floor, Grace really wanted to smack the Fucker.

Danny cleared his throat loudly as he looked at them.

"I have to use the bathroom"

Grace sighed with frustration, "Cant you hold it?"

"No!"

she walked into the bathroom and checked there was no windows he could escape from, or anything he could use as a weapon.

"Bathroom is clear, no windows or weapons" she said.

John gave the ok to let he use the bathroom, so she uncuffed him and walked to Molly and held her hand.

"Are you ok Molly?" John asked with concern.

She nodded and gave Grace a gentle kiss.

"I'm ok, nothing my sweet girl can't fix"

The bathroom door opened and Danny came out and walked over to them, he looked Molly up and down and sneered at her as he licked his lips.

"Are you sure you don't want to take a ride on this fine stud Sugar tits," he said as he reached for her hips.

"Hey- Back off" John warned.

"Why don't we go somewhere more private, I can show you what a real man can do"

Grace growled as she stepped forward, her fists clenched at her sides, Molly laid her hands on her shoulders as she tried to calm her down.

"I'd stop if I were you Asshole, unless you want to get your ass kicked by Grace" John said as he shook his head, he could see that Grace was getting close to losing her shit!

Danny laughed with amusement as he ignored the warning, again he reached for Molly with his filthy sweaty hands.

"C,Mon sexy lips, you're in for a wild ride" he sneered.

"Shut the Fuck Up" Grace snapped, he laughed at her.

"And what will a little girl do to me" He sneered.

Grace punched him, hard in the face and sent him flying onto the bed, his nose exploded and blood poured down his face as he raged at her.

"What the Fuck was that for"

Grace shook her hand as she glared at him.

"The Lieutenant warned you to back off, and you didn't listen, you put your disgusting hands on my girl, if you ever touch her again, if you so much as look at her I will make your Fucking life a living hell, Cuff him and get him out of here" she snapped.

A uniformed Officer handcuffed him and took him away, John tried hard to hide the smirk on his face, Hallie stepped forward and patted her shoulder with a proud smile, "Well Done Honey, I'm Proud of you" she said then went back to the victim on the bed.

"My Sweet Girl, Are you ok?"

Grace stroked her cheek, "I'm ok Baby, Fucking Asshole" she said as she looked at her knuckles, they were red and swollen.

"Hallie, theres a brown envelope in the top drawer with Molly's name on it, Ethan left it for her"

Hallie nodded as she got to her feet.

"I'll have it checked for prints and DNA, log it as evidence, you can have it after that" she replied.

Molly reached for Grace's good hand.

"Let's go talk to the Aunt, there's nothing more we can do here"

John waved them off so they could get back to searching for Ethan Hackett and his sister.

Watching the woman as she left, Ethan followed in the shadows, the knife in his pocket ready to slice across her throat, he'd seen her earlier talking to his girl and the Bitch, he wanted to walk in there and kill her, she had her hands on Molly, and it pissed him off, the need for revenge was burning hot in his veins, he'd followed them to The Tenderloin District, he'd seen them having sex in the car, jealousy making him see red.

As he neared the woman, whose name was Jean, he took out his knife and reached around her to hook his hand over her mouth.

She tried to scream but he dug the blade into her skin.

"Shut the Fuck up, or i'll kill you right here"

she nodded as she tried to think of a way out of this, fear shone in her eyes.

He dragged her into a black van he had stolen and shut the door, he tied her up and gagged her before jumping into the drivers seat, he drove off into the dark and found a dark alley behind the police station where his girl worked, he joined his guest in the back of the van and stripped her to her underwear, taking out his knife once again he began to cut her breasts, the Jagged X's marking her skin, he grinned as she screamed behind the gag, the sound of her fear turned him on, he moved the blade to her stomach and began cutting her there, over the next hour he left Jagged X's all over her body, including her arms and legs, when he finished he slit her throat, wrapped her in a blanket then carried her body to the parking garage where he pressed the button for the elevator, when the doors opened he dumped the body in there, then pressed the fire alarm button to keep the doors open for his girl to see what he'd done for her, with a satisfied grin, he walked away.

Molly climbed out of the car and waited for Grace to join her, they walked up the steps to the home of Ethan Hackett's Aunt, they rang the doorbell and a woman in her late 50's answered, wearing a satin robe and a coffee in her hand.

"May I help you?"

"Mrs Bailey, I'm Detective Molly Garrett, This is Detective Grace

Garrett, we are here about your nephew Ethan and his sister"
with a sigh she stepped back and let them in.
"You better come in Detectives, I had a feeling the Police would be

after them one day"
Grace raised her eyebrows at that and followed the woman into her
house where they were led to a spacious living room, there was an older
man there, with a woman in her late 20's and two little girls, around 5
years old.
"This is my husband Charles, our daughter Chloe, and Twin

Granddaughters, Brianna and Bethany"
Grace smiled as the two little girls walked over to her and Molly.
"What's your name?" Brianna asked as she blinked her pretty eyes at
them, Molly sat down next to Grace and place her hand in Grace's to
squeeze her fingers with love.
"I'm Grace Garrett, This is Molly Garrett, we are with the police" Grace

said as she smiled at the cute little cherubs in front of them. "Why do

you have the same name?" Bethany asked.

"Bethany, don't be rude" Chloe warned her daughter as she looked at the

two Detectives. "I'm sorry"

"Please it's ok, really, if you are ok I can explain" Grace replied with a
smile, when Chloe nodded her agreement Grace slipped off the sofa to
kneel in front of the girls so she could look at them.

"Molly and I have the same name, because we are married, we love
each other very very much and we live together, we wear our wedding

bands as a symbol of how much we love each other" Grace reached for
Molly's hand ands they held them out to show the girls the Platinum
Wedding Rings with a beautiful Cubic Zirconia Diamond surrounded
by Pale Purple Amethyst diamonds in the shape of a heart.
The girls gasped as they looked at the rings, Molly pulled out her wallet
and showed them a picture from their wedding, the picture showed
them in their wedding dresses with their arms around one another,
looking deeply into each others eyes and smiling with all the love they

had for one another, Grace had one hand in Molly's hair and the other on her waist, Molly had one hand on her cheek, stroking her soft skin, her other hand was placed over her heart.

The girls were staring at the picture with bright eyes, Chloe and her parents had a look and smiled at them.

"You both look so beautiful, and very much in love, Congratulations to you both, it's so refreshing to see two people who are so in love and not afraid to hide their true selfs," Sandra Bailey said.

"Ok girls, time for bed, say goodnight to Molly and Grace" Chloe told her daughters as she got to her feet.

"Goodnight Miss Molly, Goodnight Miss Grace" they said in unison as the went to kiss their grandparents goodnight.

"Goodnight Girls, sweet dreams" Molly said as she waved to them, Grace climbed back onto the sofa, wrapping her arms around her Molly gave her a kiss to her temple.

"I'm so proud of you baby" she whispered against her soft skin.

"I'm sorry if my granddaughters offended you Detectives"

"Mrs Bailey Please, don't apologise for those sweet girls, they are so beautiful, it was a pleasure to explain it to them"

"Well, you said you were here about Ethan and Kristin, Kristin died when she was 13 years old"

Grace looked at Molly who frowned and pulled the pictures from her pocket, she showed them to Sandra Bailey who gasped when she saw the photo of Kristin in her Police Uniform.

"Can you identify this woman for me please?" Molly asked and waited for the answer.

"Oh My God, That's Kristin, What has she and Ethan done? I always knew Ethan would end up hurting someone,"

Grace's phone rang and she pulled it out of her pocket,

"Sorry I better get this, It's John" she said to Molly as she stepped just behind the sofa to answer it.

"Hey John, what's up, we are just talking to Ethan's aunt- What?" she said with shock.

"Ethan has Murdered 12 people," Molly said to Sandra and her Husband.

Grace hung up the phone and and sighed with frustration, she dropped her head into her hands, she ran her hands through her hair as she turned to Molly who was watching her with concern.

"Grace, Honey what is it?" Molly asked as she got to her feet and went to her.

"The death toll is now 13, Ethan killed the waitress from the diner, he butchered her body and left her in the elevator at the Police station".

Chapter 15.

Rain was pouring down as Grace drove in to the Underground Garage behind the precinct, there were cops everywhere, John was stood there looking pissed as they climbed out of their car and headed over to the elevator, where a grisly display was left for them.

Molly turned away when she saw the butchered body laid out on the floor of the elevator, Grace shook her head and sighed with frustration,

"Fuck, this guy is seriously deranged, how long has she been here?" Molly asked with a clipped tone.

"About an hour. He set off the fire alarm then pulled the keep doors open button so she would be found quickly, is this the waitress you spoke to earlier?"

Grace nodded at John and blew out a breath.

"This is getting out of control, he's killing more people because of me!

If I hadn't escaped they would still be alive, this is all my fault!" Molly said with a sob, Grace wrapped her arms around her to soothe her.

"No Baby, this isn't your fault,"

"YES, it is. If I stayed with him then these people would be alive, i've done this to them. I can't be anywhere near you, he will kill you if your with me."

"Molly what are you talking about?" Grace asked as she turned her to look into her eyes, what she saw scared her.

Molly's heart broke as she looked at the ring on her finger, the very thought of losing Grace destroyed her soul, her chest felt tight as she realised what she had to do- she had to walk away now to keep the woman she loved safe.

She slipped the ring off her finger and placed it in Grace's hand, she leaned forward and kissed her deeply one last time.

"Goodbye my Darling, I'll Always Love You" she whispered through her tears, Grace clung to her as she began to cry.

"Molly what are you doing?" John asked with confusion as he watched them.

"No! Molly don't you dare leave me. I won't let you go baby, please don't go" she sobbed, Molly wiped her tears with her fingertips.

"I Love You Grace, I'll be waiting for you sweetheart, always and forever" Molly backed away as her tears streamed, Grace was sobbing her heart out as Molly turned and ran into the night, Grace ran after her as did John, trying to find her in the darkness but she was gone, she'd left to save them from danger.

"MOLLY! Please come back" John held her tight as she broke down, she began to shake with fear.
Hallie walked passed to the elevator that that led to the Morgue, the body was in a body bag on a gurney, her techs were working on the evidence in the elevator car.
She gave John a sympathetic half smile as she went by, she was shocked that Molly had given herself up to Ethan, she understood that they may never see Molly again, But Grace wasn't ready to hear that yet.

"Where is she?" Isabelle Garrett said as she walked into John's house with her daughters, Evie, Hannah and Brooke.
John led them into his Living room and they gasped when they saw Grace laid on the sofa sobbing her heart out, Isabelle dropped onto the sofa and pulled her baby girl into her arms, Grace wrapped her arms around her and her sobs got worse, Brooke went to them and stroked her little sisters hair, trying to soothe her, John and Deanna watched with devastation, tears were running down Deanna's cheeks as she feared for Molly's life.

"What the hell is going on?" Isabelle asked as she rocked her daughter in her arms.
John led the girls to the sofa and his wife to the cuddle chair in the corner.
He stood in front of the fire place and explained to Grace's family what had been going on.

"Molly has given herself up to a Serial Killer to protect Grace, The Kiss Me Killer is someone from Molly's past, he's obsessed with her and he's been killing people in an effort to get her to declare her love for him, he's created a fantasy that they are in love, he killed his 13th victim tonight and Molly couldn't take the idea that they had been killed because she escaped from him"

Brooke gasped, "he kidnapped her?" she asked with shock.

"He kidnapped Grace, for 2 months he tortured her and beat her, Molly exchanged places with Grace so he would let her go, Molly eventually escaped- she escaped the day they got married, they couldn't wait to get married because of what they had both been through, now Molly believes that Grace will remain safe if she walks away and gives herself up to him,"
Isabelle looked at her youngest child and wiped her eyes.

"Grace, honey why didn't you tell us you had been kidnapped, or what was happening to Molly, she's family"

"I want her back, please find her Mama, I can't live without her" she sobbed into her neck, Isabelle just held her until Grace eventually wore herself out and fell asleep, she laid her daughter down on the sofa and covered her with a blanket, then they all walked into the kitchen to talk,Alexa was in her wheelchair watching the tv as she sat at the table, she was watching a show with sign language.

"How do we help her?" Hannah asked as Deanna handed out mugs of coffee, they were going to need as much coffee as possible right now, John had made it clear that they were staying at his house until this problem had been dealt with, Baby Summer was with her other grandparents and her daddy.

"I don't know, I've sent out a city wide alert, Molly is to be found as soon as possible and Ethan Hackett and his sister are to be arrested on sight,"

"This is going to be bad, isn't it?" Brook said as she looked them in the eye, John nodded as she hung her head and sighed, "What do we do?"

Evie asked.

"Don't let Grace out of your sight, stay here with her and try to get her to eat, I need her strong, once we find Molly and Locate Ethan, I'm letting Grace take the shot, she said she wanted to be the one to kill him, I'm giving her that,"

Isabelle and Brooke looked at each other with concern, Hannah and Evie just drank their coffee, feeling worried for their sister and poor Molly who had to give up her life to save the woman she loved.

"we can't let that fucker hurt Molly, she's family, we have to find her before he hurts her"

"Agreed" John said as he pulled a box down from the top of a cupboard, he unlocked it and pulled out a gun, and a box of bullets, he loaded it, he then handed the gun to Deanna, who looked at him with confusion.

"Put this in the drawer in the living room, it's our emergency gun just in case. Don't get it out unless you feel the home is under attack, remember the code word I gave you during the Galliano Case 3 years ago?"

Deanna nodded as she took the gun, "Well i'm using it now," she headed to the living room and hid the gun in a secret drawer that Alexa couldn't reach.

"Isabelle, if something happens there is a panic room in our bedroom inside the closet, the code to open the door is 242079, get Grace, Alexa and everyone in there and shut the door, there is a working phone in there and a spare wheelchair for my daughter, there is food, water and clothes, theres also a working toilet so you wont have to worry if Alexa needs the bathroom" Isabelle nodded as she realised that the killer could possibly come here.

Molly walked through the Golden Gate Park in search of Ethan, the fucker was here somewhere, tears were streaming down her face as she wandered into the thick forest and searched for him.

"Ethan, I'm here you Son Of A Bitch, Come and Face Me" she called as she looked around, she could hear the rain pelting the trees, and the sound of what she thought was footsteps, she turned and gasped when she saw Ethan appear close to her, he smiled evilly at her as he pulled out a taser, he pressed it to her skin and everything went black.

Opening her eyes, a pain radiated through her head, the room was dark, and the smell of mould was strong, Molly tried to pull her arms free but she was chained to a bed, with nothing on but her bra and panties, she was so cold, and her vision was blurry, she could hear Ethan and his sister talking close by, or rather arguing, there was someone else there too, but this person was wearing a mask, they didn't want their identity revealed, Molly huffed with anger as she tried to figure out where her gun was, she could see her clothes were shredded up on the floor by the damp wall, but her badge and gun were gone,. FUCK! She thought as she tried to focus her eyes to see where she was, this was a different place to the last one, this cave was bigger, and it looked like it was deeper inside this time, they had abandoned the other cave to make it harder for the cops to find them.

Ethan turned to her and sneered at her, he walked over and placed his hands over her breasts, she recoiled from his touch as much as the restraints allowed, the move angered him, he slapped her hard across the face.

She screamed as the pain in her head caused her to writhe with agony, he took out a knife and ran the blade over her stomach, the blood dripping down her skin as she clenched her teeth and tried not to scream again, he watched with interest as the blood fell.

"You never should have escaped Molly, I'm going to have to punish you for that, you caused the deaths of those people, but the ultimate sin is what you did, you married that bitch, you left me and married her- do you know what i'm going to do to you for that?" he snapped at her.

"I don't care what you do to me, I gave myself up to protect my wife, I wouldn't let you hurt her again," Molly snapped back, she could taste blood in her mouth, the metallic tang made her gag, she could see that he was getting pissed off at the mention of Grace, he hated that she referred to her as her wife.

"Don't you dare mention her again, you're my wife!"

"FUCK YOU" she yelled.

he back handed her and snarled at her with anger.

"I'm going to have to beat you into submission, you need to learn your place Molly! I would't have to do this if you hadn't fallen in love with her" Ethan raged as he glared at her, she lifted her head and glared back, unblinking and seething.

"I don't love you! I have never nor will I ever love you! my heart belongs to Grace, she's my love, my life, my soul mate, I'm not into men,"

he hit her again, making her scream as her head throbbed, he ripped the lace underwear off her hips and growled when he saw her naked sex, she brought her knees up to cover herself, she knew what he was going to do to her, he was going to rape her, she fought him as he tried to force her knees apart, she kicked him hard, catching him in the chest, he made a muffled sound as he was pushed back a few feet, he turned to his sister and their guest with angry eyes.

"A little privacy please, I'd like to teach my wife a lesson!" he growled, he watched as they left and then turned back to Molly, who was trying to get her hands free from the chains, he went over to a bag on his desk and pulled out a syringe, and a bottle with clear liquid inside, her heart began to hammer as she realised what he was doing, he was going to sedate her so he could control her while he raped her.
Once he walked over to her he bent over her and stuck the needle into her neck, she tried to fight, until the sedative made her body feel heavy and sluggish, the medication soon kicked in and the world went dark.
When she opened her eyes again Ethan was laid beside her naked, and holding a Polaroid camera, he was taking pictures of her naked and chained to the bed, there was already a huge stack of photos on the bed, she had no sense of time, so she had no idea how long she'd been here, or what time it was.
The drugs were still making her feel sleepy, she turned her head away from the bright flash of the camera, she hated him for what he'd done, he'd taken her from Grace, Again.

The sound of crying woke Isabelle up at 2:15am, she sat up on the sofa and looked at Grace who was sleeping on the other sofa, she was crying in her sleep and clutching Molly's silk nightgown, it smelled like her, and she'd refused to let it go since Molly had walked away almost a week ago, she'd been gone a week and Grace was completely broken. Isabelle got to her feet and walked over to her daughter side, she sat down beside the sofa and stroked her hair gently while whispering to her that it would all be ok.

"Molly! My Molly" she sobbed, John walked through the front door and stopped when he saw Isabelle sat beside her daughter trying to soothe her, he dropped his keys in the dish beside the front door, locked the door and set the alarm, then walked over to them with a sad smile.

"Did you find anything that could tell you where they are?" Isabelle asked hopefully.
He shook his head as he sat on the arm of the sofa.

"No, nothing, The FBI are more interested in finding the sister because she has a badge and a gun, so the search for Molly falls on us. It's almost a week since she left, and we still have nothing to tell us where they are hiding."

"What about the father, you said that the father was aware of what his children were doing, and that he refused to help before you arrested him, is there anyway to force him to talk?" Brooke said as she entered the room in a pair of fluffy pyjamas and slippers, rubbing her tired eyes. John watched her walk over to her sister and kiss her hair softly.

"It was Grace who figured out he was aware of what his kids were doing, he seemed quite proud once we figure it out, before then he turned on the water works and played the disgusted father routine, but once he let slip that he had a daughter, Grace put it together quickly and had to resort to almost pouring his wife's ashes down the sink to get a response out of him, but even then all he did was curse at her"

Brooke looked John in the eye. "Take me to see him"

Brooke was sat at the table with John in the interrogation room at the police station, they were waiting for Ethan Hackett's father to be escorted in, John had pulled a few strings to get this to happen, but he didn't care, they were working against the clock to find Molly before his Serial Killer Son did something to hurt her.

The door opened and he was brought in in handcuffs, wearing a dirty orange jumpsuit, he looked old and exhausted as he sat down in front of them with a sour expression.

"Who the fuck are you?" he asked as he looked her up and down, he licked his lips.

"My name is Brooke, and your sick bastard of a son has taken my Sister in-law, where are they, my sister is Detective Grace Garrett, and she's been destroyed by your son, I want to know where your kids are hiding, because thats where Molly is, now tell me" she said, he laughed at her as he leaned on the table.

"Or what girly, what are you going to do?" he sneered, as he leaned toward her, she leaned toward him and smiled at him with an evil smirk.

"This" she said and pulled the chain under the table, his head smacked onto the table and caused his nose to explode, John's eyes widened as Brooke jumped to her feet and grabbed his head and held it against the table, she leaned over him and whispered in his ear, as he howled with pain.

"You think i'm going to let your Fucking son kill Molly and destroy my sister, you have another thing coming, now tell me what I want to know you Fucking Psycho or I will make your life a living hell!" she snapped

"You can't do this to me" he whimpered pitifully, she just smiled with an evil look in her eyes, she wasn't giving up till he had given her what they needed.

"Tell Me or I get my Husband's friend to pay you a visit, I can promise you that you will never be able to sit down again when he's done with you, you will have to spend the rest of your life laying on your stomach"

John heard something and looked beneath the table, he was peeing in his seat, John smirked as he watched Brooke work her magic, he was caving in.

"They have a place in the mountains but I don't know where, they called it their cave hideaway, its in the mountains that's all I know I swear" he stuttered, Brooke let the man go and stepped back, the guard stepped over and pulled him from his seat.

"This woman assaulted me" he said to the guard, he looked at Brooke and gave her a wink, she smiled at him.

"I'm sorry, I must have had something in my eye" he replied and dragged him out of the room to return him to his cell.

John led her out of the room and they left the Lockup and headed down to the squad room on the 5th floor.

"That was pretty impressive Brooke, Molly and Grace would be so proud of you, good job I filmed it so they could see it once we rescue her"

Brooke smiled at him, then followed him out of the Elevator and over to the bullpen.

She gasped when she saw the two desks that belonged to her sister and Molly, decorated with photos from their wedding and honeymoon at the hotel, the flowers and the trinkets they had bought one another, it hurt her heart to know that Molly was in the clutches of a madman.

John pulled the maps out of the storage cabinet and spread them on the table at the front of the room, he saw Brooke looking at the pictures, her eyes caught the picture that Ethan had taken of them making love, although that one was on the whiteboard with all the other evidence they had on The Kiss Me Killer.

"We will find her, I promise we will, now lets look at the maps based around the Mountains, that's where he said they were , now there's too much area to work with by ourselves, so we need to call in the mountain rescue team and brief them on what we are dealing with, we need to get as many teams as possible together and get out there to search"

Brooke looked down at the maps and bit her lips as she tried to figure out where they could start.

"John, its October the 1st, it's going to be freezing in those caves, you need to stock up on thermal wear and heated blankets for when you find her. she could end up dying of pneumonia, this isn't just a rescue mission, its a takedown-" she said pointedly, John nodded.

"Yes it is, we may have to shoot our way out of there once we find her, Ethan is so obsessed with Molly he will kill her if he has to, if it means keeping her forever. The primary objective is to find Molly and get her the hell out, which is where Grace come's in, she will be with me and she can get Molly out once we find her, I can hold Ethan off as long as possible"

"You said you wanted Grace to take the shot, are you still going to let her do that?" Brooke asked as she looked him in the eyes. He nodded, and walked over to the white board, he pulled two photographs down, that were taken at the hospital.

"This is what Ethan did to Grace while he held her captive for two months, he beat her with a leather belt, and carved Jagged X's into her chest and stomach, he sexually assaulted her as revenge for falling in love with Molly, he traded Grace's life for Molly's so he could have what he wanted, he tried to rape Molly, and that is why i'm giving Grace the shot, this bastard has hurt them too much, i'm tired of seeing these beautiful women being torn apart by a serial killer"

Brooke wiped the tear that was falling down her cheek, as she looked at the pictures of what had happened to her sister and to Molly, he was right, they had suffered enough.

"So lets get this plan in action, I want Molly home with Grace and this Fucking killer in the ground." she said with serious tone.

"I like how you think" John replied and they got to work on a plan, once they had the Mountain Rescue Team contacted and coming in at 10am for a briefing on the situation, they headed back to his house to get some sleep and tell the others what they were doing.
As they approached the front door they saw an envelope on the doorstep, with Grace's on the front!

John picked the envelop up and looked at it, he had a bad feeling as he ushered Brooke into the house and locked the door behind him, then set the alarm.

He walked into the kitchen and found his wife making coffee and breakfast for everyone, Alexa was sat at the table in her wheelchair eating a plate of waffles, strawberries and maple syrup.

Grace looked exhausted and worn down, she was staring at Molly's wedding ring on her finger, she had slipped it on her finger with her own wedding ring, and she refused to take it off until Molly was home so she could put it back where it belonged.

"How are you holding up honey" Brooke asked as she stroked her hair gently, Grace didn't respond to anyone, Isabelle looked at John and shook her head, meaning she'd hardly slept, she'd spent most of the night crying, and the tears were still falling.

"Grace this was left on the doorstep for you" John said as he handed the envelope to her. Grace took the envelope and opened it, a large stack of photos fell onto the counter, she screamed when she saw a picture of Molly chained to a bed,with blood on her chest where he had carved Jagged X's into her skin, she was unconscious and covered in bruises, her eye was swollen shut, and blood was round the outside of her mouth, he'd beaten her violently.

John pulled the pictures away from Grace and put them back into the envelop then into a plastic bag, they were evidence.

"Oh god no, Molly, what is he doing to her?" Grace cried as she wrapped her arms around her legs and curled up into a ball on her chair, she was falling to pieces.

John called the chief and asked him to send some officers down to guard his house, then explained why, he said 4 officers would be down within the hour.

"Deanna, Hun, Get the gun from the secret drawer and get everyone upstairs into our room, Brooke can you take Alexa and have the panic room door open ready please, we need to lock this place down, Now"

"John is that Bastard coming here?" Brooke asked with panic, John sighed and turned to her, he looked strained.

"I don't know, but i'm not taking any chances, get upstairs and keep the doors locked, I need to talk to Grace"

Brooke picked Alexa up and carried the child upstairs, Isabelle followed with Evie and Hannah close behind, Deanna brought up the rear with the gun in her hand.

John turned to Grace and put his hands on her shoulders.

"Grace, Honey I know you are in a bad place right now, but I need you to pull it together and focus, we're getting Molly back, and I'm giving you the shot!" he said as he looked into her tearful eyes, she lifted her head and looked at him, she could feel her heart pounding as she sat up and wiped away her tears.

"You wanted the shot, I'm giving it to you, don't let this fucker win Grace, we may have a location and I have a Mountain Rescue Team coming to the station at 10am for a briefing on the case and what we are dealing with, I want you there when we go searching, I want him to see you rescue Molly, right before you put a bullet between his eyes"

Grace thought about what he was doing to Molly, and she got angry.

"This is between him and me, I'm saving my girl, then i'm going to deal with him, i'm putting an end to this" she said with rage, John nodded as he watched her, their silent agreement said it all, Grace was out for blood, this nightmare ended Now!

Chapter 16.

Molly jumped when another flash went off in her eyes, she was chained to a chair in the middle of the room, she was cold, the small white dress doing nothing to warm her body, she was hungry, and thirsty, but he'd refused to bring her food until she said her wedding vows to him, he was shouting at her to smile for the camera, but all she could do was sit there and pretend it wasn't happening, she was thinking about Grace, and the last time she had felt her soft skin beneath her fingers, the memory of Grace moaning as they made love in the car was bittersweet, she missed her so much, and she wished that she could be home with her, in their own bed at their new house, making love and laughing as they decorated their rooms the way they wanted them.

"HEY! I said smile for the camera" Ethan snapped as he took more pictures, she ignored him and thought about the woman she loved, she'd walked away to save her from harm, would Grace ever forgive her for that?

Lucy walked into the room with the mystery guest, she wanted to know who was under that mask.

"Sorry to interrupt big brother, but I thought you should know that A Mountain Rescue Team has been deployed, they are heading into the mountains to search for Molly- Now how do you suppose they found out the location?" She said with distain, he glared at her.

"Dear old dad, he told them where we used to play, I think it's time we packed up and left don't you, onto the next place" he injected Molly to sedate her, and then carried her over his shoulder and turned to his sister.

"Grab whatever we need, leave the rest, lets get going before they find us"

Lucy grabbed the medical kit, the camera and the weapons, then followed him into the tunnels that went deeper into the mountains, Lucy couldn't wait till she could kill him and take Molly for herself, she hated her brother, but he was the only one who gave a damn about her.

Grace followed John into the squad room at 9:58am and saw all the cops waiting for them, The Mountain Rescue Team were there ready, and a ton of caving gear and thermal blankets were stacked up in the corner, they were going prepared.

"Officer Jackson can you run this down to the lad and have it tested for prints and DNA" John said, he nodded and ran down to the lab as quick as he could.

"Ok, people can I have your attention please, We are hunting a serial killer, he has Molly, a detective with this unit, he's hiding somewhere in the mountains and he's considered armed and dangerous, he has his sister with him, she's a police officer, she's also armed and dangerous. The most important thing is to find Molly and get her the hell out, leave Ethan Hackett to me and Grace, if you don't know, Grace is Molly's wife, she's the one who will take the shot if it comes to it, we need to find that cave ASAP, it's October, and its Fucking freezing out there, and its going to be colder inside the caves, wrap up warm, carry an emergency pack with you, keep your weapons close, and search as many tunnels as possible, let's go people we have a lot of ground to cover, and each moment Molly is down there, her chance of survival gets worse" Grace watched as everyone got them selfs ready to go out searching, she took a kevlar vest off of her chair and put it on over her sweater, them she put her coat on and zipped up, she reached into her desk drawer and took out 3 extra clips for her weapon, she slipped them into her coat pocket and then tied her hair back so it was out the way, she was getting ready to fight,

John handed her a Colt Bright Cobra 38 Special, he looked at her with serious eyes as she lifted her leg and slipped the gun into an ankle holster John was strapping to her leg.

"Keep this Gun hidden, don't use it unless you have to, this is my own personal weapon, i'm giving it to you as a backup incase we have to shoot our way out, Grace, no heroics in there, we find Molly and put a bullet in his head, then we get the Fuck out, Got it?"

she nodded and walked over to get herself an emergency pack, and thermal blanket that was rolled up with a carry strap.

Officer Jackson walked over to John with a serious look on his face, he looked worried.

"What is it?" she asked at she slipped the pack on her back, then put a winter hat on to keep her head warm, she took a hat and gloves and a jacket off of the desk that she had brought with her for Molly, along with some thick clothes.
John looked at the papers in Officer Jackson's hands and frowned.

"This can't be, there must be a mistake," John said as he read the report with disbelief.

"They ran the prints 3 times Sir, it's not a mistake" Officer Jackson said with a sure tone.

"John?" Grace said as she forced him to look at her.

"The prints on the envelope, and the prints that were found on the

pictures belongs to Hallie!"

Grace gasped at that. "What? How is that possible?"

"There's more, a fingerprint was found on one of the belts found in the

cellar where you were kept, that print also belongs to Hallie"

"Hallie was down there? While I was held for 2 months being beaten and abused she was down there with me? Hitting me with a belt then coming back here to spend time with Molly while she was grieving?" Grace shouted.
John picked up the phone and called the morgue, the assistant Claire answered the phone, sounding stressed and worried.

"Claire, put Hallie on the phone, I need to speak to her Now!" he said with a clipped tone, he was pissed.

"She's not here, she never turned up to work this morning, and she's not answering her home phone or her cell phone, her husband hasn't seen her since 11pm last night, she said she had to go back to work to run a

few tests on the latest body, but theres no tests pending"

"Claire get up here now, I need to speak to you in private, don't say a

word to anyone" "Ok, yes sir" she said and hung up. John turned to Grace who had been listening the whole time.

"What The Fuck Is Going On?" Grace asked quietly as she leaned on the desk to speak to John without anyone hearing.

"I have no idea" John replied as he sighed with confusion.

"John, Hallie has been a part of this from the start, she's been working with Ethan and his sister, it was a set up from the beginning" Grace said as she slapped the file folder onto the desk with anger.

"Fuck, I have to call the Chief of Detectives and tell him to get his ass down here, this isn't going to end well" he huffed and made a call he never wanted to make.

Claire walked through the door and over to them, she looked flustered after running up the stairs.

After John called The Chief of Detectives he turned to Claire and told her to follow them into his office, Grace closed the door behind them.

"Claire, I need you to stay calm, but what i'm going to tell you does not leave this room, and neither do you, I need you to stay in here while we are out on the search, can you do that?"

she nodded as Grace sat her down.

"Hallie's prints were found on a belt taken from the cellar where Grace was held captive for 2 months, and her prints were found on an envelope and some pictures dropped off at my house early this morning, the pictures are of Molly being beaten and abused, she's involved in the these murders Claire, and she's now a suspect"

"Oh God, is she responsible for what's happened to Molly?" she asked,

"Possibly, I don't know what Hallie has in common with Ethan or his sister, but she's connected to this somehow, I need you to use the computer in here, and do a full background check on Hallie, I want you to dig into her life from the time she first walked to who she is now, she's dangerous and she's not going to appreciate us digging into her life, if you find anything call me or John, we need to know everything!"

"Ok" Claire said as she walked round to the computer and got busy with a background search.

"Keep these blinds closed and this door locked" John warned her, she nodded and locked the door as they left, the shades were closed next and they left to begin the search in the Mountains.

The rain was coming down harder as Grace followed John through the thick dense forest leading into the Mountains, she was cold, and they had been searching the mountains for almost 8 hours now, they had searched 6 caves so far, and had found nothing, Grace was waiting for Claire to call her to tell them what she had found.

"There's a cave just ahead, looks like footprints at the entrance, let's go in slowly, get your gun out and radio for the rescue team, they are just behind us" he said, Grace nodded and pulled out her radio, she contacted the rescue team leader and informed him of where they were.

"We have a cave entrance about 50 feet in front of you, waiting for you to arrive before we go in, there's a disturbance at the entrance," Grace said into the walkie talkie, "Copy that, on our way"

Grace waited as she stood to the side of the entrance, John stood on the other side with his gun ready, he looked up when the Rescue team appeared with their emergency equipment.

"Going in in 3,2,1," John whispered, Grace followed him in and raised her gun, the team followed, with about 7 cops behind them as backup. Moving as quietly as they could through the first cavern, they headed into the tunnels and cleared each cavern they came too one at a time, as they got deeper, they could smell something, candles.

"They've been here, I can smell candles, Grace stay with me, and the rescue team, I want you 7 to take the next set of tunnels and stick together, keep your walkies on so we can contact you"

with a nod, the cops veered off to the set of tunnels to the left, John and Grace went to the right and remained quiet.

Tension was building in Grace, it was beyond freezing in these tunnels, she hoped Molly was wrapped up in blankets.

"John, I can see candle light in that cavern" Grace whispered as they got closer, John nodded and stepped inside, he cleared the room and Grace stepped inside, she gasped when she saw the bed with blood on it, and metal posts which Molly had been chained too.

There were pictures of her dressed up in various different outfits, sexy underwear that didn't even fit her, and dirty nightgowns, her hair was in pigtails again like a schoolgirl, and she had bruises on her body and a black eye. Grace saw a pile of shredded clothes on the floor, she walked over to it and kicked it with her foot, as she did her foot his something, she bent down and found Molly's gun and badge.

She picked them up and put them in her backpack, with the emergency supplies.

Grace laid her hand on the bed, it was still warm.

"Fuck, it's still warm where she was laid, they were just here," Grace

whispered. "Keep your eyes open, they couldn't have gotten too far" they set off into the only tunnel they could have taken and made their way deeper into the cold dark unknown.

Molly tried to open her eyes as she felt her head swinging from side to side, she was thrown over Ethan's shoulder, and they were moving quickly, she could see Lucy and the other person in the mask following behind them, they looked angry.

"Can we please stop for a few minutes, my feet are killing me" Lucy whined, Ethan rolled his eyes as he kept going.

"No! We need to keep going or they will find us, I'm not going to jail

Lucy, keep moving"

"I can't, I'm tired of running, they'll find us eventually, lets just give up,

Give Molly to me and get gone," she said, she hoped he fell for her lies, but from the angry look on his face she could see that he wasn't falling for it.

"Nice try,Sis! You think I don't know that you've been trying to get Molly to yourself, your in love with her- I know that, but its not going to happen, she's mine"

"When are you going to learn Ethan, she's not interested in men, she's only interested in women, I'm a woman, I'm in love with her, she can love me back, now hand Molly over to me" Lucy shouted at him,

Suddenly a shot rang out from behind, and Lucy clutched her stomach, then fell to the floor, Ethan stared at her dead body, before lifting his head up and facing the person in the mask, a gun was pointed at his head, Molly was trying to see who was holding the gun, but the sedative was doing a great job of clouding her memory.

"Put Molly on the ground and step away"

Molly tried to pinpoint that voice, but she couldn't tell if she knew it or not, she was struggling to get her head to focus, she needed to wake up and find a way to get away from them.

"What the fuck are you doing, we have to keep moving," Ethan snapped

"I SAID PUT HER DOWN ON THE GROUND, SHE'S MINE AND SHE'S COMING WITH ME"

Ethan stepped back as he realised that he was about to be double crossed not just by his sister, who was now dead, but by this bitch too, he was angry as he reached into his pocket and pulled out a flare gun and shot it toward her, she jumped back and yelled when the flare hit her leg, burning her, Ethan took this opportunity to get gone, so he turned and ran into the darkness, Molly was moaning with pain as her head was being thrown around as he made his escape.

"Bring her back to me!" she screamed as she got to her feet once more and hobbled after them.

"Did you hear that?" John asked, Grace nodded as she realised what the sound was, it was a gunshot, she took off in the direction of the gunshot and prayed Molly was ok, John followed with the rescue team right behind them.

As they were running through the dark tunnels, with only flashlights to guide them, they stumbled on Lucy's body, she had a gunshot wound to her stomach, she was dead, there was a flare on the floor that was sparking, casting the dark tunnel in an ominous red glow.

"They're here, lets keep going" Grace said as she moved over the body of Lucy, and down an incline.

"Listen, I can hear crying" John said.

They followed the sounds and came to a very big cavern with a lake in the middle and a 200ft drop off the edge of the walkway, Ethan was stood on the other side of the ledge holding a chain, he had an evil sneer on his face.

Molly was bound by chains, and being hoisted up into the air by her wrists by a deranged serial killer, who would rather kill her than risk losing her.

Grace felt her fear spike as she realised that the water below was hot, Molly was barely awake as her head was draped top the side, she was wearing a small dress and nothing more, her body was black and blue.

"MOLLY" Grace called as she looked up at her with fear.

"Back off, or I let go of this chain, and she boils to death" he snapped at them.

"Ethan think about this, let Molly go, she's never done anything to you"

"Yes she has! She ignored me at school, she didn't declare her love for me, I did all this for her, I killed those people for her, I even killed the ones who raped her, I made them pay for what they did to her" he yelled, John Gave Grace a sidelong glance to get her to find a way to get Molly down, while he distracted him.

"Yes, you made them pay, and that was good of you, but you can't just force someone to love you, Molly isn't interested in any man, she's in love with Grace, and Grace is in Love with her, they are married, and they are going to spend the rest of their lives together, you need to let this obsession go, and stop this before someone else gets hurt, don't hurt Molly because she loves someone else" John said as he tried to calm him, Grace was walking around behind the stone walls trying to find a way to get Molly down, that's when she spotted a ledge above that she could climb onto and reach over to Hook a Carabiner to the chain holding her wrists, Grace whispered something to the rescue team and the one in charge nodded.

"Here, take this, as quietly as you can, get up there and hook this onto the chain, then make sure its done tight, we can pull her over to the ledge so you can get her down" he said as he handed her the gear she'd need.

Grace climbed up the wall to the ledge and shuffled her way to the end, as she reached out Molly's head lifted up and she saw Grace reaching for her, her arms were hurting badly, and she was beyond exhausted, but her heart jumped for joy when she saw Grace reaching for her, tears began to fall as she fought the sedatives to stay awake, she needed Grace's arms round her so badly right now.

Grace took the hook that the team had given her and reached out to snag the chain, once she had it she pulled slightly and attached the Carabiner to the chain and tightened it, with a signal to the team they pulled the rope attached to it and Molly was pulled over toward Grace, with a glance below, John was keeping Ethan occupied enough to free Molly.

Once Molly was on the ledge she worked quickly to remove the chains with a bolt cutter that was passed up to her, Molly was shivering as she watched what Grace was doing, despite the hot water and the cavern filled with steam, Molly was frozen to the bone, Grace was afraid she was going into shock.

The chains finally fell from off of her wrists, they were bleeding badly, and looked to be infected.

"Oh Baby, I'm here now. You're going to be ok my darling, put your

arms around me and I can get you out of here"

Molly wrapped her arms and legs around her and Grace held her tight as she climbed down, Molly was wrapped in a thermal blanket and a heated pad was laid over the top to bring her core temperature back up to safe levels.

Grace laid her on a stretcher that the team had carried all the way in there, she leaned down and took her lips in a passionate kiss, Molly was crying now as she realised that Grace had come for her, she had walked into the caves and tunnels to find her.

"I Love You So Much Molly, we're going to get you out of here baby

just hold on ok?"

Molly nodded as she held her hands tight against her chest.
As she looked into her eyes, she lost consciousness.

"Molly?" Grace gasped,

"she's going into shock, we need to get her out of here now! She needs to get to the hospital, but we can't get her out of here in time on this stretcher, the tunnels are to narrow to navigate"

Grace wrapped her arms around Molly and picked her up, she wrapped her legs around her waist and laid her head on her shoulder and wrapped the thermal blanket and heated pad around her, she held her tight as she walked our from behind the rock wall and saw John was struggling to keep Ethan calm, that resolve snapped when he saw that Molly was wrapped up in Grace's arms, anger flared in his veins as he pulled out a gun, he aimed it at Grace but missed when Hallie appeared out of nowhere and hit him in the head with a wooden post, Hallie saw Grace was holding Molly and she screamed with fury, she grabbed Ethan's gun and started to fire at them in a rage.

Grace pulled out her gun and aimed it at Hallie, she squeezed the trigger with a steady hand and shot her in the chest, causing her to fall to the floor and her porcelain mask shattered, she was dead.

Grace cursed when she saw that Ethan was gone, and John was bleeding.

"Fuck! John where are you hit?" Grace called out to him.

"In the shoulder and the leg, I'll be fine, Get Molly out of here, she's under Police Protection until Ethan is dead"

"No Shit" Grace said as she headed for the tunnels that led them in here, they were now making their way out of there with two wounded and One dead still in the cavern and one dead in the tunnels. Ethan was still out there.

"Grace" Molly whimpered as she clung to her body, she could feel Grace's body heat seeping into her as she tried to keep herself awake. She could feel the movements as Grace ran out of the tunnels, she was stroking Grace's hair as she felt her heart beating wildly, "It's ok Darling, I'm getting you out of here, just hold on Molly, please hold on baby" Grace soothed her as she ran, the rescue team was right behind them with John being carried by two of the rescue workers.

"I see light, we're almost out Molly, it's ok we are getting you to the hospital"

as they raced out of the tunnels and into the open air, it was almost dark now and the night was cold and wet.

"There's the Rescue Helicopter," John said as he saw it landing in the park, they raced down the mountain side through the forest and into the park as fast as they could.

Once they reached the helicopter they climbed inside and shut the door, Grace laid Molly onto a stretcher and wrapped her in the thermal blanket again to get some warmth into her body, she was shaking now with severe shock, her lips were blue and so were her fingers and toes, she had hypothermia.

"We are in the helicopter baby, it wont be long now, just please hold on honey" Grace said as she leaned over and kissed her head, she stroked her hair as she knelt next to her gurney and laid her hand over her cold face.

"I Love You Grace" Molly whispered, then everything went black.

Chapter 17.

Grace was sat in the waiting room in the ICU as the doctors worked to save Molly, she had gone into shock and then her heart stopped, they were battling to get her stable as they tried to warm her body up, she was in a very serious condition and Grace was beside herself with worry, John patted her leg with sympathy, he's had the bullets removed from his leg and shoulder, after he was stitched up and given anti-bio tics to ward off any infections, he had hobbled up from the ER, to the ICU to sit with Grace.

He had called Deanna and told them they had found Molly and to get to the ICU as soon as possible.

"She's going to be ok honey, I promise"

"You can't promise that, she's been hurt too much, what if her body

can't take anymore and it shuts down, I don't want to lose her" Grace cried softly, the doors to the Elevator opened and Isabelle stepped out with Brooke, Evie, Hannah and Deanna, who was pushing Alexa in her wheelchair.

"Mama" Grace cried as she launched herself into her arms. Her sisters wrapped their arms around her too and they comforted her as much as they could.

Deanna went to John and gave him a kiss, he held her tight for a few minutes, then embraced his daughter, who looked confused by the sling holding his arm up, and the bandages on his leg.

"What happened, is she ok?" Brooke asked as she looked at the tired and distraught expression on her sisters face.

"We found Molly in a huge, cavern, she was suspended by her wrists over a boiling lake, he was willing to let her boil to death, John kept him busy so I could climb up there and get her down, her wrists are infected, she has severe hypothermia and her heart stopped, they are fighting to save her, i'm so scared Mama, I can't lose her, please tell me

she's going to be ok"

Isabelle cupped her daughters face and held her steady, he looked deep into her eyes and told her what she felt.

"Molly is going to be ok, I promise you that she's going to make it

honey, be strong for her Grace, she's going to need you"
Grace nodded as she laid her head on her shoulder.
 An Hour later the doctor walked into the waiting room, he looked at
the group that was sat there and cleared his throat.
"Molly Garrett's Husband please" he said.

"I'm Molly's wife, is she ok?" Grace asked as she jumped to her feet.
The doctor was taken aback by that, but he smiled at her and reached
for her hands.

"Yes, she's fine, she has a lot of bruises, contusions, she has a severe
case of hypothermia, her toes and fingers are still a little bit blue from
frost bite, she has infections in her wrists, and i've stitched up the knife
wounds to her body, we have her on a heating mat to try to get her core
temperature back up, she is very traumatised, but otherwise she's going
to be fine, and there's evidence of sexual assault, but no penetration,

you can see her now"

"Thank you so much" Grace said and threw her arms around him, he
hugged her happily and then led them all to her room, which was dark
and quiet as they stepped in, Molly was heavily sedated and on an
Oxygen mask to help her breathe better.

 Grace walked over to the bed and leaned over to kiss Molly's head, Dr
Maddison watched by the doorway as Grace kicked off her shoes and
climbed into the bed with her and wrapped her arms around her, he was
about to tell her she couldn't do that, but stopped when he saw that
Molly responded to Grace's body, she moulded herself to her and
snuggled closer, she tucked her hands inside Grace's shirt to touch her
soft warm skin, she moaned with happiness as she felt her lips tracing
kisses over her eyes.
"Ssh Baby, I'm here, and you're safe, I won't let anyone hurt you ever

again honey," Grace whispered to her, Isabelle walked over to them and
gently stroked her hair, her sisters stood close by and they all reached
out to touch Molly, to give her the loving comfort she needed.

"Grace" she mumbled heavily, John and Deanna stood to the side, with

Alexa watching with confusion, Dr Maddison walked to the other side to check her vitals, her breathing was improving and her fingers and toes were less blue, the heated mat was helping her, but he suspected it was Grace that was healing her.

"Grace, My Grace" she mumbled again as she tucked her head into her neck.

"Ssh Molly, you're in my arms and your safe, i've got you baby, I Love You So Much"

"I Love You" she whispered back as she finally relaxed and let the sedatives pull her into a deep and welcome sleep.

The feel of a gentle hand caressing her face woke her from a deep sleep, she fought to open her eyes as she focused on what was beside her, the bright light from the sun hurt her eyes, she groaned and squeezed her eyes shut, someone ran over to the window and pulled the blind shut, then closed the curtains, finally she opened her eyes and saw that Grace was sat beside her holding her hands, she looked so tired, but she was here beside her, and she was sobbing into her palm as she kissed her hands with happiness.

"Grace!" Molly whispered, she couldn't talk louder than that right now, she was severely dehydrated, and the pneumonia had caused a lot of stress and damage to her body.
Grace got to her feet and sat on the bed, she took Molly's lips with hers and kissed her passionately, Molly wrapped her arms around her and held her tight.

"Oh my sweet baby, you're home and your safe now,"

"Grace, you came for me! You saved me!" she whispered as she placed her hands on her face and stroked her soft skin.

"Of course I came for you, I wasn't leaving you down there with him, I fight for what's mine Molly, and your mine, baby."
Grace took Molly's wedding ring off her finger and took her hand, she placed the ring back on her finger and then kissed the delicate fingers she loved so much.

Tears slipped down Molly's face as she watched Grace put the ring back on her finger, Grace then lowered her head and kissed her gently.

"Don't ever leave me like that again, EVER, Molly you scared the shit out of me, it broke my heart when you walked away, I thought i'd lost you forever"

Grace wrapped her arms around Molly and just held her.
Molly then looked around the room, but the room wasn't a hospital room, it was a bedroom.

"Where are we?" Molly asked as she looked at the big bedroom, with a door that led to a master bathroom, the walls were painted in a soft Lavender colour with white marble floors, and a lavender rug, the bed was made from Oak, as was the dresser, and a plush brown cord corner sofa was in the corner by the fire place, there were pictures of them both from their wedding hung on the walls.

"Home, Our Home, Brooke and Hannah decorated it for us so we could bring you home, I wanted you out of the hospital and in our bed, you're under police protection now until Ethan is dead"

Molly nodded and shifted so Grace could climb in beside her, she needed her warmth right now, and her arms firmly around her.
Brooke stepped forward with baby Summer in her arms and laid the baby between them, Molly gasped when she saw the baby smile at her, she kissed her soft cheeks and stroked her hair, Grace watched as the baby turned to nuzzle her mouth against Molly's breast, she couldn't wait to have a baby with Molly, she wanted to watch her wife's belly swell with their child, then to watch her as she nursed the baby, her heart was bursting with love.

"I can't wait to have a baby with you, once your better and Ethan is dead, I want to try for a baby" Grace said as she kissed her lips softly,

Molly smiled at her as she nodded with joy. "I want that too" Molly whispered.

"I think my husband can help with that," Brooke said, as she sat on the end of the bed, Grace and Molly looked at her with confusion.

"Matthew has a lot of sperm frozen at the sperm bank, we were wondering if we should donate it to someone who can use it, because you can do that, but after meeting you at the wedding and seeing how much you love Summer, we have decided to donate the sperm to you and Grace, so you can try for a baby, he will sign over paternal rights and he has also agreed to let you formally adopt the baby so he/she will be your's legally"

"Oh my god, Brooke, why don't you use it, I thought you wanted to give Summer a brother or sister?" Grace asked with astonishment.
Brooke just smiled.

"Well, as of July next year, Summer will have little brothers or sisters to love, I'm Having twins"

Grace shot up on the bed and launched herself into Brooke's arms, she held her sister as she giggled with joy, then she bent down and kissed her stomach, Brooke laughed as she rolled her eyes, Molly was smiling as she held Summer in her arms, who was now fast asleep.

"Brooke, this is a big decision, are you sure Matthew is ok with doing this?" Molly said as she shifted to get comfortable, Grace climbed back into the bed and snuggled up behind Molly, kissing her cheek softly.

"Yes, we're sure, we can see how much you two want a baby, and you'd both be fantastic Mommies, we've already signed the paperwork, all you have to do is sign, then once your better you can begin treatment for conception, all you need to do is track your period so we can determine when you ovulate"

"Thank you so much Brooke, this means so much to us," Grace said as she looked at Molly, but Molly was fast asleep, she was exhausted, her head resting on top of Summer's and her fingers intertwined with Grace's.

Brooke smiled at her sister in-law and leaned over to kiss her forehead. She picked Summer up carefully and tucked the covers over her and Grace, she kissed Grace on the cheek.

"Get some sleep, it's been a tough few weeks, you need to be with her"

Grace slipped her arm beneath Molly and gently turned her so that she was facing her, then closed her eyes and slipped into sleep.

Molly woke up feeling cold and alone, she looked to the side and noticed that Grace wasn't there, she could see the light on in the bathroom, and she could hear the shower running, she climbed out of the bed and walked into the bathroom, Molly bit her lip as she looked at Grace in the shower washing her hair, the hot steamy water looked to inviting right now, she slipped the t-shirt off and opened the door to the shower, Grace turned and smiled when she saw her stood there, naked and reaching for her.

Grace pulled her in her arms and wrapped her in her loving embrace. They kissed gently at first, then as Molly traced her hands over her skin their kiss became more passionate, and urgent.

Grace shivered with arousal as the hot water covered them.

"I want you Grace, I need you right now," Molly gasped as she felt Grace bite down on her neck, the sensation making her flush with need.

"Molly, are you sure your ready, I don't want to hurt you sweetheart?" Grace asked as she licked her neck, making her tremble, Molly pulled Grace closer and took her mouth in an erotic kiss, stealing her breath.

"I'm always ready for you Grace, no one can stop me from making love to you, I need you so badly,"

That was all Grace needed to hear.

She picked Molly up in her arms and pressed her against the shower wall, she then reached between them and pressed her fingers against her heated core, she could feel how much Molly wanted her, she slipped her fingers inside and began a gentle massage against her sensitive walls, Molly gasped as she bent down to take Grace's breast into her mouth, she teased the tip with her teeth as she reached for Grace's centre and placed her fingers against her clit, she rubbed her in gentle circles as she put her fingers inside her, she thrust her fingers as Grace began to shake with need, Molly could feel herself trembling as she moaned.

"I need you to Come, Grace, fall over with me,"

Grace began to moan with pleasure as she kissed her deeply, "I Love You Molly" Grace said as she dropped her head onto her shoulder as Molly rubbed her clit in fast desperate circles, Grace picked up the pace as she thrust her fingers inside and Molly's Muscles tightened around her.

"I Love You So Much" Molly replied as her body exploded and Grace cried out, their cries of release echoing in the tiled bathroom, Molly dropped her forehead to Grace's as they both tried to catch their breaths. They kissed briefly before Grace reached for the shampoo and turned Molly in her arms, she lathered her hair and massaged her scalp, the sensation making her moan, Grace kissed her neck and whispered to her.

"If you keep moaning like that i'm going to have to take you again,

you're turning me on Molly!"

"Sounds like a good plan to me" Molly replied, Grace rinsed off her hair and washed her body with the vanilla body wash Molly loved, then led her out of the shower and back to bed, where she wrapped her in love and made love to her all over again.

Walking into the large kitchen and finding Grace stood at the counter with her Mom making Coffee, Molly smiled as she walked over to them and wrapped her arms around Grace from behind, Grace hummed with happiness as she leaned back into her and placed her arms over Molly's.

"What are you doing up? You should be resting baby," Grace asked as she turned to face her, Molly kissed her softly, then she let go to hug Isabelle tight.

"Hi Mama" Molly whispered, Isabelle cradled her gently in her arms as she stroked her hair, "Oh Honey, We have been so worried about you, are you feeling ok, are you in pain?" Isabelle asked her with worry.

"I'm tired, a little cold, I need to get some fleece pyjamas," Molly stated as she pulled the thick robe tighter around her, Grace handed her a mug of hot coffee, which she took great fully and took a sip.

"Ok, I know there's something you're not telling me Grace, John and his family have been here, I heard Alexa giggling, Officer Jackson was here, Isabelle and the girls are here,"

Grace looked at her with concern, she was unsure if she should impart what they had found out from Claire.

"I don't think your'e ready Sweetheart, you need more time to heal

before we get into all the details" Molly put her coffee down and took Grace's hands in her own, she looked her in the eye.

"I need to know what's happening baby, there's an armed police guard outside the front door, and one in the back yard, you told me i'm under

police protection until Ethan is dead, but I know theres more"
Isabelle sighed as she laid her hand on Molly's shoulder, she nodded to Grace to tell her everything.

"Ok, Molly honey- there's no easy way to say this, but Hallie is dead"

"What?" Molly gasped, her lip shook as she took in this information.

"Hallie wasn't who we thought she was, her name wasn't Hallie, it was Lauren Lee, she had a lot of dark secrets that she'd kept buried in her closet, even her husband didn't know who she really was"

"And who was she?" Molly asked

"She was a Schizophrenic, Molly she was down there in the cellar with me while I was being beaten and tortured, she beat me with that belt, she was involved in all of this from the very beginning, Lauren Lee was

another student who went to your school,"

"Oh My God" Molly exclaimed as she got to her feet and paced the room, she was beyond angry, she'd trusted Hallie, or rather Lauren Lee.

"She was in love with you Molly, she needed you but she couldn't find a way to have you, she knew Ethan was in love with you too so she approached him in a chat room to groom him, she needed him to do these killings so he could eventually abduct you, her plan was to then kill Ethan and have you for herself. She set the whole thing up so Ethan would take the fall if he got caught, Lucy Grant was pulled in to the plot by her sadistic brother, because she too had fallen in love with you after she joined the police force,"

"Jesus Fucking Christ! What is it with everyone falling in love with me, i'm not interested in anyone but you" Molly snapped as she ran her hands through her hair.

Grace pulled her into her arms and tried to soothe her.

"Ethan is still out there?" Molly asked with a shaky breath.

"Yes, that's why your in Police Protection, we think that he may come after you again, this time to kill you so no one can take you away from him- i'm not going to let him hurt you again Molly, i'm going to take the shot and end him once and for all!"

"So we are down to the final fight, Lauren is dead, Lucy is dead. Now it's just Ethan to deal with,"

"He could be anywhere- what if he's skipped town?" Isabelle said with a worried tone.

"He won't skip town, his pride might be a bit dented but he's obsessed enough to try again, he want's Molly and he wont walk away until he has her, he's going to go down fighting"

"If he's going down, fighting, then lets make this fight count" Molly said, Grace frowned at that.

"Molly what are you talking about?" Isabelle asked as she looked at her with concern.

"was everything from my house brought here?"

Grace nodded, "yes, we put all the boxes in the attic until you could go through them"

"I'll be right back"

Molly hurried up the stairs to the attic while Grace and Isabelle waited in the kitchen, Molly returned a few minutes later with a big box, Isabelle took it from her when she saw Molly struggling to carry it, she'd lost so much weight, and muscle tone because of everything that had happened, Grace was anxious to get her eating again so she could build her body back up to what it should be.

Molly opened the box with a knife and pulled out 3 guns and spare clips with bullets inside, Grace looked in the box and saw the surveillance equipment, and a tool kit.

"What is all this?"

"Insurance, Grace can you take Mama and the girls to John's please, I don't want them here when this goes down,"
Grace looked at her with disbelief, fear settled in her heart.

"Whoa, hold on a minute- Molly you are not going up against this Fucker, he almost killed you"

"Grace Please, I can't live like this anymore, I can't keep hiding behind these walls afraid that he's going to come after me with every loud noise, I want this over! We didn't get to finish our honeymoon, I married my best friend and I haven't even been able to celebrate with you or your family, I want us to have a baby, to settle into our new house, to Make Love just like we did on our wedding night, I want our lives back, and I want to sleep beside you without waking up feeling scared that he's watching us!"
Brushing a strand of hair back from her eyes, Grace could see that Molly had reached her limit, she wanted to end this so they could get on with their lives without fear overshadowing them.
Grace pulled out her cell phone.

"John, can my mom and sisters stay with you for a while, I think we're getting ready to put an end to this nightmare,"

"I'll be right over" John said to her over the phone.

Grace turned to her Mom, "Mama, can you pack a bag for each of you, and can you make sure all the windows are locked"

Isabelle looked at her girls with fear, she sighed with a shaky breath, "I wish you wouldn't do this" she whispered, Grace looked to Molly who was busy checking the guns and making sure they were clean and ready to fire.

"We don't have a choice Mama, this isn't going to end unless we end it! This man is deranged, and he's not going to let Molly go without a fight, so we need to fight back"

Grace said as she checked her gun, then the spare weapon John had given her when they went into the mountains, Molly took out the tool kit and began to set up the surveillance cameras in various parts of the kitchen, then quickly moved through the house setting the cameras up so she could see what was happening on a mini tablet screen that she would carry with her, once she had them set up she set up motion sensors and separate night vision cameras, she was wiring this house up so they could keep an eye on what was happening at all times, they needed to be able to live as normally as possible while they waited for Ethan to show up.

"Grace, Sweetheart I think we should leave one window open, see if he takes the bait, maybe he will find the open window a little hard to pass up" Molly said as she looked at the window in the kitchen. Grace looked at the window too and nodded with agreement.

"take some bottled water and snacks upstairs, who knows how long this will take"

John turned up a few minutes later and helped Isabelle load the bags into his car, he took one look at Molly, and put a hand on her shoulder.

"You look like shit kiddo! Are you sure you want to do this?" he asked. Molly nodded and sighed deeply.

"We have too, this is the only way to end this now, he won't stop unless we stop him John"

John gave Molly a fierce look as he lowered his voice, he had a very serious look on his face.

"Don't you dare get killed Molly, when you walked away like that it almost killed her, it took me over a week to get through to her,"

Molly looked over to where Grace was helping her Mom load the babies thing into the back seat now all the bags were in the trunk of the car, she felt so damn guilty for causing her so much pain, she felt her heart break at what Grace must have gone through.

John pressed something into her hand, she looked at it with confusion.

"This is my body alarm, its connected to my phone, its also connected to the guards outside, they will be in an empty house across the street, press it and we will know that your under fire, and I can be here in 4 minutes, the guards will be here in 2 minutes, got it?"

Molly nodded, "got it"

John kissed her forehead, then gave her a loving hug.

"I know i'm not your dad, no one can ever take his place, but I knew you when you were a happy beautiful and energetic child, I watched you grow up and I was happy as fuck when you joined the police force, I was even happier when you joined Homicide, your like a daughter to me Molly and it broke my heart to see you suffering so much, it hurt that I couldn't help you, seeing your health go down hill like that was scaring me so much, so I turned to Grace for help, I gave her a picture of you taken at my birthday last year, once she saw your picture she wanted to help you, she fell in love with you the moment she met you Molly,"

Molly bit her lip as she thought about how much she loved Grace, and all she had to fight for.

"Be Careful Honey" he said.

"We Will" she replied as she hugged him back, Isabelle walked over to them and hugged Molly tight.

Grace laid her hand on her shoulder as they watched them drive away to safety.

Once they had gone, Grace locked the house up tight and made sure all the windows downstairs were locked except the one in the kitchen, the window he would use to get in.

Molly grabbed Grace and hauled her into her arms and kissed her passionately.

"Upstairs, Now!" Molly breathed into her mouth, gasping at the sudden fire in her eyes, Grace felt a bolt of arousal shoot down to her core,

"Molly?" Grace whispered with shock, Molly swept her up into her arms and carried her upstairs to their room where she kicked the door shut and put Grace on the floor, so she could pin her against the wall, she pulled the t-shirt off her and dropped her mouth to her breasts and kissed the tight tip as she used her fingers to tease the other side, Grace gasped as she slipped her hands into her wife's hair and massaged her scalp as she writhed in her hands, the pleasure was intense and she loved the feel of her lips on her skin, even if her Bra was in the way, but oh god the feel of the lace cup against her nipples was exquisite, she groaned when Molly's hands travelled down to her jeans, she caressed Grace through the denim and smiled when she cried out wildly,

"Oh Fuck, Molly, Please Don't Stop"

Molly unzipped her jeans and slid them down her hips until she kicked them off, Molly dropped to her knees in front of her and pressed her mouth against her hot centre, she flicked her tongue out to her sensitive clit and licked her through her panties, making her squirm with need, Grace was gasping deeply as she pulled Molly to her feet and devoured her mouth, plunging her tongue inside and groaning as she tasted herself on Molly's lips, the erotic feeling making her knees feel weak as she pushed the robe off her shoulders and growled with arousal at the sight of Molly wearing a pair of Cream lace Panties, and a matching Bra, seeing Molly wearing sexy underwear turned her on, and she was ready to come just looking at her, Molly led her to the bed and laid her down, she removed Grace's Bra and Panties, but not before she inhaled the scent of her arousal, she groaned as she joined her on the bed and made passionate love to her all night.

The House was in complete darkness as Ethan approached the back door, he's spent the last 4 hours creeping around the back garden trying to figure a way into the house, he'd seen her Fucking boss leave with the Bitch's mother earlier, they had left the kitchen light on, but the rest of downstairs was in darkness, he could see a light on upstairs in what he assumed was the Master Bedroom, the window was open a little and he had heard them making love, it angered him, even more than the fucking lump on his head that Hallie had given him, after she double crossed him. Fucking Bitch, his head was still sore from that piece of wood she had used to try and cave his head in.

as he approached the house, he spotted a window open in the kitchen, perfect! He thought with a grin, it was dark now and this was the perfect time to break in and take what was his, it was just starting to rain, so he opened the window, and slipped inside.

Then he closed the window so it looked like everything was normal, he looked around and smiled, he could smell Molly in this kitchen, he loved the smell of her Jasmine perfume, his Dick got hard as he thought about tying Grace up, then taking Molly in front of her, so she could see who Molly belonged to, because it wasn't her, hell no, Molly was his, and his alone.

Walking slowly, he made his way out of the kitchen and into the foyer where the stairs were, he stepped on the first step, and began his assent to the bedrooms, he smiled as he thought how happy she would be when she saw him.

Here I Come Molly......He thought.

Grace laughed as she kissed Molly's shoulder, they had been making love all evening and into the night, it was after midnight by now, and they hadn't been able to keep their hands off one another, Molly was dressed in a long sleeved t-shirt, Jeans and sneakers, Grace had on a T-shirt, jumper and jeans, they were sat on the sofa with a coffee table in front of the, they had all the surveillance equipment up and running, and the tablet screen was right where they could see it, so they were ready, their weapons on the table.

The screen sent up a silent alarm to say one of the sensors were triggered, Grace leaned forward and looked at the screen as Molly saw that someone was creeping toward the stairs, the sound of someone on the steps, made them both go on high alert, their bed was made with pillows forming lumps to make it look like they were asleep, Molly flipped off the lamps and the room went dark, she kissed Grace on the lips quickly as they grabbed their weapons. "I Love You Grace" Molly whispered with Love.

"I Love You Too Baby" she whispered back, Molly sent her over to the closet as they had agreed and closed the doors, Molly took refuge behind a tall standing mirror, they waited as the sound of someone creeping around upstairs grew louder as they got closer, Ethan was in the house, and he was right outside their door, the doorknob turned slowly, he was trying to be as quiet as possible, but they already knew he was here, so she took the safety off and had her weapon ready to go. The door opened and he tiptoed into the dark room and over toward the bed, Molly could just make out his shape as she got closer to where he thought they were sleeping, he had something in his hand, it was a gun. He reached down to the bed and pulled the covers back, he was about to raise the gun over what he thought was Grace sleeping, but stopped when he saw that it wasn't Grace, confusion crossed his face at first, then anger registered as he realised that Molly and Grace were not in the bed, he looked around in the darkness, trying to figure out where they were, he headed to the bathroom and looked in there, but it was empty, as he creeped back over to the bed he began to panic, suddenly Grace threw on the light and stood there with her Gun aimed at his forehead, Molly stepped out from behind the mirror with her Gun aimed at his heart, "Freeze Asshole" Grace snapped. Ethan snarled at her, they had set him up!

Chapter 18

"Fucking Bitch" He spat at Grace as he clutched the gun in his hand, he glared at her with hatred as he stalked forward, waiting for the opportunity to strike.
Grace held her gun steady as she watched his movements with guarded eyes, she kept Molly in her sights, making sure he didn't take a step toward her, if he even moved in her direction then she was ready to put a bullet in his head, she had the gun strapped to her ankle, and the spare one Molly had given her earlier, the spare clips were in the pocket of her jeans.

"Don't move you Fucking Asshole," Grace said as she held her stance by the closet, Molly was poised and ready, waiting to see what he was going to do, the body alarm was clutched tightly in her hand, her finger over the trigger of her gun, her thumb hovered over the alarm waiting to send the signal for back up.

"It's over Ethan! You lost, now throw the gun over to Molly and empty

your pockets slowly" Grace said as she watched him intently, he sneered at her as he tried to decide what to do, he was getting agitated as he felt the sweat pouring down his face.

"Fuck You Bitch, Molly is mine, I'm not letting you have her"
Molly laughed at that, she looked to the one she loved so much and suddenly knew what she had to do, the only way to make him back down and surrender was to make him see what he couldn't have, she moved forward and slowly made her way to Grace, she held her hand steady on her gun as he watched her movements with hunger.

"Ethan, I'm going to put my gun away for a minute, ok? Then I can talk

to you"
Molly slipped the gun into her hip holster, then held up her hands. He continued to watch her as she walked over to Grace and stepped in front of her, Protecting what was hers from the madman in front of them!

"Ethan, I need you to listen to me, because I don't think you know what was really happening, you were set up, the person who wore the mask is the one who contacted you on the chatroom, her name was Lauren Lee, she was Schizophrenic and she had an obsession with me, just like you do, she set this whole thing up so she could groom you into killing the people who hurt me, she did it so you would take the fall if you got caught, you were manipulated into doing all this so she could then kill you once you had abducted me,"

Ethan darted his eyes between Molly and Grace, and tried to connect the dots, the woman had set him up? Fuck!

He held his Gun on them as he watched to see if they tried anything, Grace was stood behind Molly with her gun held firm in her hand, she was to the side of Molly and had a clear shot if she needed to take it.

"Molly's right, Ethan, this was a set up from the beginning, Lauren played all of us, even her husband had no idea who she really was, she had a lot of dark secrets that she had buried deep, she'd woven a big web of lies to keep her story straight, but she lost it when we deployed The Mountain Rescue Team! She Fucked up, the pictures you took they had her fingerprints on them, so did the envelope, she left them on John's doorstep, but she forgot to wear gloves, when you had me in the cellar, she was there, she hit me with the belt, her fingerprints were on the belt too,"

Molly stepped back so she was almost flush against Grace, holding the gun in one hand, Grace slipped one hand around her waist protectively, and watched his reaction, she had a bad feeling, as he took in the information that they told him, rage was vibrating inside him, he was pissed.

"I don't give a Fuck, Just give Molly to me, and I wont shoot you" he snapped as he narrowed his eyes at them, his hands were shaking as he gripped the gun, watching as Grace stepped forward and directly in the firing line should he decide to shoot, Molly wrapped her arm around Grace and tried to keep Ethan calm. "Ethan it's time to let it go, I'm in love with Grace, she's my wife, my soul mate, please just stop this shit, I'm not worth killing people over, drop the gun Ethan, please" Molly said as she looked at him with determined eyes, he watched her, and started to lower the gun, Molly almost breathed a sigh of relief, she slipped her hand onto Grace's hip, caressing the tiny bit of flesh that was exposed, Ethan saw it, and the rage ignited inside him as he raised the gun and fired twice.

The events that followed happened as if in slow motion, Grace pushed Molly to the floor, and returned fire, clipping him twice, once in the shoulder, the other was in the head, making him jerk back and fall to the floor, Molly hit the body alarm, as she scrambled to her knees and over too Grace, who was laid on the floor unconscious!

"Grace, oh god, no, Grace talk to me please,"

Molly turned her onto her back, and unzipped her hooded sweatshirt, she lifted the t-shirt and saw that Grace was wearing a kevlar vest,

"Grace open your eyes, honey talk to me," she cried, she jumped when the two guards burst into the room with their guns drawn, when they saw the suspect down, one went to check him while the other ran to Grace, he saw blood on the floor by her head, he turned her head to see if she had been shot in the head, he sighed with relief when he saw that it was from the fall, Grace's eyes sprang open as she came too, her breathing was erratic as she tried to sit up, Molly threw her arms around her as the guard held a handkerchief to her head to stop the bleeding.

"Grace, oh god I was so worried, are you ok?" Molly sobbed as she held her tight, Grace wrapped her arms around her as she groaned at the humongous headache she now had.

"I'm ok Baby, I must have hit my head as I fell, the vest caught the first

bullet, which hurts like a Mother Fucker," she stated as she tried to get up, but she went dizzy. Molly got to her feet and carried her over to the sofa, John arrived a few minutes later looking worried.

"Molly, Grace" he ran over to them and dropped to his knees at their sides.

"Girls are you ok?' he asked with concern, Molly nodded as she held Grace against her side, kissing her temple.

Grace just looked pointedly at him as she declared with a smile.

"If you don't give us a real Fucking HoneyMoon, We Quit!"

Molly and John burst out laughing at that.

"That's a deal I can't refuse, two weeks in Hawaii are already booked for you along with the hotel, all inclusive. I have the plane tickets in my car, you leave in a week,"

Grace widened her eyes at that, Molly gasped with happiness, she reached for his hand and held it tight.

"Thank you John, for sending this Angel to save me, for giving me my life back"

"Your welcome, now tell me that Asshole is dead"

Grace snorted, then groaned as pain shot through her head.

"Yes, he's dead, Grace shot him in the head. This nightmare is finally over, and I can stop waking up in the night feeling scared, and we can finally have our Honeymoon, then we can have a baby."

Grace's eyes lit up with fire at that, despite the monster headache she had, she pulled Molly into her arms and devoured her lips with desire. Molly bit her lip as she smiled at her sexily.

"Once your head is stitched up, we are going to bed and staying there until we leave for our HoneyMoon,"

Smiling at the things she was thinking of doing to her, she groaned as she laid her head on her shoulder.

"Best idea ever,"

Paramedics arrived then and they assessed Grace, all she needed was dissolvable stitches which one of them did after they cleaned the wound.

She had bad bruising to her ribs and stomach from the impact of the bullet, but she was given a clean bill of health, then she watched as they checked Ethan who was very dead, and leaving a red pool of blood on their marble floor.

Walking hand in hand along the Beach in Hawaii, Molly looked out at the Ocean and felt a sense of Peace, the last few months had been filled with fear, heartbreak and exhaustion, everything had happened so fast and Molly hadn't even had time to process everything, Lauren Lee was dead, and the dark secrets that she had been keeping were starting to come out, her marriage to Chris wasn't legal, she had a long history with drugs, and she'd killed a woman 15 years ago when the woman broke up with her for being to clingy.

There were still a lot of questions that needed to be answered, but that would wait until they got home, for now Molly was content to walk along this beautiful beach with her wife, feeling safe for the first time in 2 months.

Grace stopped walking and pulled her down to sit beside her on the soft sand, the water just inches from their feet, wrapping her arms around Molly and pulling her back into her she kissed her cheek gently, the bruises were almost gone, the infected chain marks were healing and looking better, and the cold feeling Molly had felt since her rescue had gone once they had touched down in the sunshine.

"What's going on in that head baby?" Grace asked as she caressed her arms tenderly. Molly didn't answer at first, lost in her thoughts, eventually she turned her head and looked back at her, smiling brightly.

"I'm thinking how lucky I am to have you, to be sat here in your arms and feeling so calm and at peace, i've never felt so safe, or so loved, you're my best friend Grace, my heart beats for you, my soul cries for you when I'm not touching you, I Fucking Love You Grace Alora Garrett"

Grace turned Molly in her arms and took her lips in a passionate kiss, Molly hummed with hunger.

"I Fucking Love You Molly Rose Garrett"

"I wish I had met you when we were younger, I feel like we haven't had enough time to love one another, I can't get enough of you, and I can't wait to spend the rest of our lives making up for lost time, starting tonight, I want to make love to you right here on the sand, as the sun sets, then i'm going to carry you back to the Cottage and make love to you in bed all night,"

"Oh Molly" Grace breathed as the sun went down around them.

Grace gasped as Molly ran her tongue over her skin, the candlelight casting a romantic glow over their bodies as Molly traced her fingertips over her shoulder and kissed her spine, then ran her hands to her stomach and caressed her as Grace shivered with arousal, she clutched Molly's arms as they slipped lower to Grace's waiting heat, Molly slipped her fingers inside her and bit her neck in a passionate and erotic kiss that would leave a mark, their bodies damp with sweat as Grace felt her body vibrating with each deep and loving thrust of Molly's hand, gasping as she felt Molly's breasts against her back, she moaned when Molly picked up the pace and added her thumb to her overly sensitive clit, she cried out as Molly's other hand went to her breast and teased her nipples, creating a fire inside her soul as she writhed in her arms, reaching back for Molly she held on as Molly made her body tremble as her muscles tightened and her Orgasm loomed, she gasped as Molly rubbed her clit harder,then thrusting harder as she held her tight against her, the feel of Grace's damp skin, the trembling beneath her fingers turning her on. she knew that when Grace came, she would follow.

"Oh Fuck, Molly" Grace cried as her core clamped down on her fingers, she exploded in an earth shattering orgasm, her body shaking as she gasped with pleasure, Molly came as Grace did, shaking against her as she tightened her arms around her with love, and kissed her deeply as they came down from the most powerful and erotic orgasm of their lives, they fell back onto the pillows and Molly turned her to face her, her body was flushed and sated as she grinned with complete and absolute love.

"How do you do that? How do always blow my mind like that?" Grace panted as she stroked her face with shaky hands, Molly laughed as she leaned over and pulled her lips to hers for a deep and thorough kiss.

"You turn me on Grace, that's how, I think of how much I love you and how much I want you all the time, I wont ever get enough of you, I hunger for you Darling, i'm addicted to you"

"Then Lets Overdose Together, It's My Turn" Grace said as she pressed Molly into the mattress and proceeded to make Molly scream with her own release deep into the night before they wrapped their arms around one another and fell into a deep and happy slumber.

Epilogue.

  Walking around outside the of the Holiday Cottage on the Beach, The
SandMan watched as the two beauties made love in their room, there
were some advantages to having window slats on the doors, he had a
good view of what he wanted to see, he watched for over two hours in
the darkness as they fucked like rabbits, he watched as they gasped and
cried out their release, raising the camera to the open slats he took one
picture after another, he smiled as he thought of the Masterpiece he
would create for them.
walking away into the dark night he headed back to his van parked
nearby in a dark and secluded area.
He drove too the airport and quickly boarded his flight back to San
Francisco.

4 Hours and 53 minutes later he left the airport and collected his car
from the long term parking lot, once he loaded his bags into the trunk,
he got on his way as the rain poured down in San Francisco.
He eventually arrived back at his quiet and dark hideout.
He left his suitcase in the car, but took his camera with him to his
workstation in the basement, loading up his computer he plugged his
camera in to transfer the pictures over so he could print them out.
The sound of someone crying made him look over to the cupboard in
the corner.
Walking over to the cupboard he unlocked the padlocks with a key that
was on the wall next to the door, yanking open the door he smiled when
he saw that the girl was still alive, tears stained her face, her clothes
were filthy and she looked terrified as he came close to her and dragged
her out and over to a set a chains on the wall.
She cried as he shackled her to the wall and ran his fingers down her
quivering face as she pulled away from him.

"Please, let me go, I want to go home, just let me go" she sobbed as she
squeezed her eyes shut, he back handed her to keep her quiet, then went
to his computer.
Printing out the 2 dozen photos he'd taken while they were on their
Honeymoon, he'd only been there 2 days and he had a large selection to
add to his masterpiece.

He couldn't wait to leave this one for them to find, he hoped this little puzzle made them squirm in a bad way, he glued the pictures together with a picture of the young girl in the middle with a clear message to entice them to play his game.

Save Me From The SandMan
Or I Die!

he'd set the stage, now he had to get their attention, then let the games begin!

The End..........For Now!

Printed in Great Britain
by Amazon